The sudden, strangled gasp was drawn with harsh desperation,

and it came from behind Miranda. She whirled and saw the body on the table, every muscle tensed, begin to shake. Huge arms and legs trembled convulsively. The broad chest vibrated. The corded neck was arched and quivering.

She stopped seeing a specimen at that moment. What she saw was a man on the brink of suffocation, a man straining to breathe. A man about to die ... *again.*

Dear Reader,

I just have to start telling you about this month's books with Dallas Schulze's *Michael's Father*, our American Hero title. For Kel Bryan, Megan Roarke was the answer to a heartfelt prayer—until she left him alone on the ranch, taking with her a secret that could change his life. Then it's back to Conard County with Rachel Lee's *Point of No Return*, a look inside the marriage of Nate and Marge Tate as the past returns to haunt them. Doreen Roberts sets your soul on fire in *Where There's Smoke*, while Maggie Shayne throws off enough heat to melt . . . Well, see for yourself in *Miranda's Viking*. Jo Leigh's *Suspect* matches a by-the-book cop with the most beautiful suspected murderess ever to cross his path. Finally, in *True Blue*, new author Ingrid Weaver puts her own spin on the classic tale of a good girl falling for an oh-so-bad boy.

In months to come, more excitement will be coming your way in books by authors such as Kathleen Korbel, Linda Turner, Judith Duncan and Marilyn Pappano, to name only a few of the favorite writers entertaining you every month—here in Silhouette Intimate Moments.

Enjoy!

Leslie Wainger
Senior Editor and Editorial Coordinator

Please address questions and book requests to:
Reader Service
U.S.: P.O. Box 1325, Buffalo, NY 14269
Canadian: P.O. Box 1050, Niagara Falls, Ont. L2E 7G7

MIRANDA'S VIKING

Maggie Shayne

Silhouette

INTIMATE MOMENTS®

Published by Silhouette Books

America's Publisher of Contemporary Romance

SILHOUETTE BOOKS

ISBN 0-373-07568-5

MIRANDA'S VIKING

This edition published by arrangement with Harlequin Enterprises B. V.

® and TM are trademarks of Harlequin Enterprises B. V., used under
license. Trademarks indicated with ® are registered in the United States
Patent and Trademark Office, the Canadian Trade Marks Office and in
other countries.

Printed in U.S.A.

MAGGIE SHAYNE

lives in a rural community in central New York with her husband and five daughters. She's currently serving as president of the Central New York chapter of the Romance Writers of America and has been invited to join the National League of American Pen Women. Maggie's first novel, *Reckless Angel,* appeared on the Waldenbooks bestseller list for series romance, and her second book, *Twilight Phantasies,* landed on the Waldenbooks mass-market romance bestseller list, also receiving an award and acclaim from critics. In her spare time, Maggie enjoys speaking about writing at local schools and conducting a romance writing workshop at a local community college.

To Maria Greene, who helped Rolf think like
a true Norseman, and to Anita Gordon, who helped
him speak like one. And to Gayle Callen and
Angela Bartelotte, who helped him hoist the sails for
his ultimate voyage.

Prologue

The sting of icy spray seemed determined to peel the skin from his face, despite the heavy beard he'd grown to protect it. The long, sleek *drakkar* pitched and rolled helplessly, a toy held in the unpredictable hands of an angry sea. Frigid waves reached even to the prow, battering the fierce-looking dragon's head carved there. Men struggled to capture the tattered square sail they'd attempted to furl, but the wind proved too powerful even for their muscled arms. With one vicious gust the mass of green-and-white-striped fabric was carried away and dumped into the raging waters. A sharp crack, a slow groan and the mast came down like felled timber. Rolf lurched forward, abandoning the rudder to the fury of the sea. His arms outstretched, he launched himself from the deck toward the three men. He caught one, sending him backward to land with a jarring thud. The other man had instinctively ducked his leader's attack. Rolf had lost sight of the third.

Rolf struggled to his feet against the frantic rocking of the ship. Shielding his eyes from the slashing, sleet-filled wind he saw Svein, the man who'd avoided his running leap, lying facedown with the heavy mast across his back. He ran forward, shouting uselessly into the roaring wind for assistance. He bent to the mast and bared his teeth with the effort to raise it. But the wood was smooth and wet. Less effort to cling to a slippery eel. He chanced one downward glimpse as he steeled himself for a second assault on the burden, and saw that his efforts were all for naught. Svein's agonies had already ceased.

Rolf tilted his head back and roared his anger, his fury, his frustration. All this carnage! All due to the faithless heart of one king and the treachery of another. A curse on Knut's soul, wherever it might now reside! And a curse upon Magnus, as well! Ah, but how well he knew that the true credit for this mayhem rested in one devious woman.

Rolf lurched sideways as the ship was tossed again, and he struggled to his feet, leaning into the wind to make his way back to the rudder. When the wind threatened to down him, when the bite of the ice on his face almost forced him to turn back, he needed only think of her to regain his strength, his determination. He would not surrender easily.

Adrianna. How he'd adored her. How he'd longed to have her. Fool! He'd only been following the lustful path of every red-blooded Norseman ever to lay eyes upon her stunning beauty. How gullible he'd been not to see that her beauty was but an illusion. Her flame-colored hair and wide-set, deep gray eyes were but gifts of heredity, or fate. Her slender frame and endlessly long limbs convinced a man of her fragile nature. Her graceful and rare height only added to her allure. Truly, though, her heart was as ugly as death itself.

By the gods, he'd been taken in!

As had Knut.

A frigid wave smashed into the side of the sleek dragon ship and she rocked dangerously, righted herself only to be pummeled by another. Rolf reached out, nearly blinded by the sleet and his own bitter anger, and he gripped the ice-coated rudder. He watched in mounting fury as the chests filled with the plunder of this journey slid over the side and sank beneath the waves. The booty was the result of his rage against Adrianna and against the fates themselves. For months he'd vented that rage as a scourge on the shores of every land he'd passed. Again and again his *drakkar* had swept down upon the rich coastal villages of England, of Francia, of Normandy, of Ireland, with vengeance billowing in her sails. So great had been his plunder he'd had to hide the first of it well, before returning again for more. This latest trip had netted greater riches than the first.

All of it gone now at the whim of an angry wind.

The hurricane raged around him, rain and sleet slanting so heavily he could no longer see an arm's length ahead of him. He clung to the side as his glorious ship lurched and rolled over, but to no avail. Icy water reached for him, caught him in relentless, greedy hands, and dragged him away. He felt himself enfolded in raging, biting cold. He struggled to keep his head above the waves. He would not surrender! He was a warrior! He would die at the point of a sword, not at the hand of a storm.

He refused to allow his exile to become a death sentence. He was *úrhrak,* outcast, but he would not die as one. He went under, fought his way to the surface and was pulled beneath the waves again. His body burned with cold. His muscles tightened to such a degree they began to tear themselves from the bone. His lungs screamed for air. His head pounded as if it would crack and his heart seemed about to explode.

Once more the angry waves tossed his body higher. He was allowed only one glimpse, just enough to fill him with the bitterness of irony. The barren shores of Helluland, black water and white ice, seemed to mock him. So close, he might've been able to swim it, had not the seas been so angry, so determined to take him into their final, glacial embrace.

Nei! He would not die! He was not yet ready to ride off with the beautiful Valkyrie upon the backs of their magnificent horses. Not ready to let them carry him onward to Valhalla where he'd feast and fight with the fallen, perhaps with Odin himself. *Nei!* He forced his arms to stroke against the frigid waves, forced his legs to propel him toward the shore.

Even as his body was tossed and battered, Rolf silently vowed he would not die. When he could no longer raise an arm for even a single stroke, he closed a fist around the gilded hilt of his sword, Hefnd, still secure in its bronze-trimmed leather scabbard, still held fast to his nearly lifeless body. "We have not yet finished," he whispered, though the words were drowning as they left his lips.

The last thing Rolf glimpsed before the waters swallowed him up were the barely visible shapes of the fur-ensconced Skrælingar of the north looking on from the shore. He imagined their eyes were filled with awe, and with wonder.

Chapter 1

The wind had knives in it. Razorlike shards bit into her face and stung her nose as Miranda lifted the pickax high above her head and brought it down. Its tip cracked into the solid ice, spraying her cheeks with more shrapnel. She brushed at her face with a gloved hand and paused, glancing to the right, where her father worked furiously on the glacier. The cave was here, its mouth sealed by an icy hand. The sonar equipment had confirmed it. The cave and the secrets it had concealed for centuries lay just beyond this wall of ice—a wall left slightly less than impenetrable by the recent trend of global warming. The cave was only a few inches away. Or perhaps, Miranda's analytical mind reasoned, not *the* cave, but *a* cave.

No. *The* cave. She could feel it.

She warned herself against childish optimism. It would likely put a fissure in Russell O'Shea's stone heart if this expedition turned out to be yet another wild-goose chase.

She hoped to God it wasn't. Because she knew, all too well, it would probably be his last.

Now, however, even the cool, sensible Miranda that ruled her most of the time couldn't contain the thrill of anticipation. This time, even *she* was convinced. The legend had been handed down in various forms and was still told in the remote Inuit villages of Baffin Island. The variations were wild, but the similarities were strong—strong enough for Miranda to concur with her father that a kernel of truth must be concealed in the tall tales. He believed that "kernel" to be the man buried in the hidden cave, sealed by ice.

That he was a god, who had ridden the seas upon a dragon only to be attacked by demon spirits before he could reach the shore, was, naturally, nonsense.

An unusual man, a man unlike any encountered by the early Inuit, had been pulled from the sea and buried with great honor in a cave. The gods, it was said, then sealed the cave, thus preserving their comrade for some divine future mission. Highly unlikely, of course. That his body might have been preserved by an act of nature, however, was entirely possible. It was that man they sought.

Tracking the exact location of the Ice Man had been her father's life's work and, in turn, hers. Because of that renowned devotion to this project and the sterling credentials of the Drs. O'Shea, the government of Canada had agreed to a joint expedition. They accepted the funding of the illustrious Beaumont University and the leadership of its most respected professor. Her father.

The expedition would be the culmination of his life's work. The one thing he cared about, the one thing he felt any real passion for. And it would come just in time.

She wriggled the pick free of the stubborn ice that held it, lifted it once more, and brought it down hard. And again, and again, so absorbed in the work she was barely aware of the others working similarly in other areas around her. She paused periodically to glance toward her father. Tall and far too thin, he worked a short distance from her, his long arms wielding a pickax of his own. She didn't like the slight grayness to his stern face, or the short, shallow way he breathed. She didn't like the stiff way he tended to hold his left arm and shoulder. She was certain he'd sit down and clutch his chest if he were alone. In front of her and the others, though, he'd never concede to a weakness.

She pulled her gaze from him and resumed working. With the next impact, a huge chunk of ice broke away to drop backward into a vast blackness. Miranda stiffened as a low sound, like the deep-throated howl of a wolf, filled the air. Before her eyes the hole made itself bigger. The edges crumbled and fell inward. The moaning sound grew louder as the hole grew larger, and it took a full minute for her to realize what caused it. She dropped the pickax. "Russell, I'm through!"

Her father froze in place for an instant before he rushed toward her. He paused at her side, one hand gripping her upper arm to pull her back a few steps. In moments they were surrounded by the others, all craning their necks to see and murmuring excitedly.

"It's a vacuum, Miranda." He released her arm almost at once.

She nodded, understanding as her father did, that no air had been inside the cave. A vacuum seal had been created by nature and now the fresh air was rushing in, filling the far recesses of the cave with life-giving oxygen. She stood back and watched in fascination as larger and larger chunks of ice snapped away from the hole she'd made, and the opening grew. The moan became a roar, then slowly began to fade. The rush of air eased little by little... and then it died. Swallowing hard, Miranda looked at her father.

His hard gray eyes very nearly twinkled, and the pallor of his sculpted cheeks gave way to glowing color. She wondered if he'd ever felt for another human the way he felt for his work.

"This is it, Miranda. You know it, don't you? You feel it, just as I do."

She couldn't help but smile despite the part of her that ached over his inability to show his feelings for her this way. His excitement, so rare, was contagious. "You usually call relying on feelings unscientific and foolish."

"Not when there's hard evidence to back them up." He turned from her and shouted, "Bring the lights, some rope! We're going in."

A lean, rather awkward student raced down toward one of the crop of dome tents, which seemed to have sprouted up like vegetation far below on the tundra in the glacier's shadow. It was warmer there, nearly fifty degrees unless one factored in the biting Arctic winds. This was summer on Baffin Island. Presently he returned with two huge spotlights, a length of rope looped over his shoulder and Russell's ever-present journal held to his chest. "You'll need this, Dr. O'Shea."

Russell took it and slapped the youth on the shoulder, his way of showing what little affection he was capable of feeling. "That I will, Darryl. Go on and get the cameras and other equipment. Choose five others and wait here. I'll call you when I need you." Darryl's face beamed. He shoved his round wire rims up higher on his nose, tugged his knit ski hat down over his ears, and raced away once more.

Miranda took one of the lights, flicked it on and shone the beam through the opening, now large enough to crawl through. She bit her lip and prayed silently the cave would be large and open, not cramped and suffocating. She wasn't certain she could go a step farther if it were the latter. Already her heart began to pound, her hands to shake. She chanced a quick glimpse toward her father, dreading to see that he'd noticed her hesitation. He detested weakness, and that's what her mild claustrophobia was. A weakness, but a manageable one.

The darkness within was unrelieved. The beam of her light danced over black stone walls and an equally dark floor. No dank, musty air rushed up to greet her. The place had been filled with the fresh air from outside. She smelled no hint of dampness or mildew. Best of all, the cave was huge, at least, this first section of it. Maybe she'd be all right.

"The floor's about ten feet down." She picked up a chunk of ice and dropped it, nodding when she heard it thud. "Sounds solid enough." Drawing a fortifying breath, she handed her light to her father, then scooped up one of the helmets lying nearby and flicked its light on, instead. She fastened the chin strap with care. "I'm going in." She attached the belt around her waist, giving the carabiner links an experimental tug.

Her father handed her a rope, with another carabiner attached. She snapped it to her belt and slipped over the edge. She waited until those anchoring the rope had drawn it taut before beginning to rappel down.

"I'm right behind you," Russell called out. The hiss of rope through the links was punctuated by the tap of her boots against the sheer inner wall. The distance was not great. At the bottom she disconnected, and the rope disappeared above her.

Her father dangled a flashlight a short distance above her head. She caught it, her five feet seven inches of unseemly height making it easier. His own light followed, and then he lowered himself to the floor beside her.

Miranda tucked the spare lights into a pocket, and used the one on her helmet to examine their surroundings. The light showed her a narrow, stone-lined area, like a tunnel. The ceiling arched high above it, making it a bit less likely that she'd be rendered immobile with panic as she moved through. There was only one way to go and she turned in that direction, her father right beside her.

As they moved, their steps echoed. They placed each foot carefully, testing each bit of stone beneath for safety before putting any weight on it. Miranda fought her mind's rebellion at being in the place. She tried to think of herself as the fearless heroine in a gothic novel, traversing the hollow, chilly halls of a castle. Much more romantic than being a shivering scientist moving through a dark cave in search of a well-preserved body. She moved her head and her light . . . if she were that heroine, her light would come glimmering from a candelabra . . . scanning the black walls for writings or drawings indicating they were about to find what they'd hoped for. Surely if the Inuit had believed the man to be a god, there would be something, a shrine of some sort.

There was nothing. Perhaps the Inuit thought to protect their newfound god by secreting him here.

They rounded a curve in the passage and stepped into a large open area, its ceiling a massive stone dome. She nearly gasped with relief when the stone walls expanded so suddenly. The romantic within her fancied this would be the great hall of that castle she'd been imagining. And her fur-collared parka would be instead a white muslin nightdress.

She almost laughed at her ridiculous ponderings. Next she'd be casting a pile of bones in the role of the brooding hero, who would sweep her away on a tide of passion! She chided herself. It was okay to use foolishness to distract her from her fear of small spaces. She knew such fantasies did not occur in real life, nor would she wish them to.

This was real life. Biting cold, hard work, and piles of bones from which secrets could be learned.

Miranda turned around slowly as she stood near the center of the chamberlike area, shining her beam on the walls and rock formations around her, wondering how long it had been since a human had stood in this place, seen these things. The air was frigid, fresh, and utterly still. The silence within the cave was like a living thing, a heavy leaden force that could smother them should the idea appeal to it. She shivered, took a calming breath, and continued studying the hollowed-out room, putting aside her imaginary world in favor of the real one.

Her body stilled as a tingling sensation skittered over her nape. The tiny hairs there stood upright, and suddenly Miranda knew they were not alone. She felt the presence as surely as she felt the cold air on her face. Behind her. Directly behind her. She turned very slowly. Her legs became jelly, and as all the air escaped her lungs in a slow, involuntary rush, Miranda sank to her knees.

He lay upon a table of stone, his skin as perfectly pale and rigid as if he were carved of white marble. His hair gleamed the light's reflection, making it seem silvery, but as stiff as the rest of him. It was long, and as her eyes adjusted, she saw it was a deep golden blond, rather than the pale silver it had at first seemed. His face was all but concealed behind a bushy, reddish beard that curled wildly. He wore a brown tunic over a well-worn shirt that might once have been blue but now was gray. The long sleeves of the shirt covered his arms, and the shorter tunic sleeves came only to his elbows. A wide black belt with a tarnished buckle that might prove to be silver if it was polished encircled his middle. His legs were encased in tight-fitting black leggings that clung to his form. Miranda's throat went suddenly dry as she studied thighs like tree trunks and calves apparently banded with steel. On his feet were furry boots laced tightly with leather thongs.

Her father had heard her gasp, seen her sink to the floor, and he, too, turned to stare in wonder at the slumbering giant before them. "It's him," he said in the darkness.

Miranda forced herself to stand and look at her father. "It can't be.... Russell, look at him. He's...perfect." The last word was a whisper. She shook herself. "He can't have been lying here for nine centuries."

"It was the vacuum, Miranda." He spoke with certainty. His hand came up, his forefinger extended. "Look."

She moved her gaze to the direction he pointed and saw the weapon that lay at the giant's feet. The sword's blade was at least four feet long, and from all appearances, without rust, though the iron seemed dulled with time. The gilded hilt added another foot to its length, and was decorated with intricate patterns and engraved with shapes that might have been letters, words. She moved closer, leaned over it, somehow unable to make herself touch the beautiful piece. She frowned when she recognized the symbols. "Runes." Frowning harder, she studied the ancient writing and tested her memory, as she tried to translate. "*Hefnd*. Vengeance," she said slowly.

"Look, Miranda. The battle-ax, the shield."

She looked, and shook her head in awe, knowing what her eyes were showing her, but still not quite convinced. The fanciful Miranda within would have been alive with excitement, but that one was allowed no access to the real world. She was reserved for those times with the books, late at night when she needed to fight the loneliness.

The scientist, Miranda O'Shea, was a skeptic. "All the things you'd expect to find with a Viking," she conceded. She looked closely at the sword. "It looks genuine, but—"

"What we have here, Miranda, is the perfectly preserved remains of what was once a Viking warrior... maybe *our* Viking warrior." He shook his head. "This is the find of the century. It has to be him, Miranda. The Plague of the North. The man banished from all of Scandinavia for treason against Knut the Great, and who wreaked havoc in his vengeance." He paused. "I'd say his sword was aptly named."

She turned to face her father, amazed he would believe so easily. He set his light on a stone protrusion, opened his journal, and pulled a pencil from his coat's deep pocket. He sat down near the man and began writing furiously, effectively shutting her out.

Miranda studied the giant again and an uneasiness crept over her. She wasn't sure why, but she suddenly felt she was committing a sacrilege by being here. Genuine Norseman or not, his appearance was that of a god. No wonder the Inuit had treated him with such reverence. His size alone would have made him appear like some supernatural being to them. With that glorious golden hair, in contrast to their naturally dark features, and the sword, he must indeed have seemed godlike.

It seemed wrong to defile the grave of such a magnificent man.

Her doubts made no sense. She'd come to terms with those kinds of feelings years ago. She knew that her work was for the benefit of mankind. Somehow, though, this was entirely different.

She moved closer to the man...*specimen*, she corrected herself, and examined his chiseled face. His eyes were closed, his frozen blond lashes touching his hard cheeks. He was huge; she guessed at least six foot seven, and well over two hundred fifty pounds. His arms and shoulders bulged beneath the material that covered them. His chest was as wide, she thought, as a small table. His hands had a span that could easily surround her throat without much effort.

Too perfect to be real, she thought.

Miranda tugged off her gloves and thrust them into a pocket. She reached forward and ran her fingertips over his cold, unresponsive, huge hand. She curled her fingers around his and squeezed. A shiver worked its way through her wrist, upward to her elbow, a tingling sensation so mild it was barely perceptible. She jerked her hand away and blinked rapidly. "I don't think we should take him." She'd blurted the words before she knew she was about to speak them.

"What?"

She shook herself and tried to give voice to the uneasiness settling more heavily upon her with each moment she spent here. "I just . . . I don't know, something doesn't feel right."

Russell sighed and set his journal aside. He got to his feet with an effort. "This doesn't sound at all like you, Miranda. You've never been superstitious. You're a scientist."

"It's not superstition. I'm not sure what it is. There's something wrong here. I feel it."

His face, as he searched hers, hardened. "I thought you were beyond this type of sentimental nonsense. I am aware that with a specimen that looks as . . . human as this one, well, it can be difficult. To an amateur. A beginner. A student. Not to a scientist of your caliber, Miranda. Shake it off and let's get on with this."

She wanted to tell him what she was feeling, to ask him to help her understand, to share with him. But she knew better. He cared little for feelings. His own, included.

"To leave the body would be to destroy it," he went on, no longer looking at her. "The seal's broken now. The air and the moisture have invaded the cave. There'd be nothing left if we came back in a few years. Nothing. Is that what you want?"

She frowned and shook her head. The idea of leaving the great warrior—if, indeed that's what he was—to the merciless elements was just as unpalatable as the thought of taking him from his sacred place and disturbing his rest. It was too late to back out now, and to be honest with herself, the guilt she was feeling made no sense. She'd do better to ignore it and get on with her mission.

She sighed, wondering where the weak sentimentalism that sometimes reared its head within her could possibly come from. She'd had no one with that type of bent in her life since her mother. "You're right. I don't know what's wrong with me." She forced a smile but it felt shaky. "Shall I call Darryl?"

"Go ahead, but warn him to take care. Nothing is to be touched or disturbed in any way until we've photographed, measured and mapped every inch of this chamber."

"Darryl knows all of that." Her voice, she thought, lacked any hint of enthusiasm for the task.

"He might need reminding. If he has any sense at all he'll be half-crazy when he sees this find." Russell shook his head, then sucked a sharp breath through his teeth.

Miranda tore her gaze from the man—the specimen—and knelt by her father's side when he sat down abruptly. "What is it?" She knew without asking that he was having chest pains again.

He grated his teeth; she could tell by the tight line of his jaw. "Nothing. It's nothing. Just go on with what you were doing. Get some measurements."

Fear streaked through her. Cold though he was, her father was the only living being left with whom she had any sort of connection, any bond. She didn't want to lose him, too. "Dammit, Daddy, tell me."

He glared at her. "You call me by my name. You want your colleagues to regard you as a scientist, or as Russell O'Shea's little girl?" He fumbled in his coat pocket, pulled out a pill bottle and attempted to remove the cover. She reached to take it from him as he struggled, but he jerked his hand away and managed to extract a pill on his own. She blinked against the tears she knew her father hated, but not before he'd glimpsed them. "You have to get over this, girl. One of these times the chest pains will come, and they won't leave until I'm dead. You know that. I know that. There's no use crying over what can't be changed."

She bit her lip. "I know."

"I've had a good life. And as of this minute, I've achieved every one of my goals. We don't live forever. It's just the way it is."

Miranda nodded.

Russell reached into her pocket and removed her gloves. He pressed them into her hand. "Put them on, your hands are freezing."

It was the most affection he'd shown her in years. It nearly made her sob. Instead though, she simply put the gloves on. "You'll be the most respected archaeologist in the field by the time you hit fifty. Take my word for it."

It wasn't praise. It was more like an order. "I know," she chanted from long habit.

He took his specs from a deep pocket and slid them up on his nose to resume making notes in the journal. His relaxed facial muscles were the only indication that the sudden spasm of pain had passed.

Miranda went to the entrance and passed along her father's orders.

With the jet chartered by the university, it was only a matter of hours until the warrior was safely installed in the climate-controlled room that took up half the basement of their huge Georgian-style home, two miles from Beaumont University in Mourning Bluffs, Maine. Under lock and key—or rather a high-tech, digital lock—he continued his peaceful slumber, undisturbed by Miranda's careful ministrations.

She unlaced the tunic's neck to apply the sensors to his broad, hairless chest. She ignored the shiver of unease that danced over her spine as her fingers moved over frigid flesh. She was a scientist. That shiver had been felt by someone else, someone who should be banished from this room. But for some reason, it was more difficult than ever to shut her out.

She pushed the tangled blond hair away from his face to attach more electrodes near his temples. In the adjoining room, a bank of control panels and monitors lined the walls. Here, in this refrigerated tomb, there was only the sheet-draped table, as hard, she thought idly, as the slab of stone on which they'd found him.

On another table, near the farthest corner of the windowless room, were his double-edged broadsword—Vengeance—his well-worn shield, his battle-ax, the heavy, gold pendant in the shape of Thor's hammer and the leather thong that had held it around his thick, corded neck. A small rawhide pouch rested there, too, and inside it, Norse coins. Some were round, some half circles, some pie-shaped wedges. The silver had been exchanged according to its weight, and coins were often cut to the proper heft for a purchase in the early eleventh century. She had all the proof she required now that it had been his time. She no longer doubted. She only marveled.

Miranda pulled her lab coat more closely around her and removed her gold-framed reading glasses. They steamed up every time she exhaled. Russell had fallen asleep in the control room, his journal open on the desk before him, his chin pillowed by his chest. No wonder. Neither of them had eaten or slept from the moment they'd discovered this wonder in the Arctic.

She paused near the table—his bed—and scrutinized the warrior's face. But the person looking through the scientist's eyes was the one the scientist wished would go away. She was the one who whispered very softly, as if he might be able to hear her, "I'm almost tempted to give you a shave, see what you look like without all that hair." She caught her hand moving nearer, as if about to stroke his whiskered face. She stopped herself, frowning. "Listen to me, talking to a frozen Viking. I'd be drummed out of my profession if word got out." She felt a foolish grin tugging at the corners of her lips. "I don't suppose you'll tell, though, will you?"

She caught herself in a firm grip and ordered her practical side to take over. She needn't waste time speculating about such trivial things as what his voice might have sounded like or what he'd looked like when he'd smiled. She focused on important matters, examining him closely for signs of deterioration. She saw none.

She shook her head in wonder. What had come over her? She was the most sedate, levelheaded person she knew. Oh, sure, she occasionally felt that little girl inside trying to get out, but it had never been a problem. Since when did she engage in one-sided conversations with one of her finds?

She felt silly. Lack of sleep, she supposed. Or maybe the high of helping to realize her father's dream. "You," she said sternly, "are nothing but a specimen. You're an experiment, and nothing more." Saying it aloud did nothing to make it seem true. "I suppose some part of me recognizes what else you are . . . the one man I can't scare away. Most of them find me exceedingly unappealing, you know."

Releasing a slow breath, Miranda lifted a sterilized instrument and placed it against the exposed flesh of his chest. With a single, efficient stroke, she cut a snippet of flesh the size of a saccharine tablet from him. She winced as she did it, even knowing he couldn't feel any pain. "There I go again, giving you all sorts of attributes you don't possess. I need that for the radiocarbon testing, and you certainly won't miss it. We want to know just how old you are."

She placed the sample in its prepared receptacle and frowned. "Where was I? Oh, the men who find me unappealing. Those are the ones with good eyesight, I imagine. Won't be a problem with you. I'm too tall, too thin, too clumsy. I don't suppose you notice any of that, though. My eyes are set too far apart and they're the most perfectly dull shade of dark gray." She shook her head. "Those few men bold enough to get past all my physical faults run screaming when they learn that I don't particularly enjoy sex."

She pulled a tall stool nearer the table and perched herself upon it. She studied him. "This is kind of nice. I can say just about anything to you, can't I?"

She sighed hard, wishing she were an insomniac. She wanted to do everything herself tonight—run every test conceivable before she had to share him with the world. Beaumont's agreement was to return the specimen to Canada after a year of study. So little time. But already exhaustion began to slow her. "I shouldn't be talking to you like this. I'm just overtired. You're just a specimen . . . not

a man." She tilted her head to one side. "I've never dealt
with one that seemed so. . ."

*What? So human, so real? Yes, as if you had just lain
down for a nap and might wake and smile up at me any
minute. What color are your eyes, I wonder? What is your
name?*

She pressed her fingertips to the front of her throat in
alarm. This was getting out of hand. She quickly rose to her
feet, but her eyes seemed determined to remain focused on
him. The rest of the testing would have to wait, she decided at once. She no longer felt sure of herself, or her
abilities.

Tomorrow he'd need to be bathed in fungicide to prevent any fungus growth on the body. His clothing would be
carefully, painstakingly removed. It would be studied,
tested, and eventually put on display somewhere, along
with his sword and other belongings. He would be CAT
scanned, autopsied, DNA tested. Before the professionals
were through with him they'd know what he'd eaten, where
he'd lived, how he'd died, and even the names of his clos-
est living descendants. Studying him would be the dream of
every scientist in the world. The university would charge
exorbitant fees for photo opportunities. Russell would
probably write a book on him, and Miranda would no
doubt be asked to do articles and go on lecture tours. And
after a single year of study, as per their agreement, the Ice
Man would be shipped back to Canada, where the process
would begin all over again.

She sighed once more, wondering why she felt so incredibly sad at that thought, and forced herself to leave the
room.

It was past midnight when something woke her. Some
sense of unease in the house. Frowning, she shoved back

her covers, knocking her paperback to the floor in her haste. She stepped over *Shadows of Love,* and pulled on her heavy, terry robe. She'd fallen asleep right after the dark, mysterious hero had pulled the defiant heroine into his arms for a desperate kiss. She shook her head, wondering why she felt the need to entertain herself by reading such nonsense. No one loved like that in real life. That kind of passion . . . it simply did not exist.

Then again, neither did the monsters Stephen King wrote about, and plenty of people read his books. Fantasy was fantasy. There was a place for it in life. She reached for her glasses, belatedly remembering she'd left them lying beside a large, forever-still hand in the basement.

She padded barefoot into the hall and toward Russell's room. The door hung wide. The rumpled bed lay vacant. Frowning, she switched direction and hurried downstairs. She didn't bother checking the rooms on the first floor. If Russell were up at this hour, she had little doubt where she'd find him. She walked softly. She'd just peek in to be sure he wasn't ill again. He'd be furious if he knew she was checking up on him. Her light steps took her fluidly down the basement stairs. She saw light gleaming from the slightly ajar control-room door.

As she moved through it she realized something was terribly wrong. In the space of a heartbeat, her eyes took in the disarray. Chairs were toppled, files scattered over the floor, spilling from open drawers. Then she saw Russell, crumpled on the floor, a trickle of blood spider-webbing across his forehead, over his closed eyes.

She took a step toward him, her heart leaping painfully, but whirled as she sensed the blow coming at her from behind. Her sudden movement caused the fist to miss its target and crash down on her shoulder rather than her head. The force of the blow knocked her to her knees and wrung a cry of pain from deep in her chest. She caught only a vague impression of a dark silhouette as the intruder fled. She heard heavy steps on the stairs and the door slamming hard. She blinked back tears of pain and fear, and drew a calming breath.

He was gone. She was alone now. Her gaze darted toward the still-closed door to the next room, where the Viking warrior rested. That the door remained undisturbed eased her mind. She moved clumsily nearer her father. She touched him, wincing when she tried to use her right arm. Then with her left she stroked his pale face, gently shook his shoulder. "Daddy. Wake up, Daddy, please!"

He didn't stir and she felt a cold hand grip her soul. She struggled to her feet, holding her right arm tightly to her chest to avoid the stabbing pain in her shoulder whenever she moved it in the least. She made her way back through the darkened, ordinary-looking half of the basement and mounted the stairs. She hoped her assessment that the bandit had fled was an accurate one. And she hoped to God he wouldn't try to get between her and the telephone.

Chapter 2

A siren screamed and warbled, announcing the ambulance's arrival. Miranda rushed to let them in, then led two men and a woman down to the basement where her father lay unconscious. She stood aside to let them work. Her blood pounded in her temples and her entire body trembled. She could no longer see Russell's pale skin, or his blue-tinted eyelids. She could only see the forms bent over him and hear their urgent words, spoken in clipped, choppy sentences.

"BP dropping . . . pulse erratic."

"Get that IV set up."

"Hustle. We need to transport stat."

"We have V-fib. Get the paddles. Clear!"

A percussion permeated the room. Her father's body stiffened and arced. Miranda forcibly held back the cry that leapt to her throat when he went limp once more. She should have heard her father get up and come downstairs, she thought. She should have been the one hit by the burglar.

"Still V-fib. Give him another shot. Clear!"

Miranda staggered backward, clinging to a control panel for support. "It's only a bump on the head . . . it isn't that bad . . . it can't be that bad—"

"Again! Clear!"

She knew, though, what was happening. It wasn't the blow to his head that threatened her father's life. It was his heart. She closed her eyes as hot tears oozed from between her lashes. She blinked them quickly away. She needed to keep her head now. Russell needed her, loath though she knew he would be to ever admit it. "He's been seeing Dr. Milton Fenmore."

"We'll alert the hospital, miss. They'll call him."

"He's been having chest pains, shortness of breath," she added, as the paramedics lifted her father's limp form onto a gurney and began to carry him away. "They told him to consider a transplant but he's...so damned stubborn." Her throat tightened and choked off her words. She would have followed them out, but several newcomers blocked her way. A man in a neat gray suit put one hand on her shoulder and she glanced into hard eyes that reminded her of her father's.

"Miss O'Shea? I'm Lieutenant Hanlon. Can you tell me what happened here?"

She shook her head, her gaze wandering past him toward the paramedics who were hurrying up the stairs. "I have to go—"

"I know. Believe me, there's nothing you can do for him right now. He's in good hands."

His words, while softly spoken, were firm. Miranda pulled herself up mentally and nodded.

Miranda knew this had been the longest day of her life. First, the seemingly endless questioning by the police, then the interminable waiting at the hospital. She'd left the house in the chill hours of predawn. As time passed like putty through a sieve, the warm, late-July sun traveled its course through the sky. She'd dressed quickly, without thought, and regretted it now, for the hospital corridors were chilly despite the warmth outside. Her lightweight khaki trousers and thin white cotton blouse did little to warm her. She hadn't even grabbed a jacket.

She'd left Lieutenant Hanlon at the house with Erwin Saunders, who'd rushed over at her phone call. As the head of Beaumont's archaeology department, he was frantic with worry over the well-being of the specimen. Miranda assured him she'd glanced at the monitors and found them all reading as they should. Hanlon wouldn't let anyone back downstairs until his men had finished. She'd taken care to firmly warn them both against opening the door to the cold room, where the specimen rested. Any contamination could spell ruin.

Finally, when Miranda had nearly paced a rut in the tiled floor of the waiting area outside ICU, a man with steel-wool hair around a shiny pate approached her. She recognized Dr. Fenmore at once. "Is my father—"

"He's alive, but I'm afraid that's the only good news I have for you. Why don't you sit down? Can I have someone bring you something? Coffee? A sandwich—"

She stopped him with a brisk shake of her head. The pins holding her unruly carrot-colored hair were coming loose, and the move only made it worse. She supposed she looked like the farthest thing from a scientist at the moment. "Just tell me about Russell. Is he going to make it?"

Dr. Fenmore sighed and slowly shook his head. "I wish I could tell you what you want to hear, but I can't. Miranda, we've discussed this before. You knew it was only a matter of time—'' he paused, drew a breath ''—his condition is critical. He's suffered a massive heart attack.''

For the first time since she'd arrived, Miranda sat down. Her suddenly weak knees had made the decision for her. ''What are his chances?''

''Not good. The next forty-eight hours will be crucial. If we can get him stabilized and keep him going, he might recover enough to go home, but this is going to happen again.'' He took a seat beside her. ''You ought to go home, get some rest if you can.''

She looked up into sea green eyes and thought she saw genuine kindness beyond the requisite bedside manner. ''Can I see him?''

''It will have to be a brief visit. Be extremely careful what you say to him. Don't upset him in any way.''

She nodded and walked beside the doctor through the formidable doors with the crisscrossing of wire mesh between the double panes of glass. The trek through the corridor was a short one, and then she was led into a room with nearly as much equipment as Russell's control room at home. But these monitors produced spiking lines on their screens and the one that emitted a soft but steady bleat gave her a surge of reassurance, reassurance she knew to be false.

Lying in the stark white bed, Russell looked thinner than he ever had. His skin differed little in color from the sheets. Tubes ran into his nostrils. An IV line was taped to his wrist. He had more electrode wires running under his gown to his chest than the Viking warrior had taped to his much larger one. Only *he* wasn't garbed in a thin, pale blue hospital gown.

She pasted a smile on her face and approached the bed. She closed her hand over his. Even his skin felt different, she thought. Loose and tender. How could he have changed so thoroughly in a matter of hours? Or was it just her imagination?

His eyes opened. The slate hardness was gone. They were dull now. "Miranda..."

She squeezed. "Right here, Russell. You're going to be fine. Everything's going to be fine."

He drew a weak breath and closed his eyes. "The specimen—"

"Safe and sound. No one's going to get near him. Don't worry."

He released a sigh and seemed to relax. "Be careful, Miranda. Someone wants—"

"I left Professor Saunders and the police at home. They'll keep track of things and I'll be very careful. I don't want you worrying. You know I'll take care of everything. I want you to trust me. You trust me, don't you?"

"What good...are you doing here? You can't...watch over it...if you're here."

She blinked to battle the tears that gathered in her eyes, and leaned over to kiss his cheek. He stiffened. "They said I couldn't stay long, but if you need me, I'll insist. I'll stay right beside you all night, if you want."

The way she had with her mother, she thought. She'd sat up all night, and they'd talked. Her mother had held her as if she'd never let go, and told her how much she loved her, and that she would always be with her. She longed for those comforting words from Russell.

But he only shook his head. "I want you home...with the find."

"I told you, it's safe. I can stay—"

"Anything could go wrong!" The pace of the soft beeps picked up, and Russell's face tensed.

"Okay. Calm down. I'll go home right now if that's what you want."

He sighed deeply, raggedly, and nodded. "Yes. Go home. I won't worry if I know you're there." His eyelids dropped, but popped open again. She could see he was exhausted by the simple act of talking to her. "Miranda, there's something...you don't know. About the specimen. I—" he paused to catch his breath "—my journal...it's all in there. Read it, Miranda. Tonight." He gasped, breathless from the exertion of speaking. "It's up to you now."

Her eyes burned. She was glad his were closed so he wouldn't see the flood of tears that suddenly spilled over. He would have been furious. She hadn't shed a tear in front of her father since her mother died, since that awful dawn when she'd been only twelve. But those tears had dried the instant she'd seen his reaction to them. Somehow she'd sensed his anger was only a cover for his pain. He needed her to pretend everything was fine, in order for him to be able to do so. So she had.

She'd seemed to stop being his daughter that morning. Instead she'd become his student, and then his colleague. All she'd done in her life, she'd done to please him, to gain his elusive approval...with that one brief, disastrous exception.

She brought his hand to her lips to kiss it, then thought better of it. She wasn't supposed to upset him, and physical displays of tenderness tended to drive him nuts. A hand on her shoulder interrupted her, and she turned, still clutching Russell's hand.

"He's asleep." Dr. Fenmore's voice was as soft as his touch. "It's the best thing for him right now. You ought to do as he asked and go home. I'll leave orders you're to be contacted if there's any change," he soothed. "Any change at all, or if he asks for you."

But he wouldn't ask for her. Miranda knew that without a shadow of doubt.

The house seemed abandoned, not the same one she'd left some sixteen hours ago. Her car's headlights moved over the brick exterior like trespassers violating some sacred spot. No welcoming light shone from the windows.

She turned off the ignition and killed the headlights. She murmured meaningless greetings to the two officers who stood outside the house. Apparently Professor Saunders had convinced Lieutenant Hanlon that the find needed guarding before he'd gone home.

She unlocked the house and went inside, flicking on lights as she went. Emptiness met her everywhere she looked. It was almost too much to bear. What if Russell didn't recover? What would her life be without him? She had very little except her work and her father, and the two had always gone hand in hand. They'd worked and lived together, except for that brief rebellious period, when she'd accepted Jeff Morsi's proposal of marriage just to prove to her father and herself that she could be a "normal" woman. Instead she'd only proven she couldn't be. Losing Jeff had been a narrow escape from a nightmare. Losing Russell would leave her bereft . . . utterly alone.

She pushed the thought aside, tossed her purse on the sofa, and walked down the basement stairs and into the control room. Russell wouldn't die, not yet. It was too soon, and he was too stubborn to go in the midst of his greatest discovery. And when he came back home, his first concern would be for that discovery. She'd care for it diligently. If anything happened to the find, it would kill her father faster than any heart attack ever could.

At first glance everything seemed just as she'd left it. Files on the floor and a small bloodstain where her father had fallen. She shivered and gave the monitors a cursory glance . . . then sucked in her breath.

The digital temperature panel read ninety-eight degrees Fahrenheit. Panic knocked the wind out of her as surely as a fist to the stomach would have done. The climate-control panel must have been knocked askew in the struggle. A quick glimpse at the setting confirmed her guess. Why hadn't she checked it before? Why had she satisfied herself with a glance at the readings, and not checked the settings? God, everything her father had worked for could be ruined!

She punched numbers rapidly into the panel to release the lock, threw the door open wide, and hurried inside. Only the soft glow of the minimal lighting in the windowless room guided her. The stifling heat slammed into her like a living thing. But the Viking lay as he had before. His skin seemed less chalky, but it might be the lighting or her fear making it seem so. Maybe it wasn't too late.

She turned to go back to the control panel and readjust the climate control to lower the temperature as rapidly as possible. She froze in the doorway when her gaze locked on the monitor directly opposite. The wavering white line across the screen sent her blood to her feet. She blinked and double-checked the label on the monitor. EEG. Electroencephalogram. The meter of brain-wave activity. But it had to be malfunctioning. It couldn't be reading what was there. It wasn't possible for there to be—

The sudden, strangled gasp was drawn with harsh desperation, and it came from behind her. Then silence.

She whirled and saw the body on the table, every muscle tensed as it began to shake. The huge arms and legs trembled convulsively. The broad chest vibrated. The corded neck was arched and quivering.

She stopped seeing a specimen at that moment. What she saw was a man on the brink of suffocation. A man straining to breathe, but unable to do so. A man about to die ... again.

She reacted instinctively, not taking time to dwell on the unthinkable thing that was happening. She was beside the table before she knew she'd moved. She gripped the solid shoulders, fighting to hold him still as she pressed her ear to his chest. She felt nothing there. She lifted her head, and then clasped her hands together in one balled fist. She brought them down hard on his sternum. He flinched.

Frantically she caught his whiskered face between her palms and tipped up his chin. She pinched his nose and covered his mouth with her own and she blew life into him, once, twice, again. She blew hard to fill his massive lungs, then returned to the chest, positioning her hands over his sternum to massage a long-silent heart.

A rapid thud tapped against her palm, and it seemed her own heart rate sped up until it echoed his. The fit of convulsions slowed and died. She watched in utter awe as the huge chest rose and fell, far too quickly, but regularly. Beneath her hands, now-supple flesh gradually warmed.

He was breathing.

His heart was beating.

His brain was functioning.

She stepped backward, away from him and turned in the doorway to scan the monitors. They confirmed the impossible. Not one flat line among them. Not one.

An agonized moan, so hoarse it hurt her ears, brought her around once more. His eyes were blue ... the pale, silvery blue of an icy sea, and they were staring right into hers. She saw many things in those piercing blue eyes—confusion, pain and an unfocused quality that told her he wasn't seeing clearly. He remained on his back, just staring at her, silently asking her a thousand questions, most of which she was certain she couldn't answer.

She was in awe, in shock. Life's blood pulsed through the formerly dormant body, giving color to his skin. She took a step toward him, then another. Slowly, tentatively, she approached him. He moved only his eyes, keeping them locked with hers. Beside the table she stopped. In wonder, she lifted a trembling hand, and placed it with tender reverence upon his face. Her fingertips brushed over the small expanse of his cheek uncovered by beard. "You're alive." It was no more than a whisper.

His response was to slowly lift one of his large hands and thread his fingers through her hair, pulling what few strands had remained pinned in place down to join the rest in what she knew must resemble a pumpkin orange disarray. "Valkyrie." The word came in a voice hoarse from disuse.

Her words, she knew, were foreign to him. She understood his, though. It was almost laughable. If he thought her one of the legendary demigoddesses, the Valkyries, who in Norse mythology were said to greet fallen warriors at their deaths and lead them to Valhalla, he must be incredibly disappointed. Valkyries were supposed to be beautiful, strong, sensual creatures. She saw herself as none of the above.

She stifled her amused grin and met his wonder-filled gaze. "No." She shook her head. "Not Valkyrie. Miranda." She frowned hard, searching her memory for the Islensk words. "*Eg heiti* Miranda."

She wished she had a more thorough knowledge of the language. Not that it mattered. She wouldn't be able to tell him anything, anyway. She had no idea how this had happened, but she was absurdly glad it had. Her eyes burned and she had the urge to laugh out loud. "You're alive." She said it softly, a sense of wonder in her voice. She stared down at him, wondering what he was thinking, what he was feeling. Was he in pain?

His hand clasped the base of her neck to draw her nearer. He squinted, then blinked as if to focus his vision. Suddenly the curious, reverent gleam left his eyes and they narrowed in a way that made her heart jump in fear. His hand in her hair turned cruel, twisting a lock around it until she thought he'd rip it out. His mouth curled into a sneer and he gruffly ground out, "Adrianna." It was, she sensed, an accusation.

He rose slightly and with a brutal thrust pushed her away from him. His shove was so forceful she found herself on the floor. Even as she fought panic and shock and began to get to her feet again, she saw him leap from the table. He loomed over her, spewing forth a stream of Norse words so filled with anger and bitterness she could barely believe the strength of it. How had she allowed herself to forget, even with all that had happened, who this man was? The Plague of the North. He reached down for her, his huge hand menacing.

She cringed, terror-stricken, but then he stopped. His large body swayed slightly. One hand pressed to the side of his head and he wobbled on his feet like a tree about to fall. Miranda shot up, gripping his upper arm with all the strength she possessed and slipping an arm around his waist when that first effort was no longer sufficient.

"Easy. Come on. Lie down," she said in a low, firm voice. He couldn't understand her words, but he might be able to sense her intent in her tone. She trembled with fear, but refused to give in to it. "I mean you no harm," she went on as she urged him toward the table. *"Eg er...vinur þinn,"* she managed. "I'm your friend."

He scowled darkly, and she thought he called her a less than flattering name. He still remained unsteady on his feet.

"You're sick. *þið eruð veikur.*"

He hesitated, but finally he sat on the edge of the table. He closed his eyes for a long moment and his voice was almost sad but tinged with bitterness when he spoke again. The words had the ring of despair and the lilt of a question. And again he used that name—Adrianna.

"No." Carefully she touched his face, tilting it upward so he would look at her more carefully, then quickly drawing her hand away so as not to offend him. It would be in her best interest to make him see she wasn't whoever he thought she was. He seemed as if he'd like to throttle Adrianna, whoever she might be. When his ice blue gaze, clearer now, fixed upon her face, she said softly, "I am Miranda." She tapped her chest with her forefinger. "Miranda."

He frowned and his eyes narrowed as he studied her more closely. Again he reached for her hair and she forced herself not to draw back in fear. He drew a lock forward and rubbed it between his fingers. He shook his head and leaned nearer, lifting the hair to his nose and inhaling its scent. His gaze traveled over her face and he seemed confused. Not convinced, though.

After a moment, he glanced at the room around him, his brow furrowed. Then he lowered his head and pressed a palm to it. When he noticed the electrodes taped to his chest, he frowned harder and lifted a hand to tear one free.

"No." She laid her hand over his, looked him in the eye and shook her head. "Let me. It will hurt if you just rip them off." He tilted his head, seemingly just realizing she spoke in a tongue he'd never heard. She clasped his hand and gently moved it away. He allowed it, then watched curiously as she caught the edge of a strip of tape and carefully peeled it back. As she pulled it away, she winced, knowing the sting he'd feel. She glanced up at his face to see if she'd hurt him.

To her amazement, he smiled at her. His eyes glittered with unmistakable amusement. His huge hand came up again, and imitating her, he picked at the edge of a strip of tape. Unlike her, once he had it, he yanked it free in one quick motion, not even blinking as he did so. He kept glancing at her as he repeated the procedure until his chest was free of wires and sensors. He was showing off, she thought, her mind reeling. He thought it funny that she'd been worried about hurting him. She smiled back at him. She couldn't help it.

Her smile instantly instigated the return of the angry glare in his eyes. He looked quickly around the room, made a sweeping gesture with his hand and murmured a hoarse question. What is this place? she imagined he wanted to know. Or where am I? How did I get here? She made a helpless, shrugging gesture. Then she touched his throat with her fingertips. Instantly his hand closed like a steel trap around her wrist.

She stiffened, but didn't turn away from him. God, but he didn't trust her. "Thirsty. You must be thirsty. That's all I was trying to say." With her free hand she made a circle of her thumb and fingers to lift an imaginary glass to her lips. "Drink," she told him. "Would you like a drink?"

Frowning, still looking skeptical, he released her wrist. *"Eg er þyrstur,"* he said hoarsely.

"Right. *þyrstur.* Thirsty." Miranda quickly left the room and him. She paused in the control room, her hands gripping the edge of the sink as her knees began to tremble in reaction. For a moment, the enormity of what was happening hit her like a whirlwind, but she had to keep calm, not think about it too deeply or she'd lose her mind or have a fit of hysteria. Things like this did not happen. "What in God's name am I going to do with him?"

She shook her head, filled a glass with cold water, and returned to the cold room, which had now become hot. The table was empty. Startled, she swung her gaze around the room and saw him in the corner, so large she nearly reconsidered her determination not to be afraid of him. He held the massive sword by its hilt, turning it this way and that. Miranda found herself glad she'd painstakingly polished it, to ready it for viewing by the archaeological staff tomorrow.

She swallowed hard. What on earth was she going to tell the staff? And Professor Saunders? "Sorry, guys, the find came to life. I'm afraid you can't have him." She rehearsed the words silently in her mind, and her eyes widened as she realized they would still want him. He'd be the center of study by every scientist on the planet when they learned . . . if they learned.

He saw her and came toward her, his stride not quite steady, but extremely confident. She held the drink out and he took it. He held it up, frowning harder than ever as he examined the glass and the clear, sparkling water it held. "Glass," she said firmly, tapping the outside with one short fingernail. "Glass."

He nodded slowly and, his voice still coarse, repeated the word, "Glass."

Miranda couldn't suppress a smile. She nodded. He lifted the glass to his lips and began guzzling. When he lowered it, Miranda said, "*Vatn.* Water."

He cleared his throat, and returned the glass to her. "Water," he mimicked. When her hand closed around the glass, though, he caught it and lifted it, examining her fingers with close scrutiny. He even ran the pad of his thumb over the edges of her unpainted, neatly cropped nails. He frowned. Then he released her hand and studied her face. "Adrianna?"

She set the glass down. "No." She shook her head firmly. "Miranda." She tapped her chest hard for emphasis. "Miranda." She saw that she was at least making some headway. He now wondered. She spotted her glasses where she'd left them the night before, and automatically picked them up and slipped them on.

A second later, they were removed by amazingly gentle hands. He turned them this way and that, a frown making parentheses between his brows. He drew them close to his face and peered through the lenses.

He's like a child, she thought, watching him. Like a big, lost child in a strange new world. Except that he was a dangerous child, one she needed to handle carefully.

She took the glasses from him and slipped them into her pocket. She pointed to his chest and said, "Ulf? Svein?" So far she only knew him as The Plague of the North. "*Hvað*, um, your name . . . *heitir þú?*"

"Rolf Magnusson." His voice was clearer now, and decidedly louder. He nodded, indicating the empty glass. "Water."

"More?" She took his wrist in her free hand and drew him carefully from the room and into the adjoining control room. He gazed curiously all around, eyes widening at the bank of monitors with their flat white lines and the rows of buttons and dials and switches. He was more amazed, though, when she turned on the faucet and water flowed into the sink. He watched her, and a second later, he moved her aside to stand where she'd been.

Setting his sword aside, he turned the knobs first one way and then the other, making the water flow, hot then cold, and finally making it stop. He studied the stream, following it to the drain. Dropping to his knees, he next examined the pipes beneath the sink.

He frowned, nodded slowly, and rose to take the glass from her hand. She willingly let it go, and watched as he filled it on his own. He held the glass beneath the faucet until it was spilling over his big hand. He reached again for the knob and turned it off. For a long moment, he regarded the glass in his hand. Finally he brought it to his lips and tilted it up as if he'd down it all in one gulp as he had before.

This time she put a hand over the one holding the glass. "Slow," she told him. She pushed her other hand in a downward sweep and repeated, "Slow." She placed a palm on his stomach by way of explaining that he'd give himself a stomachache if he drank too quickly. It was as hard as rock and warm beneath her fingers, even through the thin tunic he wore and the shirt beneath it. She looked up quickly. His eyes seemed to darken. He held her intense gaze for a long moment, and it was Miranda who finally looked away, baffled by her sudden shortness of breath and the odd tension coiling somewhere within her.

He studied her as if she'd done something unexpected, then he drank, slowly this time. It was remarkably easy to make him understand her, she thought. When he finished, he set the glass carefully on the counter. "Rolf." She tested the name. "Rolf Magnusson." What now, she wondered.

The sound of footsteps on the stairs alerted her, and when Rolf saw the way her eyes flew wide and her body went rigid, his powerful hand closed around her upper arm, jerking her behind him as he lifted his sword and sent a fierce glare through the doorway, into the darkened basement.

"No, Rolf. *Nei!*" she whispered urgently. She tugged at his arm until the sword lowered. She reached around him to close the door until it was only open a crack.

"Miss O'Shea?"

"Who is it?" She clung to Rolf's tensed biceps, praying he wouldn't decide to behead the man with a single swipe of Vengeance before he could answer.

"Officer Phillips, miss. I was knocking for quite a while. Got worried when no one answered, since the lights are still on. Everything all right?"

Rolf emitted a low grunt and his expression told her what he thought of her restraining hand. "Fine, everything's fine. I'm afraid I can't talk to you now, though. Some of the controls got knocked out of whack earlier and I have to get them back in order. Sorry to be rude."

"No problem. Anything I can do to help?"

"No, thank you. Good night, Officer Phillips." She sighed in relief when he responded in kind and she heard his steps returning up the stairs. She listened until the door slammed. Then her entire body sagged at the close call. She hadn't realized until this very moment what she was going to do with Rolf. It shocked her now that she had. Her entire life had been devoted to science. The decision she'd made, though, was the opposite of the one the scientists of the world would wish for. It was more like the one the romantics of the world would approve. But there was only one decision she could make. She couldn't allow him to become the hottest new guinea pig in the world. She simply couldn't. She had to hide him from everyone . . . she didn't know how, but she had to do it.

Rolf's hand closed on her shoulder and she winced. He turned her toward him, his frown deeper than ever. His fingers closed on the collar of her blouse and he pulled it to one side, snapping the top two buttons and baring the shoulder he'd inadvertently hurt. He saw the bruise she knew had formed there, the one she'd received from the intruder. His face turned thunderous and he spewed forth a stream of words she didn't understand. As he spoke he motioned with his sword toward the stairway and the last phrase sounded as if it might have been a question.

She wondered if he were asking whether Officer Phillips had given her the bruise, or whether she'd like the man dissected for his crime. Either way, she knew she had to disabuse him of the notion. Funny, she thought, that he would pull her hair the way he had, shove her around like that, yell at her for whatever this Adrianna had done, and then get so angry at the knowledge that someone else had harmed her. She touched his face, bringing his gaze back to hers. "*Nei*, Rolf. It wasn't him. *Nei*." She touched the hand holding the sword, putting a slight downward pressure on it, and he lowered the weapon, looking none too pleased about it.

She nodded in approval and smiled. His gaze dropped to her bruised, exposed shoulder and softened. Gently he touched the purplish skin with two fingers and murmured something low and soft.

She pulled her shirt together hastily, feeling the blood rush to her face at his show of tenderness. It was an odd feeling, having someone so angry on her behalf, one she didn't remember ever having experienced before. Of course Russell would have been upset if he'd known the intruder had harmed her, but not like this. Rolf had been ready to do battle... all over a little bruise. All right, not so little from the way it ached, but still... She shook herself and took one of Rolf's hands, or as much of it as she could grasp.

She looked up into his eyes. "I'm not going to hurt you, Rolf. I'm your friend. *Eg er vinur þinn.* You're going to have to trust me."

He watched her closely, his eyes going from hers, to her lips as she spoke, to her throat and back to her eyes again. He licked his lips after a moment, pressed two fingers to his thumb and tapped his lips three times. *"Eg er svangur."*

"Hungry? I'm hungry, too." She touched her lips as he had. "I am hungry. Say it, Rolf. I am hungry."

"I am hungry." His mimicking ability was astounding.

She nodded encouragingly. "Now say my name. Miranda. *Endurtakið.*Repeat it, Rolf. Miranda." She had no doubt he understood what she was asking of him. He seemed keenly intelligent.

He studied her for a long moment, his eyes narrow with suspicion. At last, sneering slightly, he gestured, lifting one hand, four fingers touching the thumb. He flicked the fingers open with a sarcastic little snap and whispered, "Adrianna."

"Can't pull one over on you, can I?" She shook her head, rolled her eyes to show her displeasure, but still gripped his hand and drew him through the basement and up the stairs.

Chapter 3

Rolf's body felt oddly weak, and strange tingling sensations still radiated through his limbs, though not as severely as they had at first. His mind seemed fogged. He knew not where he was nor how he'd come to be here, let alone why he felt so peculiar.

The woman—Adrianna, he was certain—was behaving strangely, speaking in this odd language, pretending not to understand him. Without a doubt the language was of her own creation. Did she believe she could deceive him, the man known throughout the North for his gift with languages? He could learn any tongue there was in a single night of study—enough to communicate, at least. Given a week he'd be as fluent as the natives. Adrianna knew that. Everyone knew that. Before his name had been ruined by her slanderous tongue, Rolf had been summoned to England by King Knut himself to act as translator to visitors from other lands. So what game was the lovely Adrianna trying to play?

He watched her as he sat at her table and ate the cold roast fowl she placed before him and drank the milk, wishing it were mead. He nibbled the oddly shaped, sliced bread and he studied her. There was something...something different about her. Her eyes were the same deep gray of storm clouds, set far apart and fringed in rich auburn lashes. But they were filled with some turmoil he had yet to understand. She covered them with a strange shield. Disks of what she'd called glass, though clearer and smoother than any he had ever seen, held in place by thin metal the color of tarnished gold. They seemed to distort the vision, those eye shields. Her fiery hair, wild now that he'd tugged it free, had at first been pulled tight to the back of her head as if in an attempt to tame the unruly waves.

In fact, her very mannerisms seemed to have changed. Adrianna had always dressed provocatively and moved with a sensual grace designed to tease and entice men. Her eyes forever threw sparks to her admirers, and her lingering gazes and sidelong glances had been perfected to an art.

She was different, obviously troubled about something, seemingly oblivious to her own charms. She wore strange, loose-fitting leggings and a simple white shirt without adornment or sashes. She hadn't even bothered to scent her hair with henna, though it did carry a scent all its own.

And there was more. She was treating him oddly. There was such uncommon softness in her voice, and a hesitancy in her slightest touch. She looked at him with an awe visible in her eyes, even beyond the unrest he saw there.

The strangeness of this place puzzled him, as well. Rolf rose now to examine it. Already the food seemed to be restoring his strength. He began with the water-spurting device, which he recognized, though it differed slightly from the one below. This one had a wooden box built around it to conceal the pipes beneath, with swinging doors and shelves within for storage. Other wooden storage boxes were fastened to the walls. He opened these, one after another, and found strange vessels that appeared to hold foodstuffs, and stacks of dishes made of a shiny, hard substance.

A tall metal box held more food, but this one was cold inside. There was a niche cut into its door and a lever within. Rolf closed the door and touched the lever. At once several small bits of ice spilled over his hand and onto the floor. He jumped in surprise, then swung his head around at the sound of a feminine laugh.

She hurriedly clapped a hand to her lips, but her eyes sparkled with mirth. Rolf felt a warm spiral of anger begin to curl within him. So she found him amusing, did she? As he glared at her, she rose and moved to stand beside a wall. She pointed to a small protrusion fastened to it. She moved a little appendage, and said something. The small lamps suspended above the table went out. Rolf stared in wonder, for when she moved the thing again, they lit once more. He frowned and stepped nearer the lamps. Their flames, he'd first thought, were only concealed beneath the painted shades of glass. Now he saw there were no flames at all, only oddly shaped globes which emitted a blinding white glow.

"How is such a thing accomplished?"

She only shrugged, again feigning near ignorance of the tongue he spoke. How long would she persist in this game?

He sighed in disgust and returned to the food. He needed every bit of it. He felt weaker than he could ever remember feeling. Mayhap he had been ill. Might Adrianna have nursed him through some long sickness? He glanced up at her quickly. *Nei.* Such selflessness was not in her.

There had been a moment in the rooms below when he'd forgotten her black soul. When he'd seen the ugly bruise marring her perfect, lily skin, an anger had risen within him. He'd wished to discern the name of the one responsible, and to make him pay for such cruelty. It made no sense. She'd done worse to him by far than bruise his flesh. She'd borne false witness against him, accused him of murder. She'd stood by and seen him banished from Norge, and as a result he'd—

Rolf dropped the leg of fowl he'd been eating. His head came up fast as he fought for the memory. A sudden shiver raced through him and he felt again the sting of ice lashing his face, but only for a moment. The sensations faded fast and he was left wondering what had become of his vaunted memory.

Then there was softness, her hand covering his, her eyes filling with concern. Her voice was plaintive as she spoke his name and asked a question. Did she wish to know what troubled him? He searched his mind again, but found only a deep well of darkness. The journey from Norge across the North Atlantic was nearly forgotten. He knew he'd embarked on that journey, but its memory was as elusive as that of a dream one tries in vain to recall.

"Rolf?"

He studied her face, so soft, and her eyes, so intensely searching his. Truly she had never seemed as beautiful as she did at this moment. How could she be here? If he'd ever completed that journey, then he should be in the wilderness of Helluland, among the Skrælingar by now, far to the north of Vinland with his crew of other outcasts.

How could she be here?

In answer to her queries, he only shook his head and returned his attention to the food. As he ate, he recalled her brief lesson below and that she had said she, too, was "hungry." He pushed the platter of fowl toward her and repeated her words as he remembered. "Adrianna... am hungry."

"No." She shook her head firmly, giving him no mistake as what her no meant. "Miranda. Miranda is hungry. Rolf is hungry."

"Adrianna is," he stubbornly repeated. "Rolf is." He frowned. "I am."

She nodded, but he could see a flare of anger in her gray eyes at his refusal to use her newly acquired name. He sighed his relief. At least she would now give him a lesson in her make-believe language. Did she insist on using it, he might as well learn to speak with her.

She pointed at him with her graceful finger. He wondered briefly why she'd cut off her nails. They had once been her pride. "You are hungry." She made a motion with her hand indicating them both, and went on, "We are hungry." She picked up a piece of fowl and placed it between her full lips. Rolf watched her eat the food. His own appetite had vanished.

Every once in a while he looked at her in a way that sent shivers down the back of her neck. They weren't from fear, because she no longer saw the anger she'd seen earlier. His gaze would simply intensify... to an unbelievable degree.

The rest of the time she could only marvel at his obvious wonder and occasional delight with everything he encountered. He didn't pretend not to be impressed, as most of the men she knew might have done. Especially her father. Rolf's feelings were out in the open in full view. Especially the sudden frustration he'd seemed to experience a few minutes before. She wasn't certain of its cause, but she saw that he was troubled about something.

As they shared the meal, Miranda began his English lessons in earnest. There was so much he would need to know if she was going to pull off this charade. First and foremost, she needed to be able to communicate with him. His ability to learn astounded her. In a single sitting, she taught him to conjugate the verb "to be" and to name every object in the entire kitchen. In fact, by the end of the meal she was pointing to things and asking "What's this?" and getting perfect answers every time.

She'd been amused by his reaction to the fork. It was alien to him, but he was curious, so she showed him its use. He only shook his head, his expression telling her more eloquently than words could, how ridiculous an instrument it was. With elegant grace he continued picking up the fowl in his long fingers and placing it between his lips. Watching him, she nearly conceded that forks were useless.

She longed for some time to sit down and think through this crazy decision of hers. She longed to analyze and plan, to weigh the consequences of her actions, to make a list of pros and cons and to prepare for the possible results of such a deception. But she couldn't. She didn't dare leave him alone at this point. It was vital that she find a way to communicate with him as quickly as possible, and equally vital that she think of a way to hide his presence from the police and Professor Saunders. That was the only thing she knew for certain. She couldn't let anyone know. She couldn't let him fall into the hands of ambitious scientists who would see him only as the opportunity of a lifetime. They would justify his incarceration and resultant torment as being for the greater good.

With two police guards right outside the door, she realized her predicament was precarious at best. If they saw Rolf...

"Clothes," she whispered, mostly to herself. "We need to get you some clothes." She looked at him frowning at her and tilting his head to one side. Shaking her head, she picked up the telephone and dialed Darryl's number. If she could trust anyone at all it would be her father's sidekick, assistant and devout worshiper. He answered on the first ring.

"Darryl, it's Miranda O'Shea." She smiled as Rolf tilted his head and frowned again.

"How's the professor?" Darryl asked without preamble, genuine concern in his voice. "I called the hospital, but they wouldn't tell me anything."

Miranda swallowed hard. Guilt reared its head inside her. She'd actually forgotten about her father for a little while. How could she? "He's not good, Darryl. Not good at all."

She heard the young man swallow hard. "Will he—"

"The doctors don't know yet. They're doing everything possible, but..." Her throat swelled and her words faded out.

"Man, I'm sorry. What about you, Ms. O'Shea? Are you all right?"

She sighed. "I'll be fine. But I do need a favor and you're the only person I can ask." Rolf was standing now, staring curiously, coming nearer.

"Sure. You know I'll do anything I can. What is it?"

Rolf positioned himself right in front of her. He reached out a hand to the phone on the wall, fingers touching the buttons and causing tones to sound in her ear. She pushed his hand away and shook her head at him. "A friend of mine just arrived from Norway, er, Iceland."

"A friend?"

"Colleague, actually. He's a...um..." Rolf was tugging the phone from her ear, and she had to struggle briefly to regain it. She caught his questing hand and held it in hers, trying to send him a silent message with her eyes. "...historian." She rushed on to cover her stammering explanation. "He didn't know about Russell, of course. Anyway, he's staying here and the airline lost his luggage."

"You gotta be kidding me."

"No, I'm afraid not. The thing is, he hasn't got a single thing except the clothes he's wearing—" Rolf gripped the phone with his free hand and pulled it from her ear. He bent his head lower, listening, eyes going wider. She tugged the receiver back in time to hear the last part of Darryl's offer to take Rolf shopping.

"Actually, he speaks very little English and he's really timid about going out in public. Do you think you could just pick up a few things for him? I know it's a lot to ask, but—"

"Come on, after everything you and the professor have done for me? It's nothing. Here, let me get a pen. What size is he?"

She knew his measurements by heart, so an educated guess wasn't difficult. "You'll have to go to a big and tall shop, I imagine. Do you want to stop by for my credit card?"

"I'll just use my own and bring you the bill."

It was the answer she'd been hoping for. Time was of the essence here. God only knew when the police outside would take it into their heads to check on her again. "As long as it's okay with you," she said. "If you could just grab a couple of casual outfits and some basic necessities, I'd be grateful. And I hate to say it, but I need them in a hurry."

"No problem. I'm glad I can help out."

As soon as Miranda hung up, Rolf had the receiver in his hand, holding it to his ear and punching buttons at random to hear the tones they made. She reached up, depressed the cutoff, and motioned with her hands for him to stay where he was. She ducked into the living room and picked up the extension. "Hello, Rolf. This is Miranda." She saw him step into the doorway, receiver in his hand, and stare first at it, then at her. *"Gott kvöld, Rolf."*

His face broke into a broad smile. He spoke into the mouthpiece as she had, his voice deep and resonant, caressing her ear. *"Gott kvöld,"* he replied.

She smiled back at him and replaced the receiver. He did the same. The scientist in her was steadily shrinking. This was going to be an adventure. "Come on, Rolf. You need a bath. And a shave. If we disguise you, we can say the specimen was stolen and that you are my dear old friend from Iceland. Old Norse is still spoken there, so it ought to be believable." She looked at him and shook her head. "More believable than the truth, at least."

He frowned at her and muttered, *"Eg skil ekki."*

She took his arm, quickly glancing into his eyes to see if he would object. He didn't seem offended by the contact. She drew him toward the stairs. "Come with me, Rolf."

He did, albeit reluctantly, as she guided him up to the second floor and along the hall. He stopped often to peer into each room they passed. In the bathroom she forced herself to take her time, to show him the tub and the basin, the hot- and cold-water settings, to teach him the words for these things. His patience seemed as boundless as his curiosity. She started the water running in the tub, and while it filled she located a pair of scissors, a razor and a can of shaving cream.

She swallowed hard and brought him to stand before the sink where he could see his reflection in the mirror. He jumped at first, but she saw that he understood what it was and gradually accepted it. In a moment he was studying his reflection with interest. Mirrors in his time had consisted of nothing more than small disks of polished steel. This one must be quite a surprising change.

"Rolf?" He looked at her, his blue eyes wary and searching. She lifted the scissors to her own face, moving the blades on an imaginary beard. Very slowly she moved them toward his face.

Rolf drew back fast and shook his head. *"Nei!"*

"All right. It's all right." She spoke softly, feeling as if she were soothing a confused, frightened child. The poor man had traveled thousands of miles and nine centuries from everything he'd ever known. He'd died and been resuscitated. The last thing on his mind would be the need to shave, but she had to force the issue.

She approached him, setting the scissors aside, lifting her hand to show him it was empty and then moving it closer, slowly, until she let it rest gently on his face. "Trust me, Rolf," she said softly. "You've got to trust me." She glanced down at the scissors, then back at him. She fingered the thick whiskers and grimaced slightly. *"Gjörið svo vel?* Please?"

He frowned and turned toward the mirror once more. He studied his face, threading his fingers thoughtfully through the curling reddish beard. When he looked at her again, she saw his reluctant compliance even before he sighed and said, *"Já."*

He stepped forward again and stood with unbelievable patience while she trimmed and trimmed and trimmed. It seemed to take forever to get the beard down to a manageable thickness. He watched in the mirror as she worked, but his eyes were as often on her reflection as on his own. Eventually she whittled enough hair away so that he wore only a thin coating of it on his face. He now had the look of a dangerous rebel rather than a lumbering mountain man.

He was much more attractive with the shape of his face visible. Not that she would be foolish enough to let herself actually feel an attraction to him...even if she were disposed to that type of thing, which she most certainly was not. She didn't even like men.

Finally she set the scissors aside and lifted the razor. She showed him what she intended by smearing lotion on her own face and scraping it away with the razor. Rolf glanced into the mirror, running one hand thoughtfully over what remained of his beard. He nodded once and turned to her.

Miranda smeared the lotion over his face, feeling the tickle of his whiskers against the sensitive hollow of her palm. It seemed such an intimate act, rubbing her hands over his face this way. But of course it wasn't. It was simply something that needed doing, and who else was there to do it?

She could let him shave himself. He would manage. Shaving had not been unheard of, even in his day. She frowned and glanced down at the razor. No, she didn't want him cutting his face to ribbons just because she was ridiculously shy about touching him. Besides, she'd never shaved a man before.

She rinsed the scented lotion from her hands and lifted the razor to his cheek. In careful, steady strokes, she began to remove the bristles from his skin. Little by little his face was revealed to her. First the shape of his cheeks, then the wide, firm line of his jaw, then his square chin with the cleft at the center.

When she finished she took a wet cloth and dabbed the remaining cream and loose whiskers from his face. She stopped, staring mutely up at him and blinking down her shock. The man was incredible, the most undeniably handsome man she'd ever encountered, bar none. She knew she was gaping like an idiot, but she couldn't take her eyes from him.

He grinned and she caught her breath. He had dimples in his cheeks!

Okay, that's enough, she told herself firmly. *With all I have to worry about it's positively insane to be standing here, staring at him this way. So what if he's gorgeous? Lot's of men are gorgeous. What does it matter to me? I'm frigid, remember?*

He glanced into the mirror, running one hand over his now-smooth face. He looked at her once more, nodding in approval. *"þakka þér fyrir."*

"þakka þér fyrir," she repeated. "Thank you. Repeat, Rolf. *Endurtakið.* Thank you."

"Thank...you."

She smiled. She couldn't help it. He seemed so pleased with himself. "You're welcome."

"Ahh, yor welcome," he echoed. *"Verði yður að góðu. Já?"*

She was fairly certain he'd just repeated "you're welcome" in Islensk. "Yes, that's right." She couldn't contain her pleasure. He really was good at this.

His gaze intensified then as he studied her. His smile died slowly, and he searched her face. One hand rose slowly and covered her cheek. He shook his head. "Adrianna?"

"No. Miranda." She put as much emphasis as she could manage behind the words. His eyes narrowed, seemingly roving her face in search of some proof of her identity. She knew of none she could show him, none he would understand, at least. Instead, she reached for a spare toothbrush and proceeded to give him another lesson in modern hygiene. He actually seemed to enjoy brushing his teeth. But even while he did, he kept his eye on her.

She shut off the water in the now-brimming tub, forcefully dismissing the lingering effects of his probing stare. She pointed. "Bath. Rolf, take a bath." He didn't move and Miranda reached up to his already unlaced tunic and tugged it slightly. He seemed hesitant, but he pulled the tunic over his head. She nodded. "Good, now the shirt." She touched the shirt as she had the tunic. "Take it off."

His eyes glittered with some secret amusement, but he obeyed, removing the shirt and standing bare-chested before her. Her gaze fixed itself to that muscled wall of chest, then moved downward over rippling pectorals and a tight, flat belly. His skin was utterly hairless, with one exception. Sparse golden hairs inches below his navel traveled a narrow path downward, disappearing into the waist of the leggings he wore.

The raw masculinity of him hit her like a solid blow to the solar plexus. She couldn't seem to draw a deep-enough breath for a moment, or to take her stupid, stubborn eyes from his bare skin. With great effort, she forced herself to meet his gaze. She saw his knowing look and perhaps a hint of something else, as well. She was humiliated and looked away. She pointed again to the tub and repeated her earlier words. "Take a bath, Rolf." Her throat was tight.

Lifting one foot he very nearly stepped into the water, leggings and all.

"No!" She gripped his arm, her discomfort momentarily forgotten, and drew him back. She shook her head in exasperation. She knew perfectly well his people had been fond of bathing. He must know what she asked of him. Honestly, there was so much to be done and so little time. She tugged at the ties that held his leggings tight at the waist.

His hand covered hers, stilling it.

She looked up slowly and gasped. His eyes blazed with some unnamed, but obviously potent, emotion. In a second he'd closed his arms around her, drawing her flush against his warm, naked chest. She brought her hands up, trying to put some space between them, but to no avail. His body forced hers to bend backward as he leaned over her. His mouth came so near to hers she could feel his every breath. He whispered, "Adrianna..."

"No," she began, but too late. His mouth claimed hers with ferocity. He forced her lips open and thrust his tongue inside, ravaging her mouth the way his people had ravaged the coasts of England in his time. One hand moved upward, to cup the back of her head and hold her face more tightly to his for his brutal, punishing kiss. His other hand dropped lower, cupping one buttock and squeezing hard, painfully hard. His hips moved against her and she felt the rocklike arousal pressing into her stomach.

She forgot that he was confused and out of his time. She forgot that he was huge and could probably break her neck with one hand. She only knew a rush of panic and a need to escape. She lifted one shoe-encased foot and slammed it down hard on the top of his bare one.

His hold on her relaxed with his shock, just enough for her to avert her face from his. She tried to pull free of him, but he gripped the front of her shirt and shot a rapid stream of Norse words at her, words she was glad she couldn't understand. Anger rose to displace her fear. She brought one hand stingingly across his face and tore loose from him, her blouse ripping down the front as she did.

And then Rolf froze. For a long moment he stood stock-still as if paralyzed. When she dared glance up, she saw that he was staring at the dark, berry-colored birthmark on the upper half of her right breast. It was the size of a silver dollar, but kidney-shaped. He blinked twice, shook his head and lifted his gaze to her face. Whatever he saw there seemed to confuse or confound him. He scowled harder than ever and released her at once.

She glared at him, despite the hot tears she felt pooling in her eyes. She fought down the waves of nausea that swamped her, but to no avail. The fear had been too real, and she whirled, falling to her knees in front of the toilet, and violently emptied her stomach.

For a moment she remained there, trembling. His hands on her shoulders urged her to her feet, and then he pressed a damp cloth into her hands. She couldn't look at him. She swiped at her face and flushed the toilet. She pointed to the tub. "Take a bath." The words were bitten out. She turned and left the room without another glance at him.

She went downstairs and into her father's study. She reached up to the top bookshelf and pulled down a tiny key.

It opened the top drawer of the tiger maple desk, the drawer where Russell kept a tiny, antique derringer. Miranda checked to be sure it was loaded and was about to tuck it into her pocket when she paused and thought hard. Could she really take the life of a nine-hundred-year-old, living, breathing Viking? Hiding his existence from her colleagues was bad enough, but to destroy him utterly? She slipped the gun back into the drawer and pushed it closed. She didn't think he'd attack her again. If he did, she'd drive a letter opener into his leg, or give him a dose of hair spray in the face. If he got to be too much to handle, perhaps she'd have to let someone else in on the secret. For now, though, she'd manage on her own. She wouldn't allow her nightmarish memories to drive her to act hastily.

She looked down at her torn blouse and exposed skin, and felt her stomach heave once more. She fought the sensation and this time she won. She supposed she ought to be grateful for the birthmark she'd always hated. Apparently Adrianna, whoever the hell she was, didn't have one.

Rolf bathed. Did the woman wish so badly for him to bathe, then bathe he would, no matter that it seemed a waste of his time. Bathing was the last thing he wanted to do. He was eager to learn more about this place, this land, the language... the woman.

She was not Adrianna.

At least, not the Adrianna he'd known. He imagined himself a fool to believe she might not be Adrianna at all. He suspected he might well be about to entangle himself in another web of her deceptions and lies. But even when she'd been trying to win his trust, Adrianna had never treated him as gently as this one had. She'd never looked at him as this one had.

Miranda. Adrianna's twin? Or one of her plots? Her emotions showed clearly in her eyes. When she looked at him in awe, it was clear. Equally obvious when she felt concern or worry on his behalf. And then, just before he'd mauled her like an angry bear, she'd looked at him with desire so potent it had altered her stone gray eyes to the color of molten steel. A desire so real he could feel it emanating from her.

He thought of the Adrianna he'd known, of her deceptively innocent eyes and ready supply of tears. Her true emotions, did she have any, had never been apparent. Never.

But Miranda, or whoever she was, had desired him. Unlike the woman in his past, she'd been unable to hide or alter the feelings that showed in her eyes.

No doubt he'd cured her of that malady. It wounded his pride that she would react to his kiss so violently. It stung to think he repulsed her to such a degree. But as he soaked in the hot water that eased the burning aches in all of his limbs, he gave the matter more thought.

If she were repulsed by his kiss, he had only himself to blame. For at the time he'd been certain she *was* Adrianna. He'd been certain the longing so plain in her eyes was no more than another of her tricks. He'd been angrier still that his body had felt a response to her heated gaze and trembling touch. Would he never learn? He'd thought to teach her a lesson she would not soon forget. Oh, he guessed he'd done that and more. Only the lesson had, perchance, been taught to the wrong woman.

He shook his head slowly and closed his eyes in disgust. He supposed it was well to know where he stood with the woman. She'd done nothing but show him kindness and patience, despite her fear and dislike of him. If she was Adrianna, perhaps this was her method of atoning for past wrongs. If she was not Adrianna, Rolf was deeply in her debt. True, he hadn't requested her hospitality, had no idea how he'd come to be in her house, and could not find the words to ask her.

No, not any more than he could find the words to explain his actions. Or should he feel the need to explain? For even were she not the woman he had believed her to be, she had been the cause of his lust. Did she not desire to enflame his passions, why had she looked at him as she had? Why had her eyes moved scorchingly over his body?

Rolf had never lifted a hand to a woman in his life. And now he'd done so. Twice, he reminded himself, whether she'd been deserving of it or not. He knew he'd been far more rough than was decent. Even were she Adrianna. He was far bigger than she was and had ten times her strength.

Mayhap she would order him away now. Mayhap she would summon her man to defend her honor, did she have one. He'd seen no evidence of it thus far. Was she alone in this place, then? What of Steinholf, her *faðir*? Of Kalf, her *broðir*? *Nei*, the more Rolf pondered it, the less sense it made. He'd known those men, known them well. Never would they have allowed their cherished and spoiled Adrianna to travel alone to such a strange and remote place.

For more than an hour he soaked and he considered. When the water became too cold to allow such laziness to continue, he put an end to it. He rose slowly from the water, stepped onto the floor and reached for the huge, soft "towels" she'd left for him. After a vigorous rubdown he conceded that he felt a good deal better. He glanced around in search of his clothes, disconcerted to find she'd taken them. What was he to wear?

He anchored the towel around his hips and went in search of her, wondering how she would react to him now. How could he make his peace with her when he knew so few words of her language? Were he only able to locate some writings, or find his way into a room filled with talking people. He had endless questions and he must gain answers.

He moved over the softly padded floor of the corridor and down the stairs. He found her in the largest room, the one with the overly stuffed seats all around and the curious box that seemed to be the focal point. She had several packages spread on the largest seat of all and was pulling garments from them. She looked up quickly when she sensed him standing there.

Her eyes wavered beneath his gaze and he saw, for a moment, the fear within them. But she averted them quickly. She reached over to the small wooden stand in front of her and picked up a large knife with a long, curving blade. She studied the item for several moments then caught his gaze again as she slowly replaced it, at her side this time. She'd delivered her message without uttering a single word. Did he touch her again, she fully intended to run him through.

Rolf glared at the blade and then at the woman. She thought to tame him with threats, did she? To frighten him? *Him?* The notion infuriated him. Not that he thought her capable of doing him harm. She could have no chance to outwit or outfight him.

"Come here, Rolf."

He heard the words and committed them to memory, yet still wondered at their meaning. She used her hands to explain, and repeated the words. Rolf moved nearer, spying his sword and sheath leaning against a small table. He made no move to pick them up. He could reach for them quickly enough should the need arise. That is, should some enemy burst in upon them. To deal with her, he'd need no more than his two hands. Possibly one.

She handed him a small garment, colored like cranberries, but he only stared at it, frowning. Surely she did not intend that anything so small go anywhere on his body?

Sighing, she bent over and demonstrated the way to slip one's feet through the two small openings. She handed him the garment once more, saying the word, "underwear."

Rolf lifted his brows as he took them from her. She nodded. "Put them on, Rolf."

He shrugged, hooked a finger beneath the knot in the
towel and jerked it free. She turned her back to him at once.
He awkwardly stepped into the underwear and pulled it up.
The garment fitted like a second skin, and he supposed
when she turned back to face him that she must not be
pleased. She could see as much of him with the garment in
place as she would have been able to without it. Her eyes
wandered downward only briefly before she quickly adjusted her gaze and handed him something else.

They reminded him of heavy, outdoor leggings. But they
were blue and of a sturdy fabric he did not recognize. He
pulled these on and learned they were called jeans. They
had no string at the opening. There was only an odd metal
contraption with countless tiny teeth. He peered at it.

"Zipper," she told him. She hesitated, then finally
squared her shoulders and stood very close to him. Too
close, for her scent filled his nostrils at once. She grasped
the little piece of metal on the zipper, her hands so near to
him he fought the urge to cover them with his, and to press
himself against them.

Thor save him from his foolish notions! How could he
continue to desire the one who'd so betrayed him?

She pulled the zipper upward. He smiled, distracted for
a moment from her charms by the cleverness of the device
as he watched her fasten the button at the top. Her fingers
seemed to burn him as she touched his skin. When he
looked into her eyes once more he saw how it disturbed her
to stand so near to him, to touch him. Truly, Adrianna or
not, she feared him now.

He walked away from her, trying to accustom himself to
the odd feel of the snug-fitting jeans. He moved this way
and that, bent at the knees and straightened. He finally
came back to her, nodding. He liked them very much. But

why, he wondered, was she showering him with gifts after threatening him with a blade?

She gave him little time to wonder. She handed him a shirt made of a soft, pale blue fabric with buttons down the front. He put it on and fastened the buttons, discovering more at the wrists and fastening them, as well. She fixed the collar to her liking, her touch light and fleeting upon the skin of his neck, then she quickly stepped away. "Sit down."

He did. He'd learned that particular phrase in the kitchen.

She remained standing, obviously still not wishing herself too close to him. She handed him two soft white items, and after inspecting them, he deduced their use and pulled them onto his feet.

Rolf was beginning to feel decidedly uncomfortable accepting not only food and shelter, but now bright new clothing from a woman he'd treated roughly, despite that she likely deserved it. Despite even that she'd brandished a blade large enough to eviscerate him.

He thought it over and decided he ought to offer some form of payment. At the very least as a balm to his pride. He rose, ignoring her questioning glance, and crossed the room. Through the door and down the stairs he went, to the place where he'd first awakened to find her standing over him. He hurried into the room where he'd lain, knowing she was on his heels, no doubt wondering at his intent. Rolf snatched up the pouch that held his coins and turned.

Miranda stared, curious and perhaps afraid. Rolf caught one of her hands in his and turned her palm upward. He dropped the pouch into her hand, met her gaze for one moment, then moved past her and back up the stairs.

Chapter 4

Miranda fully intended to tell him exactly what she thought of his manhandling . . . just as soon as she could communicate with him. She'd combed her father's library, and found a volume on runes with a page translating runic symbols to their equivalent English sounds. She also dug up an Old Norse, or Islensk/English dictionary. The language had changed little over the centuries since Rolf had spoken it.

He used the brush she'd given him, while she gathered the necessary things from the study for his lessons. She tried not to notice that he looked like he'd stepped off the pages of some bodybuilder magazine. She fought with the fool inside her, who kept picturing him garbed in the finest red satin, or worse yet, bare-chested, astride a mighty black stallion, charging into battle, his muscled arms effortlessly wielding his broadsword, his golden hair flying behind him. She managed to dismiss the vivid image just before she groaned aloud.

He no longer shot her suspicious, angry glances every few seconds. She thought his gesture—giving her his pouch of coins—might have been as much an apology as a payment for the clothes. But she didn't want to think about it. She didn't want to think about him at all, certainly not as a man. Only as an experiment. One she was selfishly keeping all to herself. After his assault upstairs, she thought she would have gladly dropped this entire idea, but she knew she couldn't. For her father's sake, she would see this through. He would no more want to see Rolf incarcerated in a government-funded lab than she did. She had started on this insane path and she would follow it to the end.

She ardently denied that, on some primal, animal level, the memory of his tongue ravaging her mouth sent shivers up her spine.

When Rolf saw the books, his expression changed completely. His eyes rounded and he very nearly smiled. Miranda stifled a feeling of shock as she watched him pick them up, one after another, riffling pages, scanning them. For a moment she was so enthralled watching his reactions that she forgot she was supposed to be afraid of him. If she had any sense, she would be. She wondered, briefly, why she wasn't.

"Rolf?" He looked up reluctantly. She held out the book in her hand, opened to the rune chart. That would help him with pronunciations more than anything else. When he immediately sat down, carelessly sweeping boxes and tissue paper and the rest of his new wardrobe onto the floor to clear himself a space on the sofa, she almost laughed at his enthusiasm.

She gave him time to study the chart while she busied herself writing the words for every object in the house that came to mind. She included all the words she'd taught him so far, and soon he was moving nearer to her on the sofa, peering over her shoulder, watching every stroke of her pen.

She fought the sudden surge of awareness that made her want to move away and move closer, all at once. From the corner of her eye, she glanced up at him. He wasn't in a lecherous mood just now. He wanted to learn, wanted it desperately from what she could see. And slowly, tentatively, she began to teach him.

She no longer worried about the police officers outside. If they came in and saw him, she could cover it. At least he looked more like an ordinary man now. No, she thought vaguely as he repeated the word he'd just painstakingly written down. Ordinary, he'll never be. Suffice it to say, he might pass for someone of this century—unless he reaches for his sword and starts offing with someone's head.

She could handle the police. She knew she could. But what if they asked how he got in? What if someone wanted to see the dead Viking in the basement?

I'll handle it. Whatever comes up, I'll simply have to handle it.

He could no longer believe her language was one of her own creation.

It was nearly dawn and Rolf saw that her eyelids were heavy. She must be very tired, yet she refused to rest. She seemed as eager to teach him as he was to learn. With each stride he made it seemed a little more of her dislike of him disappeared, to be replaced by a growing excitement. Each minor goal he reached filled her with delight. She seemed amazed at the amount he'd learned in a single night.

He wished he could tell her that he'd learned many, many languages in his lifetime. Some called him the wisest man in Norge. He'd made it a point to study and learn the languages of every people he'd encountered and he'd encountered many. He hadn't been overly boastful of this knowledge. It wasn't that he was more intelligent than others that made learning new tongues come so easily to him, he knew. He'd always believed it had to do with his ability to remember things precisely after seeing or hearing them only once.

His gift with languages was legend among his people. He'd been much admired for it...until the judgment and his subsequent exile. Despite his position, Adrianna's word had not been doubted. She was the daughter of a jarl, after all. The only thing that made his exile bearable, he recalled, had been his ambition to learn the ways and the words of the elusive Skrælingar of Helluland.

That thought brought a flash of memory, men struggling with the broad-striped sails of a dragon ship. The feel of icy sea spray stinging his face. The riotous rocking of the vessel, and the hideous howl of the wind. The sudden snap of the mast, and the sound of tearing fabric. The water closing its frozen hands over his body, dragging him downward, covering his head, filling him—

Thor, help him, he wished to recall that last voyage! He remembered clearly only what preceded it—Adrianna's treachery. He remembered hoisting the sails, and setting out across the North Atlantic. He remembered his thoughts about the Skrælingar, and his burning anger toward Adrianna for her betrayal. Had not Kalf been his friend, he'd have fought her before the council. He'd have found a way to prove his innocence did he have to fabricate it, as the wench had fabricated his guilt. But to do so would have only served to transfer his sentence to his friend, for Adrianna had accused Rolf only to free her *broðir*. Besides, with Knut dead, and his sworn enemy, Magnus on the throne, proving Rolf's innocence would not have bettered Rolf's predicament. Knowing Rolf was loyal to Knut would only give Magnus more reason to banish him.

Exile would have been Kalf's death. He was strong neither in body nor spirit. And knowing how he'd been used and made a fool of, Rolf had too much pride to make the knowledge public. So he'd set out in exile, seething with anger and bitterness, and his memory faded where the open sea began. Except for these puzzling glimpses.

Her head fell softly upon his shoulder. Her hair touched his cheek, and he could smell its delicate scent. For an instant he stiffened, surprised by the intimate nature of the contact. Then her deep, steady breathing came to his ears and he knew she slept. He tilted his head slightly to the side so that he might brush his face over her satin hair, just once. Despite all of Adrianna's faults, she had been beautiful beyond compare. She still was, for surely, he thought, no woman could look so much like her and not *be* her. By Odin's justice, he wished her heart were as lovely as her body, her face.

Gently, Rolf moved her from him, easing her down to the cushions even as he rose to make way for her. She continued her slumber undisturbed. He took the decorative blanket from the back of the large seat—sofa, he revised in silence—and placed it over her. For a long moment he studied her, the way her auburn lashes rested against ivory cheeks and the peculiar pouting lips, slightly parted and moist. He reached to the back of her head and silently, carefully, removed the pins she'd replaced in her hair, one by one. When he finished, he threaded his fingers through the fiery curls and shook them softly, until they framed her face and cloaked her shoulders.

She made a very tempting offering this way, no animosity in her eyes, no fear. Rolf stood straighter and turned from her. He had much to accomplish while she slept and he would do none of it here. Did he remain in the presence of this sleeping temptress he would continue to stare at her until she woke, he knew he would . . . at the least. At most, he might bend nearer, gather her pliant body up to his and taste her sweet lips once again.

He pawed through the garments he'd tossed to the floor and found the odd-looking shoes made of cloth, with laces up the front. The bottoms were soled in some strange material he'd never encountered before, like leather but thicker, with an odd, elastic texture and a funny smell. He pulled these onto his feet and then gathered a selection of the books she'd brought to him.

In silence he moved through the house and located other printed works with softer covers and larger pages. Some were glossy, others larger still, unbound and all black-and-white. He used one of the sacks she'd taken his clothing from to hold the volumes, wincing at the rustling sound it made as he packed them inside. But she didn't stir. Lastly, he belted his scabbard around his waist. He would not go in peace without Vengeance at his side.

He longed to go without. He had no notion of what land this might be, with its magical speaking devices and flameless lamps. He suspected he was not in the North, for he felt warm and saw no fire to account for it. He peered through the door in this room and saw the men beyond it. Her servants, he assumed. Or guards of some sort. He felt no desire to attempt conversing with them, given his extremely sparse knowledge of their tongue. Instead he sought another exit. He found it in the lower level—a square of glass, surrounded by a frame of wood. He forced it open easily, despite its strong locks, and squeezed through its narrow space.

Miranda woke with the absolute certainty something was wrong. Terribly wrong. Her groggy suspicion was confirmed when she sat up straighter and looked around. There were still books, and page after page of notebook paper filled with her printing and Rolf's. The boxes and bags from Wilson's Big and Tall still littered the floor along with their contents. The only thing missing was Rolf. Her heart sank as her gaze moved toward the coffee table, where the sword had rested. "Oh, God!"

She leapt to her feet and rushed through the house, first into the kitchen and the formal dining room beyond, then back when she didn't find him. She checked the study, then ran up the stairs, calling his name in a hoarse, urgent whisper. She checked all the bedrooms, the bathroom, even the closets. He was nowhere to be found, and panic began to seep through her limbs like ice water.

She took the stairs two at a time and yanked open the front door, half-expecting to see the severed bodies of two police officers on her front step. Both men looked at her, startled. "Morning, Miss O'Shea," one attempted.

She smiled weakly, her gaze surreptitiously—she hoped—sweeping the length of the driveway and the front lawn. "Have you, uh, seen anyone this morning?"

"No, ma'am. You expecting someone?"

"No." She ducked back inside and slammed the door. "Where the hell are you, Rolf?"

The only place she hadn't checked was the basement, and she hurried down there now, scanning every corner. Just when she was sure he'd vanished like mist, she spotted the opened window in the control room. A cool, early-morning breeze wafted in from the sea. Miranda didn't wait to hunt for her coat. She scrambled up onto the counter and slipped through the opening.

He wasn't in sight, at least not on the back lawn. A brisk wind whipped her hair and Miranda hugged her arms and started off for the path that wound through the small patch of woods to Mourning Bay's craggy shore. Please, she thought, please, for God's sake, be here, Rolf.

The dimness of the path added to the chill, but she soon emerged at the other end into the brilliant sunlight. The cries of sea gulls, high-pitched and shrill, came in riotous chorus. Whitecapped waves rolled in toward the shore and crashed against the rocks below. The aroma of dewy grass and the ever-present fishy smell filled the gradually warming, morning air. Rolf sat with his back against a tree, facing the sea. He had an open book on his lap, and she knew from the intense concentration on his face that he wasn't just looking at it. He was reading it. His long golden hair moved now and then with the breeze.

She gaped for a moment. Then she twisted her wrist to see how long he might have been gone. Seven a.m. She'd fallen asleep about three hours ago. She moved nearer and was able to see the astonished, confused way his eyes sped over the lines of print.

She stepped on a twig and it snapped. Rolf was on his feet in a single motion, sword drawn and poised for battle. The book fell to the grassy ground, its pages fluttering in the sea breeze. Their gazes locked. Then slowly he lowered the sword, slipping it back into its sheath. Rolf bent, picked up the book and held it out to her. He shook his head. "This . . . not my world."

She closed her eyes slowly and opened them again. "No."

Again the book was allowed to fall from his huge hand. He took a single step forward, gripped her shoulders and searched her face. "*What* world? How I am here? Why?"

She swallowed her fear, only to have it replaced by a heartache for what he must be feeling. She knew she had to explain to him what had happened but she was still unsure she could make him understand. God, that he could speak to her at all, so soon, was nothing short of amazing. "Rolf, come back inside. I'll explain."

He released her shoulders all at once and spun away from her, his fingers pressed to his temples. "I have seen . . . ships." He gestured toward the rolling sea. "Small, fast, they . . . roar." Again he turned, one arm extended toward the ribbon of pavement visible beyond the house. "Wagons, no horses. Move alone. The speed..." He shook his head, looking as if he'd like to scream.

Miranda's fear vanished. She put her hands to his big shoulders and turned him to face her. "It's all right, Rolf. I can explain it... all of it."

He shook his head. "I know not... ex-plain."

"To make you understand."

He closed his eyes and the pain was so apparent on his face, she felt it as well. "Make me un-der-stand. *Minn faðir? Minn broðirs?*" His eyes opened once more, scanning hers in desperation. "Tell me!"

"I will, Rolf. I will." Without thinking, she reached up and gently stroked his face, as if calming a frightened animal or reassuring a lost child. "First, know this. I am your friend. Do you understand? *Vinur þinn.* Your friend."

His eyes narrowed. "I have no... friend..." He lifted both hands palms up. "... here."

"Yes, you do." She took his hand, tugged him toward the path. "Come with me, Rolf. Please." He sighed heavily, but he followed.

They clambered back through the window. He didn't question it. Up the stairs, across the living room. She drew him into the study, all the while wondering just where to begin. She was still in shock over his ability to speak to her, to understand her.

She paced toward her father's desk and was sharply reminded of where Russell was right now, how precarious his situation. She needed to see him this morning, but they wouldn't let her in before nine, anyway. Right now Rolf was waiting for answers. He stood just inside the doorway, watching her, impatience and frustration clear in everything from his taut, drawn facial muscles to his poised-for-action stance.

"Tell me."

She sighed and looked around her, wondering how to start. She spotted the globe and went to it almost desperately. She turned it slowly with one hand. Pressing a finger on Norway, she glanced back at Rolf. "Do you know what a map is? A drawing, showing—"

"*Já.* I know this. Go on."

She blinked at his sharp reply, but made herself continue. "This is called a globe. It's a map of the world." His brows drew together. "The world, Rolf, is round, like a ball."

He shook his head. "Round, yes. But flat. Not a ball."

"It's true. Men have traveled all the way around it."

Looking doubtful, he drew nearer and studied the globe with perplexed interest. "This world of yours... truly is ball?"

She nodded. "Look. Here is Norway... Norge." She moved her finger to Denmark, then Sweden. "Danmark," she pronounced carefully. "Svíaríki." He stared in what she thought was disbelief.

For a long moment he studied the shapes of Western Europe and Scandinavia. Then he sought her gaze. Lifting two hands to encompass the room, he whispered, "And this?"

"It's called the United States." She moved the globe, tracing a path across the Atlantic and stopping at the east coast. She pressed her fingertip to coastal Maine. "We are here." Slowly she moved her finger north, all the way up through Canada and across Hudson Strait to Baffin Island. "Here is where I found you."

"Found me?" He looked up quickly at her words.

"Yes. What were you doing there, Rolf? Why did you sail so far from your home?"

His face darkened and his eyes seemed shuttered all at once. "There was storm," he said, avoiding her question completely. "*Minn drakkar...* went down. I see Helluland..." He shook his head, pressed fingertips to his temples. "I do not..."

"Remember," Miranda supplied.

He nodded. "*Já.* I only... remember... cold, cold water, pull me down." She closed her eyes slowly, feeling the horror of what he'd been through crash over her like one of those frigid waves. "I think...*já*...I see Skrælingar on the land."

Native North Americans, all of them, be they Inuit or not, were Skrælingar to Rolf. So the Eskimos of Baffin Island—his Helluland—had seen the ship go down. "They thought you were a god," Miranda said slowly. "The Skrælingar, we call them Inuit, called you 'the god who rode the seas upon the back of a dragon.' They'd never seen a ship like yours, Rolf."

Rolf nodded and he gazed at her intently. It was obvious he was listening, believing her. "They pulled you from the water. They took you to a cave..." He frowned, obviously not sure what the word meant. She scanned a shelf, located a book on geology, and riffled the pages until she found an illustration of stalactites and stalagmites. She showed it to him and he nodded in understanding. "A cave, inside the earth." She laid the book down. "They put you on a bed of stone, and they left your sword, your battle-ax and shield at your feet."

"Ax and shield? The ones below?" She nodded.

"*Nei,* not mine. Only this..." His hand closed on the hilt of his sword.

"Maybe the ax and shield were found and thought to belong to you."

He nodded thoughtfully. "Skrælingar take me to cave. Why?"

She sighed and licked her lips. "They believed you were dead."

"Fools!"

"Rolf..."

He waited, and when her gaze fell before his, he gripped her shoulders. "Tell me all."

"I'm trying. It isn't easy." Tears welled up and blurred her vision for no other reason than the emotional blow she was about to deliver. "You were not breathing, Rolf." He shook his head, and she demonstrated, inhaling loudly, exhaling. "Breathing." She placed her hand on his chest, just over the pounding beat. "Your heart...was silent."

His eyes narrowed and he grimaced in disbelief. "I am not understanding. You say, I *was* dead?"

"Today we know that a person is not really dead when the heart and breathing stop."

"How one is dead, and not dead!" He whirled away from her, stalking across the room. "You make stories!"

"It's not a story, Rolf, it's the truth." She drew one hand over her eyes in frustration and moved behind the desk to sit down. "There is life in the brain. This is fact. We know it beyond doubt." He turned, looked at her from across the room. "The brain..." She tapped a forefinger on the side of her head. "A person is not dead until the brain dies, too." She struggled to find simple words to explain a complex concept. "The brain dies only a little at a time. Bit by bit, you understand?"

He walked slowly back toward her. "Go on."

"If the brain is cold, the tiny bits do not die. They are preserved. The cold water kept your brain from dying, though your heart had stopped."

He drew a long, deep breath. "You say much...difficult to believe."

"I'm just getting started." She bit her lip, knowing he hadn't caught any of that rapidly spoken comment. "There is more, Rolf, that will be even harder to believe."

"Harder than dead, yet not dead?"

She nodded. Rolf moved forward and took a seat in front of the desk. With one palm-up gesture he invited her to continue, and she did, despite the pain she saw in his eyes, the frustration.

"As you lay in the cave, a glacier—that's a large mountain of ice—moved over the cave's mouth and sealed it. Your rest was undisturbed for a very long time."

His eyes went stony and held hers prisoner in an iron grip. "How long?"

Miranda's throat went dry. She cleared it and forced herself to continue. "The Inuit who put you there have died. They told the story to their children. When their children died, it was passed to their grandchildren, and so on. My father heard the story and decided to try to find you."

Rolf got slowly to his feet. "How long?"

"Please—" she held up both hands "—I need to explain first. My father is a scientist. So am I. We study people of long ago, how they lived. We teach the young people all that we learn. Do you understand?" He nodded, clearly impatient with her.

"There is much to be learned from the past. Things that can help the people of today. We spent years searching for you, Rolf. And then we found you, in that cave. We brought you here to study you, to learn from you. We, too, believed you dead."

Finally, it seemed, she had his interest once more. "Is not right, to bring dead man, *útlendur,* to your house."

"We didn't see you as an outsider, Rolf, only as an incredible discovery. We put you in that room below and kept it very cold to keep your body from ruin. But something went wrong. The room grew hot, and as your brain warmed, it began to work again."

"My brain began . . ." His eyes widened, searching her face. "Upon the hard bed, below. I . . . remember this. I cannot . . . breathe. I believed . . . I am in the sea." He frowned, struggling for the memory. When it came, she knew, because his gaze suddenly narrowed, growing so intense it felt as if it were piercing her. "You...your lips on mine. Your breath in my..." He pressed his fists to his chest.

"Lungs," she supplied. "Yes, I blew my breath into your lungs. I saw that you were alive and couldn't breathe. So I helped you to breathe."

He muttered in his own tongue, then confronted her angrily. "Was not it enough to give shelter, food?" He tugged at the shirt he wore with a thumb and forefinger. "The garments I wear? I owe to you my life, as well?" He slammed a fist on the desk in his anger, and she jumped to her feet.

"You asked me to tell you all of it."

He glanced at her with an impatient shake of his head. "You have my...thanks, lady. Only I like not...owing to another. To you, I loathe it."

She blinked back the effect of the stinging remarks. "Because I look like Adrianna?"

He glared at her. "I am unsure you are not Adrianna. She would much like such a game, to cause my mind to leave me."

"You know I'm not Adrianna. You saw the mark on my breast."

His smile was bitter. "You put it there...with the juice of berries, I think." He came around the desk, his anger like a burgeoning flame in his eyes. "I will see again, this...mark you give to your breast."

It was the way he reached for her that induced the panic. It was so menacing. She wouldn't allow herself to be abused that way. Not again. In one quick movement, Miranda jerked the desk drawer open, yanked out the tiny gun and brought it up between them. "If you touch me again, I will kill you."

He stopped short, staring down at the gun, head tilting slightly to one side. "What is this?"

"It is a weapon far more deadly than your sword, Rolf Magnusson. It shoots a small lead ball at such speed the human eye cannot see it. It will put a hole through your body faster than a blink of the eye."

He lifted his gaze to hers. "I do not believe."

"Take another step, and I'll give you all the proof you could ask for."

He shook his head. "You lie not so well as once you did, Adrianna." He took a step toward her, and Miranda closed her finger on the trigger.

Chapter 5

The shot blew a hole in the globe and sent a shredded mess of litter to the floor on the other side.

Rolf jerked in shock, his eyes widening when he saw the damage. He exclaimed in his own language, but Miranda was beyond paying attention to him. She heard only the two police officers shouting, then the door crashing open and her name being called. She'd panicked and maybe ruined everything in the process.

"Oh, hell. Rolf, listen to me. You have to hide, quickly. I'll explain later, but for now you have to trust me. If those men see you here I'm going to be in a lot of trouble. Please." As she spoke she hustled him toward the closet in the rear of the room. She opened the door and shoved him inside.

"Rolf Magnusson hides from no man."

"Those men have guns, too," she told him quickly. "Please, I'm begging you, just stay here and be quiet." She tried to close the door, but he held it open with arms of iron. She glared at him. "Don't forget how much you owe me, Rolf. I saved your life."

That seemed to do the trick. He stepped farther back and let his arms fall to his sides, but as she pushed the door closed he caught her wrist. She looked up fast, hearing the approaching steps of the officers. "These men...they mean you harm?"

She gaped for a moment, shocked he'd show any concern at all for her safety, as much as he seemed to despise her. "No. They're here to protect me."

He nodded and pulled the door closed himself. Miranda spun around just as the study door swung inward and the two men came in cautiously, guns leading the way.

She stepped away from the closet, praying Rolf would behave, and shrugged. She offered the men her most sheepish expression. "Honestly, I'm such a klutz. I didn't realize it was loaded." She lifted the gun as she spoke and moved toward the desk, dropping it as if it were soiled.

The officers visibly relaxed, darted each other a speaking glance and holstered their weapons. One spotted the destroyed globe and barely suppressed his laughter. He elbowed the other, who did chuckle.

"You all right, Miss O'Shea?"

She nodded. "I feel utterly foolish, but no harm done."

"I assume you hold a valid permit for that weapon?"

"Actually I don't. My father does, though. It's his gun. I was just checking on it. I felt a little nervous after the break-in."

The first officer frowned. "Ordinarily I'd have to confiscate the weapon...but under the circumstances..."

"Better let her keep it, Roy," said the other. "You never know."

"Yeah. I have to advise you, Miss O'Shea, that if you use that weapon, you'll be in violation of state law and subject to criminal charges. You understand?"

"Yes, of course. I'm sorry I scared you like that, really."

"Just lock it up and leave it alone and you'll be fine."

"Doing so as we speak," she assured them, opening the drawer and shoving the gun across the desk until it fell in with a loud thunk. She slammed the drawer shut and patted the desk's surface, looking for the key. When she came up with it, she inserted it in the lock.

The police officers nodded, apparently satisfied, and turned to leave. As soon as the outer door closed she rushed to the closet and opened it. Rolf stepped out, replacing his sword in its scabbard as he did. He'd been ready to come out fighting at a moment's notice, she realized a little shakily.

She sighed and shook her head. "That was close."

Rolf stood rigid, searching her face. "Never have I seen such weapons," he murmured.

"Things have changed. You were in that cave for a very long time, Rolf."

"I do not wish to believe this story you tell...." His gaze moved over her face. "You are so like Adrianna ... yet different. Your eyes, so ... hers showed only what she wished. And she ... never so feared my touch."

"I don't fear it, I just don't want it."

"*Nei*. It was fear I saw in your eyes. I believe you rather would kill me, than—"

"We were talking about you."

He ignored her. "Have you had a man before me, lady?"

"Do you want to know how long you rested in that cave or not?"

His intense blue eyes probed her soul one last time before he shrugged and looked away. "You may tell me. I may choose not to believe."

"Fine. Do you know what a year is?"

"Four seasons. I read many books while you sleep."

"Do you know our numbers?"

"Numbers?"

She returned to the bookshelf, scanned it and finally found a book with sufficient pages. She opened it, and showed him the page number in the upper right corner. "Numbers."

"Ah. Those I have begun. I will learn numbers today."

She hesitated, frowning at him. "How do you learn so fast?"

"I remember all things. Your words. Say them and they are locked forever in my...brain. I know more tongues than any man in Norge."

"Your English seems to improve by the minute."

"I do not know...minute. But I learn more with every word you speak. Now, these years, each four seasons. How many years did I rest?"

She bit her lower lip. She flipped the pages over until only the cover remained open. "If each page is a year..." She captured pages one through nine hundred between her fingers. "You slept for about this many pages."

He stared at the book, then at her. He shook his head slowly, taking a step from her. "*Nei*. You lie. You are Adrianna! You—"

"Who ruled England when you went on that last voyage, Rolf?"

He watched her warily, as if she were going to try to trick him somehow. "Knut died the year of my voyage. As I sailed, his *sonir* by Emma, Hardacnut, claimed the throne, as did his *sonir* by Ælfgifu, Harald Harefoot."

"England is now ruled by a woman, Queen Elizabeth."

"Lies!"

She shook her head, again scanning the books, grateful for her father's endless library. She found the one she wanted, and opened it to the pages listing the rulers of England and their lines of descent. She set it before him and he looked as she pointed. "Here is Knut . . . the year he began ruling is here. One thousand seventeen. These are the rulers who succeeded him, beginning with Harald Harefoot. Knut's wife, Emma, was exiled then. Harald died in one thousand forty—five years after you left Norway—and Hardacnut took the English throne without a fight. While he was busy in England, though, Magnus of Norway took Denmark, if my history lessons serve me. Hardacnut died after only two years on the throne, and England was then ruled by Emma's son from her first marriage, known as Edward the Confessor."

Rolf's brows lifted. "The *sonir* of Æthelred?"

"Yes. Look for yourself. There have been many on the English throne since then." She pushed the book closer toward him and Rolf took it, studying the pages solemnly for a long moment.

"Stodva!" He closed the book with a bang and turned from her. "You seek to drive me from my mind. Only Adrianna would—"

She came around the desk, putting a hand on his huge shoulder though he refused to look at her. Her throat burned as she realized what he must be suffering and she hated to add more to the burden, but she had no choice. "You know I'm telling you the truth. You wish it wasn't so and you are angry that all of this has happened. But you know it's true. You saw the little ships without sails and the wagons without horses. These things did not exist in your time and you know it. There is still more I have to tell you, so you have to stop arguing with me and listen." She paused, swallowed hard. "I'm sorry. I know this is hard for you, but we have to talk about these things now."

He shook his head, so much dejection in his eyes she could hardly bear to look at him. "If what you say is true, *mínn* . . . my *faðir*, my *broðirs*, all are gone. Therefore, it cannot be true."

She felt a hot tear brim over and run down her cheek. Her heart constricted in her chest. She hated inflicting this kind of pain on him, would hate doing this to anyone. Given her own father's precarious hold on life, she knew too well the loss Rolf was feeling. "I'm sorry, Rolf. I'm so very sorry."

He looked up, saw that tear and spoke slowly, his gaze penetrating. "Adrianna has tears for no one. Tears to her are...were...weapons." He squeezed his own eyes tight, tilted his head back. "Odin, why? Thor...speak to me! Do you yet live or have all the gods died, as well?" She gulped back a sob that only seemed to tear further at the man's heart.

"*Nei*, you are not Adrianna, are you?" He faced her once more.

She shook her head. "No, I'm not."

He looked at the floor. "So I must believe." He walked slowly from the room, scattering bits of the globe as he went. He reached the sofa, sat down and let his head fall back so he faced the ceiling, though Miranda knew he wasn't seeing it. "Speak what you must. I will hear."

She had followed him into the living room and now stood near the sofa. Why were her instincts telling her to sit beside him, to pull his head to her breast and cradle him there? She swallowed hard and remained standing. "There are other scientists, Rolf. Many, many others. I have not let them know that you are alive. They all believe your cold body still lies below on the table. They all want a chance to look at you, to study you."

"They will be saddened, no doubt."

"They would be overjoyed if I told them. But I'm not going to. Even my father doesn't know."

He frowned and brought his gaze level with hers. "Why?"

"They would give anything to find out how you were preserved for so long, without harm done to your mind or your body. Nothing like this has ever happened before."

"I will tell them all I can."

She shook her head. "They wouldn't question you. They'd lock you up in a room like the one downstairs and they'd study you. They'd cut small pieces of your flesh to see if they were different. They'd want to look inside you, inside your brain."

He grimaced. "What sort of men do such things to one another?"

"They would say it was for the good of many, to learn all they could about you."

"I will not allow it. Do they try to take me, they will know the sting of Vengeance."

"What is Vengeance against the weapons of today?"

He looked at her for a long moment. "Yet you think to keep me from them?"

"I *will* keep you from them." As she spoke she felt the firmness of her conviction. She saw his eyes narrow upon her as she went on. "Rolf, we cannot let them know the Norseman below has been revivified. We have to say you are of this time, a friend, visiting me from Iceland."

He released a short burst of air. "And what tell you them do they wish to see the Norseman below?"

"That someone came here while I slept and took him away."

"*Nei.* It is you who are losing the senses. Who would believe such a tale?"

"Rolf, before you woke, someone did come here while I slept. I don't know who it was or what they wanted, but my father was hurt as he struggled with them below. He thought they were after you. That's why the men stand guard outside right now." He only frowned. "It will be easier to convince them of the lie than it would be for them to believe the truth, Rolf. They would never guess it, because they believe such a thing impossible.''

Rolf stubbornly stood his ground. "I hide behind no woman. I will stand and I will fight."

"No." She stood fast and held his gaze. "My father spent years trying to find you, and so did I. After all that I will not allow you to simply let them take you, and make no mistake, Rolf, they would take you, or kill you."

He closed his eyes and sighed. "Better had you left me in the cave of the Skrælingar, Miranda." When he looked at her again, he seemed resigned. "I will do as you ask for a time. You have given me much, Miranda. I pay my debts."

Rolf felt as if the very life force had been drained from his body. He'd lost so much in such a short time. His exile had been disheartening enough, but at least he'd known his family had been alive and well. Now... He shook his head. It was very difficult to believe they were gone. Gone like early morning mist rising from an emerald sea with the sunrise. Gone, along with everyone and everything he'd ever known. The pain was nearly crippling.

Oddly enough, it seemed this woman, this...Miranda, shared in his pain. She seemed genuinely distressed at having to reveal so much to him all at once. The glimmering sheen covering her storm-cloud eyes had to be genuine, for she fought against it, repeatedly blinking, pressing her knuckles to tightly closed lids, and averting her gaze altogether.

She touched his shoulder, shaking him from his reverie. Her eyes had darkened to the color of deep slate as they dug their way into his. "Are you all right?"

"I am a warrior."

She frowned, making three tiny crescents appear right between her auburn brows. "That is not an answer."

"But it is," he replied. He consciously straightened his spine and sought to busy his mind with something else. "You have spoken of your *faðir*. Where is the man, that I might thank him?"

He didn't miss the flicker of agony in her eyes, though she turned from him quickly enough. "He is in the hospital. That's a place where our sick and wounded are cared for. We have men and women called doctors. These people spend many years learning to heal and they work at the hospitals to tend the unwell."

He nodded. She spoke slowly, carefully, as if speaking to a dull-witted child. He would not correct her just yet, however. Better that he understand every word. "He is ill?"

Her words sounded forced through a small space. "He was hurt the night someone broke in here. He was struck on the head, and his weak heart gave out."

No wonder the woman seemed to be in pain. The idea of her facing some unknown intruder, alone except for a weak parent, sent a jolt through Rolf. "You were here, then?" Rubbing her shoulder with one hand as if unconsciously, she nodded. So, she'd got the ugly purple bruise at the hands of this intruder. He wondered at her valiance. Did she fight to protect him, though she thought him dead? No, more likely the woman fought in defense of her *faðir*. She must love the man greatly. "We will go to this . . . hos-pee-tal. I would speak with him."

She nodded, her mind clearly elsewhere. "Yes, we do need to go to the hospital this morning. But it is not a good idea for you to see him just yet. It would be a shock for him to see you. Shock is not good for a weakened heart. It might kill him."

Her words made perfect sense. Truly she was learned in many things. "I would not wish to harm him. We go now? I am eager to see more of your world."

She shook herself from her lingering worry and faced him. "First, we bathe. In this time it is customary to do so every day, rather than once a week as your people preferred."

Rolf frowned. "I do not know 'week.'"

"Seven days is one week. Each day has a name. Today is Tuesday."

"Tuesday," he repeated slowly. "But this 'seven . . .'"

She held up the corresponding number of fingers. "Seven."

"Ahh."

She looked thoughtful for a moment. "Our biggest problem is going to be the two police guards outside."

"Dismiss them," he told her quickly. "Are they not your servants?"

Her lips curved upward into a slight smile. "No, I have no servants. They serve the public, like soldiers. Their job is to protect all who live here, and to stop the lawbreakers. They stand watch in case the intruder I told you about tries to come back. The problem is, they'll know you didn't come in from outside and they'll wonder where you did come from."

Rolf studied her as she paced and pondered. Odd it was, to have a mere woman taking such pains to ensure the safety of a powerful fighting man.

She snapped her fingers. "Okay, I have an idea. You'll have to listen carefully and do exactly as I say, or it won't work. That photographic memory of yours will come in handy."

He shook his head. He did not know "fo-to-gra-fik" but he would look it up in the large book of words. It eased his own wounded spirit to see her with color in her cheeks. He thought she might not be fully aware of it, but she was finding joy in the challenge of keeping her secret. It showed in her eyes. A glitter of excitement, a silvery sheen. "Tell me what I must do," he said.

She spoke firmly. "Not until after we shower and change. I'll use the bathroom first." She waved a hand at the chaos that surrounded them. The boxes and wrappings that had held his clothing littered the floor, along with many more garments. The books and papers they'd used in their studies last night covered every surface, along with writing implements of various types. "While I'm gone, you can clean up this mess."

Rolf felt his eyes widen. "You say you have no servants, lady. Do not think to make me your first."

She bit her lip and drew a long breath, as if exercising great restraint. Finally she spoke. "You have no servants, either, my friend. And in this century, women do not spend their time picking up after men. We each serve ourselves. Those are your clothes."

He nodded, wondering whether she spoke true, or was simply being difficult. "Those," he said, pointing, "are your books."

Her silken brows rose in two perfect arches and she seemed to chew her inner cheek. Finally she shrugged. "Fine. I'll take care of the books. You take care of the clothes...and their wrappings. There's a guest room at the top of the stairs and to the left." She turned to walk up the stairs without awaiting his answer.

"Miranda." At his voice, she stopped and faced him, one hand on the rail at her side. "Which way is this...'left?'"

She smiled, fully this time, and came down the two steps she'd ascended. To his surprise she reached out, clasped his hand in hers and lifted it. "This is your left hand." She gripped the other, her skin supple and warm. "And this is your right. If you face this way, then that's left." She gestured as she explained. "But if you turn around, left is that way. You see? Left is always to the same side as this hand."

She still gripped both his hands and she stood close to him. Her head came to the center of his chest and she had to tilt it back to look at him as she spoke. Rolf found himself suddenly very sorry he'd made her afraid of his touch. Now that he knew she was not Adrianna, he wished for the opportunity to erase his earlier behavior. Of course, he couldn't be certain it would matter. After all, she'd vomited. Such a response certainly indicated a strong aversion to him, one that might have been there even had he not handled her roughly.

Besides, he reminded himself harshly, he could not be certain yet that her heart wasn't as corrupt and unreliable as Adrianna's had been. If he'd learned anything from her betrayal, it was not to give his trust again so easily. A beautiful face and ivory skin did not necessarily reflect the soul they hid beneath them.

But if it were true that one could see a person's soul through the eyes, then hers must be pure. Pure and complex and very, very deep, he thought as he searched the gray orbs thoroughly. He noticed for the first time the thin ribbons of jet radiating outward from the pupil, and the deep, dark blue outline surrounding the storm gray irises. Her lashes were long and thick, a sable color, but tipped with auburn like her hair, giving them the impression of radiance. He did not recall Adrianna's eyes as having been so lovely, or so deep. He felt as if he were being drawn into them, as if he were in a quagmire from which he had no desire to escape. As if...

She blinked and lowered her head and the spell was broken. She released his hands and stepped back. "I, um, we have to get going."

"Miranda," he began, with no idea what it was he wanted to say.

She glanced up at him with a plea in her eyes that silenced him at once. She gave her head an almost imperceptible shake, taking another step away from him. Her eyes were wide and smoky with confusion. He lifted one hand, palm up, a silent entreaty, for what, he knew not.

She turned and fled up the stairs. Fled, yes, it was the appropriate word. She ran from him as if he were the wolf, Fenris, or the Midgard serpent. Or the Plague of the North, he thought grimly. Which, indeed, he was.

Chapter 6

She had to push it out of her mind. Her plan to fool the police wouldn't work if she were not convincing. And she couldn't be convincing if she were distracted by that freak storm of sensation she'd felt an hour ago.

God, but it had been powerful. The way he'd stared into her eyes as if he were searching for something. Not just searching, desperately searching. For a brief, unsettling moment she'd felt herself longing to give him what he sought, though she didn't even know what that was.

But it was foolishness. She felt sorry for him, that was all, and naturally she wished she could ease his pain. Any decent person would feel the same.

She licked her lips, checking quickly over her shoulder to be certain Rolf was out of sight in Russell's study. Between the two of them, they'd restored the living room to order. No sign of his presence remained. She gripped the doorknob in a white-knuckled hold.

"Miss O'Shea?" The officer on the right bobbed his head at her. "Anything wrong?"

"It's chilly out here. Why don't you two come on in for a coffee break?" They hesitated. "The house is so empty with Russell in the hospital."

That did it. Flanders and Morgan couldn't have been more willing to share a cup of coffee with her. She led them straight to the kitchen where the machine was just gurgling its last few drops into the carafe. Miranda casually closed the door that led to the living room and proceeded to pour the coffee. She rattled the cups and silverware, walked heavily, and deliberately scraped the chairs over the kitchen floor, all to cover any noise Rolf might inadvertently make slipping outside.

She thought she'd covered everything. She'd told him step by step what to do, what to say. Knock on the door, act like a friend she hadn't seen in a long time, shake the officers' hands when she introduced him. She'd even given him one of her old suitcases, stuffed with enough towels to give it convincing weight. Nothing could go wrong. What cause would anyone have to doubt her?

Still, when his oversize paw thumped on the front door as if trying to knock it from its hinges, she came out of her chair as if it had suddenly burned her. Both officers, she noted in alarm, leapt up as well, hands on their pistol butts. A little breathlessly, Miranda attempted, "I wonder who that could be?" Weak, pathetic and ineffective.

"Whoever it is, he doesn't sound friendly," Flanders said.

"Better let us get it, ma'am," Morgan added.

They made their way cautiously toward her front door. Flanders stood to the side, while Morgan reached for the knob. They glanced once at each other. Flanders nodded and Morgan jerked the door open.

Rolf's brows arched up. He'd obviously been expecting Miranda to open the door. She quickly inserted herself between the two officers. "Rolf! Why, it's only Rolf, my dear old friend from Iceland." The officers looked quizzically at each other, then at her.

Meanwhile, Rolf stepped inside, dropped the suitcase and swept Miranda into his arms, lifting her off her feet so high she found herself looking down into his face with her hands braced on his shoulders. He whirled her in a circle, moving forward as he did, stopping only when they were in the center of the room. "How good it is to see you," he blustered. He lowered her slightly. "Have you no kiss for your dear old friend?"

She fumed. The officers had heard him, of course. They stood near the door, which was still wide open, wearing amused expressions. "Damn you to hell," she muttered through grated teeth. She lowered her head and brushed her lips over his. He caught the back of her head with one hand and captured her lips between his, holding them there with gentle suction. His hand on her head exerted minimal pressure and she could have easily pulled away, except that it would look strange to the police. His lips moved against hers, around them, in an oddly sensual way. He sipped at them as if they expressed some succulent fluid, as if he were thirsting for it. Then he broke the contact and set her on her feet.

As she slid down the front of his hard body, Miranda felt a bit light-headed and breathless, though she wasn't sure why. Nerves, she supposed. It wasn't often she tried to pull one over on officers of the law. Rolf kept one arm around her shoulders, an act she was simultaneously angry about and grateful for. She wasn't sure she'd be too steady on her feet just now without the added support.

Facing the officers, she tried to keep her voice even. "Officer Morgan, Officer Flanders, this is Rolf Magnusson, a friend and, uh, colleague."

Morgan stepped forward and extended a hand. Rolf looked at it blankly for a moment and Miranda jabbed her elbow into his ribs. He held her so close to his side she was certain neither of the other two noticed. Rolf extended a hand and clasped Officer Morgan's. Morgan grated his teeth through a forced smile and his jaw went tight. After he took his hand away, he repeatedly flexed and bent his fingers. With a studious frown at Morgan, Flanders refrained from offering his own hand for similar punishment.

God, she wished this were over. "More coffee, anyone?" Oh, beautiful. That would speed things up. Why not invite them for breakfast?

"We'd better get back outside, ma'am. Thank you, anyway."

"Nice meeting you, Mr. Magnusson," Morgan added. They both nodded at Miranda before ducking out the door and closing it behind them.

She pulled herself from beneath the weight of Rolf's arm, and faced him with her fiercest scowl. "I didn't say anything about kissing me! What did you think you were doing?"

"You did not vomit this time." The man had the audacity to grin, twinkling those dimples at her until she felt like slapping him.

"Where did you learn a word like 'vomit'?"

"I looked it up," he quipped, still grinning.

The oversize jerk. "Not that it's any of your business, but I only vomit when I'm assaulted."

"I do not know 'assaulted.'"

"Mauled," she clarified. When he still frowned at her, she added, "forced."

"Forced?" His face changed. The smile died utterly. "I have no need of such methods. And you—" he stopped midsentence, his frown deepening, his gaze boring into hers "—you speak as if you—"

"It's time to go. Visiting hours begin soon." She reached for her jacket, a casual black suede one with brown leather patches at the shoulders and elbows. "I've explained to you about the car. Just follow my lead, and remember, act like you've been getting into cars your whole life. All right?" She glanced up at him, but he still had that speculative look in his eye.

"Have you had a man before me, lady?"

Miranda stiffened, averting her gaze. She didn't like the question and it was the second time he'd asked it. She had no intention of answering, no matter how many times he asked. Moreover, she'd like to know what the hell he meant by that "before me" part. "Do you want to ride in the car, or not?"

"I wish to know the answer to my question." He waited, but she turned her back and strode out the door. He followed her in silence, but she felt those piercing eyes on her the whole time.

She leaned over to open his door, then moved around to the driver's side. He settled himself on the small seat, dwarfing the car with his size. A Toyota simply wasn't designed with the Viking warrior in mind, she thought. He stiffened a bit when she fired up the engine. She'd explained what to expect, but she supposed riding in a car was still quite an ordeal. He must feel the way she would if she traveled by way of the space shuttle.

"Watch me," she told him as she reached for her seat belt, pulled it around her and snapped it in place. "Now you."

He glanced over his right shoulder, pulled the belt around him and snapped it in easily. He lifted his brows. "This... car. It moves so fast one needs be restrained?"

She chuckled in spite of herself. "No, Rolf. These are for safety, so if I have to stop fast we don't crack our heads on the windshield." She tapped the windshield when she said the word. "Are you ready?"

He nodded, his jaw still tight, and watched her as she shifted into gear and pulled out of the driveway. His hand clutched the small armrest as the car began to move forward, but gradually he relaxed. By the time they reached the hospital he was asking questions. Was the pedal what controlled the speed? Did the wheel choose the direction? What was the meaning of the numbers behind the glass on the dashboard? Why did she stop at the red light? He had extracted a promise from her before they entered the hospital corridors. That she would teach him to drive. And soon.

The Intensive Care waiting room hadn't changed overnight. She led Rolf to a padded seat and pressed him into it. "I'm going just beyond those doors." She pointed. "I won't be long." She hated leaving him alone in the waiting area while she went in to see Russell, but saw no alternative.

"Do not trouble yourself, Miranda. Go, see your *faðir*. I will wait."

She nodded her gratitude and hurried through the double doors and to her father's room. Dr. Fenmore hadn't been available for an update and she had little idea what to expect. She braced herself and walked in.

"Miranda." Her father tried to sit up when she entered, but she quickly went to his bedside, pressed her hands to his shoulders, and kept him from completing the motion. He looked terrible, his face a sickly gray, his skin drawn, bloodless.

"Easy, Russell. I'm right here."

He shook his head slowly. "Go home. Stay with the find. I told you—"

"It's under guard. Stop worrying."

He relaxed, but only slightly. "Did you do as I said... read my journal?"

She pressed her two fingers to the center of her forehead. "Actually, not just yet. I was planning to do it right after this visit."

"Not the blue one, Miranda." He spoke very slowly, taking deep, uneven breaths between the words. "The real one. The real one."

She frowned. "I didn't know you had more than one."

He only nodded.

"Russell, what are you talking about?"

"I... kept it secret. I wasn't sure. Didn't want to be... laughingstock... but I thought he might be... the one ... they called ... Plague. You know. We had no proof."

He stiffened and drew one arm up to his chest. Miranda's heart leapt and she reached for the call button on his pillow.

"No... listen." He touched her hand, stopping its progress. "I'm... not going to... make it. Been... like this all night. Exhausted."

"Don't you dare say something like that to me, Russell O'Shea!"

He shakily held up one hand to silence her. "Can't... talk so much. Can't breathe well." Again, he drew the deep, unsteady breaths that so frightened her. "It's all in the journal... the real one. So much more. Th-the plunder. Still hidden." He grated his teeth, seemingly forcing himself to continue despite her protests. "So much more to do, Miranda. You have to... finish. Finish it!"

She closed her hand around his and reached for the button with the other. "I'm calling a nurse. You're getting worse by the minute." She depressed the button with her thumb and released it as panic seeped into her heart.

"I waited for you," he rasped. His eyes brimmed now, watering from the force of whatever pain he must be in. He sighed, shook his head. "Wish that damned...elephant...would get off...my chest."

She thumbed the button once more, holding it down this time. "Hold on, Russell. Someone will be here any—"

He winced suddenly and the EKG monitor leapt unnaturally.

"To hell with it, I'll get them myself." She rose to go to the door, to shout the halls down until someone came to help him.

"Wait!" He gripped her hand with surprising strength.

She faced him just as the door burst open and three people in white seemed to rush through at once. One gripped her shoulder. "Daddy?" She couldn't help calling out to him like that. She did so now as his grip on her began to relax. She did so in a voice choked with emotion and with eyes suddenly blurred by tears.

"Remember..." He gasped the words now, and Miranda struggled against the hands that were pulling her from his bed. Her hand slipped from his. "Jules...Verne." His hand went limp. His eyes closed. The EKG's intermittent beep became a steady tone, and as she was pushed toward the corridor, Miranda lurched toward him, fighting the hands that held her back.

"No. Don't make me leave him," she heard herself plead. "Daddy!" None too gently, she was forced into the corridor despite her loud protests. "No! Let me go!" The door was closed in her face. Miranda cried her father's name as if she could somehow hold him to her, even though she felt him being torn away.

Chapter 7

Neither the heavy double doors nor the countless men and women in white coats stopped him when he heard her cry out. In less than a heartbeat, Rolf skidded to a stop before her. She stood beside a closed door, her back pressed to the whitewashed wall. Her eyes were dilated to an unnatural degree, the gray no more than a narrow band around the black of her distended pupils. She stared straight ahead, but he was certain she wasn't seeing. Her breaths came quickly, as if she'd just run a great distance. Her lips trembled and her skin was pale.

Confused, Rolf looked around her. He'd thought someone must be attacking her when he'd heard her scream. Now, though... He looked through the small pane of glass in the door beside her, and he became aware of the steady, high-pitched tone emanating from within that room. More of the white-garbed individuals hovered around a bed, so that the still body upon it was barely visible.

Rolf stepped closer, eyes narrowing as he watched the urgent movements of the people in the room. Then the activity slowed. One man's gaze lifted to that of his colleagues and he slowly shook his head. A woman turned, touched a button, and the irritating bleat halted, leaving silence in its wake.

Beside him, Miranda emitted a low, anguished groan, barely audible though he stood very near her. Her knees seemed to dissolve, and with her back still pressed to the wall, she began to slide downward. Rolf stooped quickly, catching her beneath the arms and hauling her up. Even that effort did little good. All of her bones seemed to have melted. Her head hung as if no longer connected to her body.

He knew without being told that the man in the bed was her *faðir* and that he had died. Despite the animosity he'd felt between them, he experienced a stabbing pain in his chest solely on her behalf. Without thinking about it, he pulled her limp body tight to his hard one, and he held her.

He felt her trembling in his arms and he wished in vain for words of comfort to spring to his lips. Instead he remained silent, for there were no words that might help her now. He understood her grief. He still felt his own, spawned by her revelations this morn. For the moment he thought the best he could do for her was to take her from this place. But as he stepped away from her, her arms shot around his waist and her face pressed once more against his chest.

His shock at her action was exceeded only by his shock at the response it stirred within him. A rush of emotion shot up from his toes to the nape of his neck, shaking him. For just an instant, he felt an instinctive urge to protect her. Normal under the circumstances, he presumed. His size and strength alone would be enough to stimulate this protective instinct. Was it not natural for the strong to defend the weak? With her in this heightened emotional state, the impulse became even stronger. But it was nature working. Nothing more.

He battled the sensation and won. He managed to hold her tightly to his chest, to press soothing hands to her trembling shoulders and back without feeling a thing in his heart. He had no intention of allowing himself to fall prey to the wiles of another Adrianna. The feminine weapons of weakness and tears, be they genuine or false, would no longer work upon Rolf's emotions.

The man he'd noticed before, doctor, he reminded himself, came through the door, his expression grim. When his hand touched Miranda's back she stiffened. Her chin rose slowly and she squared her shoulders as she turned to face him. To Rolf's surprise, her eyes remained dry. Wide, yes, and overly dilated. But dry. She had not shed a tear.

"I'm sorry, Miranda. We did everything we could."

"I know." Her voice was low, but level. "I'll make arrangements for—" she cleared her throat "—everything as soon as possible."

"Are you all right," the doctor asked. "Do you need anything? A sedative?"

Rolf didn't know what a "sedative" was, but Miranda shook her head indicating she did not require one. When she turned to start off down the corridor, her hand closed on Rolf's upper arm. She held to him tightly, though he had the impression she was not aware of doing so. She kept that rigid posture all the way through the double doors and into the waiting area he'd previously occupied. Then she froze and her grip tightened still more, as four men rose from their seats and approached them.

Without intending to, Rolf took a step that put him between her and the group. They certainly looked harmless enough. An aging gentleman with a dignified air and snowy hair and beard, a skinny youth who wore eye shields like

Miranda's and an adult male, of average size, with brown hair and eyes. On second thought, that third one had a decidedly belligerent gleam in his eye. The fourth man was dark of hair and powerfully built. It was he who came forward, moving past Rolf as if he had no fear... or no sense. As Miranda stepped from behind Rolf, the man put his hands upon her arms and searched her face.

Rolf cursed himself for acting hastily and on instinct yet again. Next he'd be doing battle on her behalf.

The two other adult men eyed him warily, while the youth seemed to turn to stone in his tracks as his jaw dropped.

"It's all right, Rolf," she said in that deep, calm tone she had no business using after what she'd just witnessed. She stepped away from the dark-haired man's touch, and nodded to the one with the pointed white beard and snowy hair. The man was too thin, save a paunch at his middle. "This is Professor Erwin Saunders, head of the archaeology department at Beaumont," she told Rolf. "I've told you about him." She smiled shakily toward the youth. "And Darryl Watters, a student. He is, that is, he was..." Her voice seemed to thicken and she stopped speaking all at once.

Rolf's gaze left the youth to focus on Miranda. Despite her determination to stand tall, she was slipping. "Your father's assistant. You spoke of him, as well." Rolf nodded toward the boy, who still gaped. His skin had gone milky and he looked as if he would faint. "I am Rolf Magnusson. I am visiting from Iceland." He recited the lines Miranda had taught him, giving her time to recover her composure. This latest revelation of her character stunned Rolf. Tears and weakness he could witness and remain unmoved. But steely strength and stubborn pride? These were qualities he'd become accustomed to finding in warriors, not women.

To his surprise, the one called Saunders extended a hand to him. Rolf lifted his own hand, to find it gripped firmly and pumped twice. "Good to meet you, Mr. Magnusson."

Miranda cleared her throat and faced the man nearest her, the one who felt it his right to touch her so freely. She glanced once at Rolf before her gaze flew back to the man. "This is Fletcher Travis, archaeologist, numismatist and all-around genius. It's been so long..." She shook her head, blinking rapidly. "Russell would have so loved to see you again, Fletch."

The man, this Travis, frowned suddenly. "Miranda? Is he—"

Rolf watched her. She met the man's gaze squarely, chin lifting still higher. A convulsive spasm moved in her throat. "He's . . . gone."

Travis put his arms around her and hugged her, but only briefly. Saunders lowered his head, eyes closed, while the youth, Darryl, finally snapped out of his stupor. He covered his face with one hand and turned away from the others. From the look of things, Rolf thought the boy was crying, but he couldn't be certain. The fourth man, the belligerent one whom he had yet to meet, seemed unmoved.

Saunders wrapped Miranda in a firm embrace the moment Travis released her. She hugged him in return, but, Rolf noted, she didn't bury herself in Saunders the way she had in Rolf's arms. She hadn't clung to Travis in such fashion, either, and for that he felt inexplicably glad.

"I can't believe...when? Is there anything I can... You'll take some time off, of course...and I... Oh, Miranda, I am so very sorry." The old man stammered and it was difficult for Rolf to follow his words, but the meaning was clear.

"Under the circumstances, Professor Saunders, don't you think it would be in everyone's best interests to move the find?'' The angry man spoke without emotion. ''Miranda isn't going to be up to having hordes of scientists and students, not to mention the press, trooping in and out at all hours.''

Rolf disliked his tone. For though he attempted to sound concerned for Miranda, Rolf heard another motivation behind the words.

''Well, I hadn't thought—'' Saunders began.

''You'd like that, wouldn't you?'' All at once, Miranda's eyes blazed and she took a step nearer the man. ''Just where would you suggest we move him, Jeff? We all know there is only one other place with the facilities to preserve—''

''That's right. We have the facilities at Cryo-Life. You're going to shoot me for that?''

''You're not taking him,'' she said slowly. ''This project was my father's life's work, and I'll be damned if I'll hand it over to you!''

''I'll be there whether you like it or not. C.L. paid dearly for the right to have access to this find, and I'm going to make sure they get their money's worth.'' He took a step closer, and Rolf felt sorely tempted to throttle him. He wasn't certain why. Perhaps the way the man's small brown eyes moved deliberately over her body. ''If you don't mind my presence in your little basement lab for the next twelve months, then I have no objections.''

She blinked, and for the second time since he'd known her, Rolf saw fear in her eyes. The first time had been when he'd brutally kissed her in the tiny bathroom. She tore her gaze from the man's and glared at Saunders. ''Is this true?''

''Your father knew about it, Miranda. It was a financial decision. We needed the funds.''

''So badly you were willing to sell out to a company that exists only to bilk sick people out of their life's savings?''

Her voice rose as she spoke, and the fire blazed again from her eyes.

"We're scientists, just like you," the one called Jeff fairly shouted. "We offer terminal patients an option."

"Hand over your money and we'll freeze your body," Miranda shouted right back. "We don't know how to thaw you out yet without killing you, but don't let a little thing like that bother you. We'll figure it out while you're on ice. What kind of an option is that?"

"Their only option, at the moment. And a find like this one could give us the answers we still don't have. Saunders says it's perfectly preserved. I need to get my hands on a cell sample, see whether there's been any crystallization of the cell walls."

"Not one cell." Miranda forcibly lowered her voice. "Not if I have to stand guard over him myself."

"You really think that would bother me...Randi?"

She turned deathly white when he called her that and one hand came flying upward. Rolf caught it deftly before she could slap the man senseless, as no doubt she'd intended to do. Gently he pulled her aside, while Fletcher Travis gripped the dog by one arm and growled at him, "Get off it, Morsi. She's been through enough. Open your mouth again and you'll lose a few teeth."

"Now, gentlemen, please. We're all on the same team here. There's no need for this bickering." Saunders's soft manner and overly flamboyant use of his hands for gesturing made his words all the more weak.

Miranda ignored them and glared at Rolf as angrily as she had at the other man. "Why did you do that?" She slid her gaze to the hand still gripping her wrist.

Rolf kept his voice low. "Miranda, I know not why you hate the man. Only that you have been dealt a terrible blow and are not thinking clearly."

"I'm thinking just fine, thank you."

"Then why do you argue the fate of a…a find which no longer exists?"

She blinked quickly, then slowly closed her eyes and kept them that way as she released all the air from her lungs. She bit her lower lip and shook her head. "God, what was I thinking?"

"Dr. O'Shea?"

She turned at the young man's call. Rolf wondered how she held on to her composure with all of this hitting her at once. He further wondered about the silent turmoil he sensed between her and the dog, Jeff Morsi, not to mention the closeness he felt sure Miranda shared with Fletcher Travis.

"Your father did know about this," Darryl went on, finally rejoining the rest of the group. His eyes were still damp and terribly red rimmed. "He hated it, but he agreed to it. Said there was no choice. He was planning to tell you about it, but… well, I guess he knew how you'd react."

"Miranda, if you want the find left where it is, I'll respect your wishes," Saunders said gently. "But you have to know we can't delay. We only have possession for one year, and there is so much to be done. The studies need to begin right away."

"Right away," she repeated in a monotone.

"Yes. It would be inhuman of me to expect you to take part at a time like this. I'll take your place, if you like. But we simply cannot delay."

"You… want to begin… today?"

He nodded, dropping a withered hand upon her shoulder. "We can do the initial exam and testing with just the three of us, if it will help. I've brought Travis in to examine the coins that were recovered. He's the best in the field. Russell would have approved. The press release can be postponed until tomorrow, but no longer, I'm afraid. And then the entire archaeology department is going to expect an opportunity to view it." He licked his lips. "You don't even have to be present if you don't want to, Miranda. But I'm afraid we have to begin today."

"Right," Jeff nearly sang. "Cryo-Life has a signed contract with Beaumont. We're to be allowed initial inspection of the find today, and today it will be. We'll follow you home, Randi."

Her head swung around and the glare in her eyes was fierce. "If you ever call me that again—"

"You'll what?"

"What *she* will do should not be your first concern, Morsi." Rolf hadn't meant to step to her defense, but he'd remained silent for as long as he cared to. Regardless of his feelings—or lack thereof—for Miranda, he instinctively disliked the swine. And Rolf's instincts about men were rarely wrong, though his record with women was far less intact.

Rolf drew Miranda with him toward the stairs they'd ascended when they'd arrived. She accompanied him without resistance and when he glanced down, he caught her studying him with a puzzled frown rippling the bit of flesh between her brows.

Chapter 8

"You are tired, Miranda."

She agreed. The pain crushing her chest was damn near unbearable. That she'd known her father's heart condition was severe, that she'd guessed it to be terminal, helped very little. Always the knowledge that he might still be with her if not for the break-in lurked in her mind. It wasn't fair.

"I...want to thank you." She glanced at Rolf as she drove the Toyota toward the house. "You were a great deal of help to me back there."

"I did nothing."

She swallowed hard, her mind going back to the moment when she'd heard that low, steady tone stop utterly and found herself held in those massive arms. He might think he'd done nothing. He would probably never know just how much he'd really done.

"You did, you just aren't aware of it."

He studied her face for a long moment. "You are grate-

ful I stopped you from striking Morsi? Is it for this you
thank me?''

She carefully pasted a stony expression over her face.
"No, I'll never thank you for that.''

"What is he to you?'' Rolf persisted.

Face impassive, or as impassive as she could make it,
Miranda forced words to her lips through a rapidly constricting throat. "Nothing. He is nothing.''

"I think you lie.'' When she looked at him quickly, he
shrugged. "Women do. I am not surprised.''

"You have a low opinion of women.''

"You have a low opinion of Morsi,'' he countered.

"I have reason.'' She returned her gaze to the street.

"As do I.''

She didn't respond to that, but drove in silence, her mind
numb, her soul empty. She felt unreal, like a shell of a person, a hollow plastic mannequin.

"You care for Fletcher Travis,'' he stated after a moment.

"Very much. He is one of my best friends.''

"A friend only?'' He looked at her and she nodded.

"A friend only. We've never been involved romanti-
cally. Why are you so curious?''

He only shrugged and was silent for a long moment.
"What of the boy?''

Miranda turned again and saw the troubled look in his
eyes. "Darryl?''

"He knows, Miranda.''

Still numb, she struggled to speak. "What do you
mean?''

"He was your father's assistant. This means 'helper'?''
At her nod, he continued. "He was with you when you
found me in the cave of the Skrælingar?''

"Yes.'' A slow trepidation made a home inside her and
Miranda was shocked that she could feel it there.

"He looked upon my face?"

"Your face was covered with whiskers. Your eyes were closed. Your skin was like a plaster sculpture. You looked nothing like you do now."

"He knows. Watch his eyes, Miranda, and you will see it there."

She sighed and absently pressed her fingertips into her right temple, making small, brutal circles. "Are you sure?"

He nodded. *"Já."*

"All right. I'll talk to him, find out if he is suspicious." She lowered her hand, but the throbbing in her head continued. "He won't say anything if I ask him not to. He's a good person, Rolf. My father adored hi—" The last word was cut off by a sudden sob that leapt into her throat. She choked on her effort to suppress it and bit on her lip until she drew blood. She blinked away the stinging tears before they could escape and wished her throat would stop burning and spasming.

"Why do you do this?"

"Do what?" she asked, not comprehending.

Frowning harder, he studied her. "You do not behave like the women I have known."

"I'm not like other women." Without meaning to, she'd quoted her father. She hadn't realized just how thoroughly his words had embedded themselves into her thought processes. She wasn't like other women. She swallowed hard. "I am not ashamed of it. Would you prefer it if I fell into a sobbing heap at your feet?"

Shaking his head, he replied, "I dislike tears."

"Tears are healthy. It simply happens I prefer to shed mine in private, as I'm sure you do, as well." She blinked. "I imagine you're feeling the same way I am right now. Or worse. You've lost your entire family, your world."

He averted his gaze. "I am a man. A warrior. I will withstand the loss."

She sighed. "Men feel sadness and heartache as much as women do, Rolf."

"*Nei,* this is a lie."

"You can deny it to yourself, but not to me. Men have spent centuries denying they had emotions. Today we know better. Men have even been known to cry when they're hurting."

Rolf's face hardened. "Never will you see Rolf Magnusson spill tears like a woman!"

She shrugged. "And you ask me why I'm not crying. Sounds like you understand already."

He frowned across the space of the car's interior at her. She studied his face and saw the sadness in his eyes. She wondered how much of it was his own, and how much was there strictly for her loss. She was certain part of it was for her. She knew he must be feeling a pain nearly identical, if not more intense, than her own, whether he would admit it or not.

She'd pulled the car partially into the driveway and come to a stop as the force of his pain and her own became unbearable. "I know you're hurting, Rolf, and I'm sorry."

"Make the car move, Miranda. The others come."

She glanced into the rearview mirror and saw two bigger, sleeker cars waiting in the street with their signal lights flashing impatiently. She finished pulling into the driveway and out of the road. They pulled quickly in behind her.

As she reached for the door handle, Rolf caught her arm. She paused and looked around at him. His face grim, he spoke in a low, deep voice, slightly hoarse. "I did not say I have no pain, only that I could withstand it." He met her gaze, his own steady. "I know what you are feeling, and I, too, am sorry."

Before she could formulate a response, he was opening his door and getting out. He waited for her to join him before walking to the front entrance. Miranda watched his gaze narrow and wondered why only briefly. All at once she realized that the two officers who'd stood guard at the front door were no longer there. As her stunned eyes moved upward, she noted the pry marks on the door itself. She reached up to touch it and jumped when it swung slowly inward with a slight groan.

Rolf's hand closed on her shoulder to pull her back. He stepped past her and peered inside. "Stay here, Miranda," he whispered, before ducking into the house and vanishing from her sight.

"The hell I will," she whispered right back as she slipped in behind him.

The first sight to greet her as she walked into her living room was that of Officer Morgan's still body, and the pool of deep crimson beneath his head.

Miranda froze. Her gaze remained glued to the poor man's pale face even as the others came in behind her. In some far-off region of her consciousness, she was aware of Darryl gasping for breath, and then the sound of his inhaler. She heard Jeff swear and reach for the phone to call the police, then Fletcher shouting at him not to touch anything. She heard Erwin Saunders's shocked exclamations. Yet she only stopped staring when a pair of large hands gripped her shoulders and turned her from the sight. "No one is here now," Rolf told Fletcher. His grip on her tightened. "Miranda?"

She looked up, saw Rolf's eyes searching her face. He kept saying her name over and over, shaking her slightly. She swallowed hard and forced her mind to obey her commands. She fought the shock that wanted to take control.

"What is happening? My God, is this all a nightmare? Has the world gone completely insane?"

"Take her into the study, Magnusson." Vaguely she recognized Fletcher's confident voice. "You've already got the phone in your hand, Morsi. Go ahead and make the call.

No one touch anything. There might be fingerprints, or some other evidence." Fletcher knelt beside the police officer as Rolf attempted to tug Miranda into the study.

"Police are on the way," Jeff announced, holding one hand over the mouthpiece.

"Tell them to send an ambulance, too. This cop isn't dead."

Miranda felt a whirlwind of confusion sweep through her mind. She felt Rolf's gaze capture hers. She saw something in those blue eyes, something to cling to, to keep her afloat in the sea of insanity engulfing her.

"My God, the find. Saunders, do you think..." Jeff's words trailed off as he raced through the room and into the basement. Seconds later his voice came wailing back to them. "It's gone! My God, it's gone!" Fletcher and Professor Saunders immediately bolted down the stairs to join him.

Darryl gasped deeply, hoarsely. Then again and again, wheezing more loudly with each exhalation. Miranda finally broke eye contact with Rolf to glance in the younger man's direction. He struggled to lift the inhaler, but dropped it. His wide eyes remained on Rolf as he fell to his knees, patting the carpet in search of the medication.

Rolf released Miranda and knelt beside him, closing one hand over the inhaler and handing it to Darryl. He took the shaken student's forearms and helped him stand, then eased him into a chair. "You are ill? What is it?"

The youth kept looking up into Rolf's eyes while he fitted the inhaler to his lips and sucked two spurts of medication into his lungs. Miranda forced herself to move forward. "He has asthma. It affects the breathing, Rolf. That's a drug that makes it better," she explained, calmly, she thought, given the upheaval in her mind.

Darryl's breathing eased. He glanced around him and saw that he was alone with Rolf and Miranda. His eyes still wide, he stared from one to the other and back again.

"It is the shock of finding Officer Morgan that makes you ill?" Rolf asked.

At his words, Miranda came to her senses. What on earth was the matter with her? She moved away, still listening to their conversation, but belatedly attending to the unconscious man on the floor. He probably has a family, she thought sadly, tugging a blanket from the sofa and tucking it around him. A wife. Children, perhaps. She lifted his feet and propped them up with throw pillows, then stationed herself near his head and pressed two fingers over the cut on his right temple until the flow of blood slowed to a trickle. She kept the pressure on and watched his chest rise and fall.

Darryl remained agitated, his eyes never leaving Rolf's face now. "It's you—" He began panting once more, and lifted the inhaler for another shot.

"Me? I cause this fit?" Miranda looked up to see Rolf shake his head. "There is no need, boy. Those who call themselves my friends have in me a loyal protector. Those who are my enemies die mercifully swift deaths." He eyed the youth's awestruck face. "Choose."

"Ch-choose?"

"Rolf, you're frightening him," Miranda attempted, but found her words ignored.

"Choose," Rolf repeated. "Friend or foe, young Darryl Watters?"

Darryl sat up straighter in his chair and held Rolf's gaze. "Friend. Unless—"

"You place conditions on your friendship?" Rolf growled, but so low that no one else could have heard unless they were as near to him as Miranda. "Go on, boy. Tell me of your conditions."

"Unless...you hurt Ms. O'Shea. If you do, then I'll—"

"You will what?" Rolf glared at Darryl, but the slightly built young man glared right back, though his knees were knocking together.

"Rolf, that's enough," Miranda nearly shouted.

"I'll make sure you pay, that's what. And I don't care who or what you are," Darryl whispered. "She's been through enough."

Rolf's expression eased. He nodded his approval. "On that, at least, we agree." He cupped the back of Darryl's head with one large hand for a moment. "I am proud to call such a valiant one friend," he said quietly.

Darryl sighed his relief and tucked the inhaler into his pocket. He continued staring in awe at Rolf, though. "Are you, really—"

"He is, Darryl," Miranda managed to interject. "But you can't say a word to anyone. Promise me. I'll do my best to explain it all later."

Darryl swallowed hard and nodded. "Did your father know—"

Rolf held up a hand and Darryl fell silent. Then Miranda heard the others trotting back up the basement stairs.

"So the only things missing are the body and the sword?" Lieutenant Hanlon paced the living room, a notepad in hand. His forensics team were combing the basement for evidence, while he did his best to make sense of the situation. A large car of white with flashing lights atop it and a piercing cry had carried the wounded man away only moments ago.

When Rolf had searched, in case the swine still lingered here, he'd discovered that Miranda's home had been truly ransacked. Every drawer had been opened and emptied, along with every cupboard and closet. Beds had been stripped, the cushions removed from every seat, the furniture overturned.

"And every file we had on the find," Miranda reminded Hanlon.

"Which is my point exactly," Jeff Morsi snapped. When all heads turned in his direction, he pointed at Miranda. "You all heard her say she'd keep this find to herself if she could. Looks like that's just what she's trying to do."

Rolf rose slowly, his gaze pinning Morsi to the spot. Miranda must be on the verge of insanity with all of this. She did not need this man's insults to push her still farther. Travis was quick to grip Rolf's shoulder. Before he could pull away and lift Morsi by his throat, Miranda leapt to her own defense, surprising Rolf yet again.

"You're a fool, Jeff! The find would be ruined in a matter of hours outside that climate-controlled room and you know it."

"Suppose you have another lab somewhere, one we know nothing about?"

"And what did I use to pay for it? My incredible looks?"

Her sarcasm wasn't lost on anyone in the room, not even on Rolf. Yet he could not, for the life of him, understand it.

Jeff Morsi sneered. "Right, I forgot. You couldn't buy a ticket to Tuckahoe with the entire package, could you?"

Rolf's fist moved so rapidly no one saw it coming, until Morsi was flat on his back with blood spurting from his nose. Lieutenant Hanlon, Fletcher Travis and Darryl all gripped different parts of his body, but he gently extricated himself. Miranda stood motionless, staring wide-eyed at him. "I will not strike him again," he said to reassure them. In truth, he thought he just might.

"Obviously we're all tense here." Erwin Saunders helped Morsi to his feet, and handed him a white linen handkerchief. "I'm sure Jeff is sorry for that remark, and that Rolf is sorry for striking him. Correct?"

Morsi eyed Rolf warily. "Sure. I'm sorry, okay?"

"I am not. And do you insult the lady again you will know the full extent of my wrath, Morsi."

"I imagine Cryo-Life would have the kind of facilities to maintain a find like this one, wouldn't it, Mr. Morsi?"

Morsi, pressing the hankie to his nose where it rapidly became soaked with crimson, glared at the lieutenant. "Is that an accusation?" He spoke like an old woman with a congested nose.

"I'd need a motive, and not being a scientist, I can't think why a company trying to develop suspended animation for sale would want to steal a nine-hundred-year-old body. Maybe somebody else here can, though."

Darryl cleared his throat. "The body was perfectly preserved. If even one viable cell were found, it would be a boon to Cryo-Life. They'd want to take the body apart bit by bit to find what had allowed life to remain..." His voice trailed off. He glanced at Rolf and swallowed.

"Which is precisely why my father and I have opposed allowing anyone from Cryo-Life to take part in any stage of this project, and why we adamantly insisted they should not be permitted to touch the Ice Man, even before we discovered him. It is also why I said what I said at the hospital. I'd sooner let you cut me up than him." As Miranda spoke those defiant words, she slipped her hand into Rolf's and her fingers closed around it. He was so shocked he nearly gasped aloud, but managed to contain himself and simply stare at her in wonder.

"Is that why you hid it, Miranda? To keep me from cutting it up?" Jeff removed the hankie, glanced at it and pressed it back to his nose. "Would you rather see it ruined than benefiting human beings the world over?"

"Human beings the world over would benefit from the proper study of the man, how he lived and what he did. They won't benefit from some witch doctor like you taking the life savings of cancer patients in exchange for dropping their bodies in dry ice when they die."

"Is that a confession?"

"You know damn well it was no confession. It was a simple statement and it was the simple truth. You people at C.L. aren't scientists, you're con artists!" Rolf's free hand came down on her shoulder, gently, but firmly enough to remind her of his presence. It seemed to have a calming effect. She drew a breath, stiffened her spine. "You're welcome to search the house, Lieutenant. My office at the university, too, if you want."

"Searching the house will be necessary, I'm afraid," he explained. "But not because we suspect you of anything, Miss O'Shea. Just to try to ascertain how the specimen was taken out of here and when and by whom."

"You don't even *suspect* she might have done this?" Morsi all but shouted, earning him Rolf's most speaking glare.

"Why should he suspect her?" Fletcher Travis asked. "Russell and Miranda O'Shea have been members of this community and tenured university professors for a combined three decades. It isn't as if they would sell to the highest bidder and skip the country. Besides, I know the passion and the years they've given to this project. Neither of them would risk it just from pure selfishness. They knew years ago they'd be compelled to share the specimen, if they ever discovered it."

"Yes, that's true, but not with me," Morsi countered.

"And I still didn't know I'd have to share it with you, Jeff. Not until you so tactfully broke the news in the intensive care waiting room."

"It makes little sense to me to believe Miranda would wreak such havoc with her own house," Rolf began, his voice level and firm. "It would seem to me the dog was looking for more than just the . . . the speciman."

Professor Saunders paced the room, nodding. "He's right. Anyone who knew about the specimen would have known where to find it, without trashing the house this way, and they certainly didn't expect to find it under cushions or inside drawers. They took all the files on the find. I would assume that's what they were searching for."

"Were the files hidden, Miranda?" Fletcher Travis touched her arm as he asked the question, concern for her etched on his face.

"They were in the file cabinet. Whoever did all this was looking for something else."

Lt. Hanlon nodded. "My thoughts exactly. Now we know Miss O'Shea wasn't responsible. Witnesses place her at the hospital at the same time Officer Flanders got that bogus message saying there was an emergency at his home. The rest of you, I'm sorry to say, don't have such solid alibis."

"I told you, I was alone at home up until I left to meet Travis," Saunders stated.

"And Travis was eating alone at a crowded diner," Hanlon reminded them. "And Morsi was stuck in traffic, and Darryl was sitting by the lake, studying. Any one of you could have clubbed Morgan over the head, forced the door and dragged him inside before trashing the house. Any one of you could have taken the body, but I don't seriously suspect you did. Until I know more, I'd like you all to keep quiet about this. The fewer people who know about it the better, from my standpoint."

"I suppose it's lucky we haven't yet announced the find to the press," Saunders observed.

"You got that right." Almost offhandedly Hanlon added, "An unidentified body turns up, most likely someone's going to call it in. If they think it might be a nine-hundred-year-old body, the citizens will be cutting it up for souvenirs." He nodded when several disbelieving pairs of eyes turned his way in shock. "Oh, yeah. Wouldn't be the first time. People are sick." He cleared his throat. "Professor Saunders, you can go on home if you want. I'll keep you informed. Mr. Morsi, you can leave, too, but I'll be wanting to talk with you later, and maybe take a tour of Cryo-Life, if you can arrange that. Mr. Travis, you won't be leaving town in the near future, will you?"

Fletcher Travis shook his head.

Professor Saunders prepared to leave. "Darryl?"

"I'd like to stay, Professor Saunders. I can walk back to campus later."

Saunders nodded and left, Jeff Morsi stalking out the door close behind him. Hanlon turned to Miranda. "We'll be doing a thorough check outside first, Miss O'Shea. See if there's any evidence of a body being dragged. I doubt they carried it. According to these notes the stiff was as big as—" he glanced around the room "—as Magnusson, here." Darryl choked loudly and spun around until his back was toward Hanlon. Hanlon looked curiously at the young man, then shrugged and stepped outside.

Fletcher peered thoughtfully at Darryl, then shot a speculative gaze at Rolf. His brows crinkled deeply, and he shook his head from side to side as if dismissing some errant notion. He came forward and offered Rolf his hand. "If you hadn't decked Morsi, I would have. He had it coming." He glanced at Miranda. "I'm glad you're here for her, Rolf." Rolf shook Travis's hand, wishing he didn't instinctively like the man. Travis hugged Miranda once more. "If you need anything—"

"I know," she said softly. "Thanks, Fletch."

The moment the door closed, Darryl looked at Rolf and grinned a bit uneasily, still staring at Rolf in awe. "It's true, isn't it. It *is* you."

Rolf nodded. "Do not forget the men downstairs and those just outside," he said gently. "Miranda asked me to keep this secret, and because I owe her my life, I agreed. Only now do I begin to see that she was right to do so."

"Damn straight. Morsi and his bunch would do just what she said they would—cut you to ribbons." Rolf saw now, that in age, Darryl was man grown, but in size and in mannerisms, he still seemed little more than a boy. Darryl pushed his glasses up on his nose. "See, usually when a body undergoes extended periods of conglaciation, there's crystallization damage to the cell walls. Despite the gelidity and the vacuity that preserved you, you must have been exposed to some chemical compound—theoretically a naturally occurring one—that kept your cell walls intact, unaltered. Might've been ingested, or maybe the contact was topical. Either way, they'd kill to know what it was."

"Darryl, easy. Rolf is just learning English. He's not ready for Anatomy 101." Despite the softness of her tone, Rolf thought her voice sounded lifeless.

"You would do well to rest in your bed, Miranda."

"I have too much to do. Arrangements to make, and—" She pressed a palm to her forehead and closed her eyes tiredly. "If I keep busy, I won't have time to think, you know what I mean?"

Rolf did. "I know," he said.

"I have some calls to make. I'll use the phone in the study."

Chapter 9

"**S**he puzzles me."

Darryl replaced the receiver, apparently realizing that his detailed explanation of its use was being largely ignored. Rolf had watched Miranda leave the room and his gaze still lingered on the doorway to the study.

"Dr. O'Shea?"

Rolf drew his gaze back to the youth and nodded. "She has no man. This is common among your women?"

Darryl shook his head. "She's unique. Her father was always telling her so. I heard him say once that a husband would only hold her back."

"Hold her back?"

"In her career," Darryl explained. "Her work, you know?"

"And does Miranda believe this is true?"

Darryl tilted his head to one side, looking doubtful. "I don't know. If she does, she didn't always. She and Jeff Morsi . . . Maybe I shouldn't be telling you this."

Rolf's spine stiffened. He felt a tremor of anger rumble deep inside him, but he knew not why. "I have eyes, Darryl. I can see there is something between them."

Darryl chewed his lower lip and nodded. "Yeah, pure hate."

"Why?" Rolf leaned forward in his chair, his elbows resting upon his knees. His gaze scanned the young man's face. He did not understand his need to know all about Miranda. No, no more than he understood the feelings she stirred within him. He wished with everything in him to take away her pain. Why?

Darryl squirmed in his seat. "They were engaged once. Planning to get married," he hurriedly clarified when Rolf only frowned. "It was two years ago, when I was just a freshman."

"She intended to wed that worm?" Rolf stood without meaning to. He shook his head in disbelief, not merely at the information, but at the rage he felt in reaction to it. "Why did she not?"

"I don't know. Half the campus had theories, but no one really knew. It was . . . like things changed overnight. Dr. O'Shea avoided Jeff like the plague, and he acted like he couldn't stand the sight of her." Darryl lowered his voice. "A friend of mine said that Jeff told him she was frigid. Can you believe he'd say something like that about her?" He looked up at Rolf. "I'm glad you hit him."

Rolf made a mental note to look up the word "frigid" when he had a moment later on. Right now he had to concentrate on keeping up with the conversation, and on keeping his anger in check. Why should he wish to feel the tip of Hefnd sink deeply into Morsi's throat?

Darryl coughed a little. "A lot of people believe she is. She gets jumpy if a man even looks at her, and as far as anyone knows, she hasn't had a date since she broke it off with Jeff."

"Date? What is this?"

"You know, when a woman goes somewhere with a man. Like out to eat, or to a movie or dancing or something." Rolf shook his head, still not quite clear on the date thing. Darryl sighed. "Well, it's like ... In your time, when you met a girl you liked, *really liked,* what did you do?"

"You mean a woman I wanted?" Darryl's face colored slightly, but he nodded. Rolf gave his answer some thought. "I assume you refer to a woman of some virtue, rather than a wanton. In that case, a man would first seek the permission of her *faðir*. He then could visit her on occasion. Perhaps bring some golden bauble to her on returning from *i víking*. He might coax her into going walking, or perhaps take her for a short ride on one of the small ships one day."

"That would be a date," Darryl said, snapping his fingers.

"If that is so," Rolf replied, "it is difficult to believe the story you tell about Miranda. Adrianna was never without a half-dozen men groveling at her feet."

"Adrianna? Was she—"

"A woman I once knew. The most sought-after woman in all of Norge, some said. Her beauty could blind a man to all of her faults. She used men, tricked them to suit her purposes and then sent them on their way. She was an artist at ... I believe the word is ... flirting. She dressed and acted and even spoke in ways designed to entice men, to make them crave that which they could not possess."

"We have a few like that," Darryl acknowledged. "Although I've always figured you couldn't hate them for it. If men are stupid enough to fall for it, then who's really to blame?"

Rolf scowled suddenly. That had to be the oddest point of view he'd ever heard, and yet in a way it made sense. He had believed himself a fool to allow Adrianna to use him, had he not? "So Miranda does not use her beauty in such a way?"

"Use her..." Darryl fixed Rolf with a look that made him feel he'd missed something important. "In case you haven't noticed it yet, she doesn't seem to know she has any. I bet it would never occur to her to use her looks to get ahead. She probably believes she is completely unattractive. The way she dresses and keeps her hair all bundled up, she's managed to convince a lot of other people of it, too."

Rolf thought for a moment. "Yet she walks proudly, with confidence."

"I figure that's because she's good at what she does and she knows it. That's what people see when they meet her. A plain, but keenly intelligent scientist. You don't notice her looks until you get to know her better." Darryl shot a wary glance toward the study, then looked back at Rolf again. "You want to know something else? I think she likes it that way. Those rumors about her being an ice queen. Well, she hasn't said or done a thing to stop them."

"I see." Rolf studied the young man, weighing his words. "I think you, too, have this keen intelligence. You see much."

"I minor in psychology." He shrugged as if that explained everything.

Hours passed. Hours in which the police finished their work and left, and in which Darryl finally ran out of questions for Rolf and went his way, as well. During all that time Miranda had emerged just once. She'd come from the study only to pass through the living room and go up the stairs. Rolf had approved, thinking she'd decided to get some rest. But as he'd patiently told tales of long ago to Darryl, Rolf had begun to feel uneasy.

When he finally was alone, he mounted the stairs and strode purposefully to Miranda's room, only to find her bed empty and undisturbed. He needed only to follow the nearly inaudible sounds of movement to find her.

He pushed open a door and stepped into her father's bedroom. Miranda stood before the bed. Suits of clothes lay spread before her. Jackets, ties for the neck, crisp white shirts, knife-creased leggings. She moved slowly, her head tilting first one way, then another, as she moved a striped tie from a blue jacket to a gray one. She nodded decisively and picked up the gray jacket.

"Miranda, you need to rest."

She didn't react to the sound of his voice. Had she known he was there? But she didn't answer. Instead she brought the jacket close to her face and inhaled its scent. "It still smells like him, you know. That specially blended pipe tobacco, and a hint of Skin Bracer after-shave."

He felt her grief and knew she ought to give it release, but not here, he thought. Not here in this room surrounded by vivid images of the man she had lost. He went to her, took the jacket gently from her hands and laid it on the bed. "Come down with me. You need food and then rest."

"I can't. I can't eat. How can I eat when my father—" She bit off her words as a sob threatened and liquid diamonds began swimming in her eyes.

"Finish it," he instructed. "When your father..."

She sniffed and shook her head, but when she lifted her gaze to meet his the tears came again. "Is dead," she said in a choked voice. "He's dead." The tears spilled over and she turned her back to Rolf. Her hands came up to cover her face, and her shoulders shook with the force of her sobs. When she could draw a breath, she spoke in broken sentences. "Go away. Leave me alone. I don't...need an audience."

"No. Whatever an audience is, I have no doubt it is not what you need." With one decisive movement he stepped next to her and swept her up into his arms. It showed him the true extent of her turmoil that she didn't yell at him or struggle. She remained all but limp, still trying to avert her tear-streaked face from his view.

This proved it. He'd been mistaken about her from the start. He saw that now. She wouldn't use tears as weapons. She was loath even to have them seen. Rolf carried her down the stairs and into the kitchen, where he lowered her into a chair. "Now, cry. It is good, I think."

She sniffed a little, her distress seemingly lessening. "I thought you hated tears."

"These ones are needed."

She blinked and swiped the moisture from her cheeks with the backs of her hands. "I can't cry with you standing there watching me."

"You wish me to leave, then?"

She looked at him for a long moment. "No. I guess I don't."

Rolf turned from her, confused by the tone of her admission, and opened the refrigerator. He removed a brick of cheese and a couple of apples and oranges. "In my village, when a warrior fell, we would join together, his comrades and his family. The women prepared much food, and all would feast the night through in the fallen man's house, telling stories of his heroic deeds until the dawn."

He closed the door and moved to the sink where he located a sharp knife. He began slicing the cheese and the fruits and stacking the wedges on a plate. "I missed the feasting for my father." He pronounced the word carefully, just as she did. "My brothers, as well." He set the filled platter before her and returned to the cold box for milk, and to the cupboard for glasses. "It is the way a warrior gives release to his grief. Mine is still within."

He turned to find her watching him, eyes red, but drier now. "I'm sorry."

Rolf eyed the platter of fruit and cheese in the center of the table and smiled sadly. "It is not much of a feast."

She sniffled and rose from her chair. In a moment she was pulling vegetables and thinly sliced meats from the refrigerator, and stacking these artfully onto what she called kaiser rolls, which she first smeared liberally with a tangy white cream she called mayonnaise. She placed the completed meal onto two small plates and placed one at her seat, one at his.

Rolf sat down when she did, noting with some satisfaction that the anguish in her eyes had subsided somewhat. When she spoke, her voice was almost normal. "You could tell me about your father," she said slowly, "if it would help."

"It would, I think. But you must tell me about yours, as well."

She closed her eyes for a long moment, then blinked them open. "I'll try."

Rolf looked pleased. "Good. And there is one other thing you need tell me, Miranda." His tone was deliberately serious. When her dark auburn brows rose in two perfect arcs, he jabbed a forefinger at the food before him. "What do you call this meal, and how does one eat it?"

Her full lips turned up at the corners. A second passed, and then she laughed very softly.

Midnight. They'd moved to the living room and Rolf had insisted on building a fire in the hearth, though she explained about central heating and argued that it was a warm night, anyway. Miranda rested in her father's favorite chair, a worn corduroy recliner. Her feet were up, her head back, and she held a cup of steaming cocoa in her hands, as Rolf went on with his tale.

"Of course the man was drunk. Had no business being on a dragon ship with that much ale in his belly. But Svein was never known for his wisdom. A fight ensued, and the fool lost his balance and plunged into the icy waters.''

"That's terrible."

Rolf agreed. "Yes. Svein had a wife and seven children. My father threw himself over the side. Had I known what he intended I would have tried to stop him. When I saw him in the water I tried to go in after him, but the other men held me fast. I was but—'' he hesitated, mentally counting ''—twelve years. It was my first time on my father's *drakkar.*''

Miranda brought the recliner down and leaned forward in the seat. "What happened?''

"Father caught hold of Svein. Nearly drowned the way Svein floundered about. Finally my father hit him and, while Svein was senseless, dragged him to the side. A rope was tossed over and both men were brought back onto the ship.''

Miranda relaxed then. "You must have been very proud of him,'' she said softly.

Rolf smiled. "My chest was puffed up for the rest of that trip.''

She tried to imagine Rolf at twelve, but failed. Twelve . . . it had been a painful age for her.

"I see the sadness again in your eyes, Miranda. Tell me.''

She was amazed at his perceptiveness. "I was twelve when my mother died. It was ovarian cancer. By the time we learned she was ill, it had progressed too far. A month later she was gone.''

"And you stepped into her place, cared for your father.''

"Yes. I began working with him right away. It was as if we both needed something to focus on.'' She curled her legs beneath her in the chair and sipped the cocoa. "At first I just helped transcribe notes, but I became fascinated with the work. When I was fourteen I went with him to a site in

England, one of your people's burial mounds. My first dig." She smiled fondly at the memory. "We sifted the dirt, Rolf, and found bits and pieces of the past."

"And you loved this . . . sifting?"

She nodded hard and felt another smile tugging at her lips. "I still do. The sifting, the exploring. It's been my life."

"And what of Morsi?"

"Jeff?" She blinked and averted her gaze. "If you don't mind, I'd just as soon not discuss that with you. It's . . . personal."

"You wished to wed him." It was a flat statement, given without inflection.

"Darryl has been talkative, hasn't he?"

Rolf shrugged. "That you despise him is obvious. His manner toward you suggests . . . familiarity."

"You *are* mastering the language in a hurry."

"I learn more with every word I hear. What did you do to anger Morsi so much?"

"What did *I* do?" She took a deep breath, set her cup down onto an end table and sat up straight. "What makes you so sure it was my fault?" She sighed and rolled her eyes. "That's right, I forgot. You dislike women, don't you?"

"More distrust than dislike. And I did not accuse you of anything. Only asked how you angered him. He looks at you with murder in his eyes, you know."

"Yes. Just the way you looked at me when you thought I was this Adrianna."

The blow hit home; it was obvious in the tightening of his jaw. He was silent a long moment. "You could be her twin," he finally said. "If you resemble her so much within as without, then it is no wonder Morsi would like to wring your neck."

Miranda flinched. "What did she do to you, to make you so bitter?"

"Ahh, we have two questions now. No answers. Will you tell me the truth about Morsi, if I tell you of Adrianna?"

It was Miranda's turn to be silent. In her mind, for just a moment, she felt again Jeff's hands on her, tearing at her clothes, hurting her, hitting her. She blinked rapidly as tears of humiliation burned in her eyes. "No." She rose and moved toward the stairs. "I'm going to try to get some sleep."

"Is it so shameful, then?"

She whirled on him, her face burning with anger. "Oh, yes, it is. So shameful I've never told a soul. Not even my father. But you don't want to hear it. You'd rather sit there and let your cynical mind conjure up a list of crimes to credit me with."

"If you refuse to tell the truth, I am left with little alternative. I believe you were not always the pillar of virtue Darryl sees today."

"And you can judge me for that? You, who spent your life ravaging coastal villages, murdering and robbing and raping—"

Rolf stood so suddenly that Miranda jumped backward. "You know nothing of my life. You cannot read a man's soul by sifting the dirt on which he trod. You cannot know a man by finding some trinket he left behind. And I will not defend myself, or my people, to you!"

Part of her wanted to cringe, or to turn and run. But another part, a part she hadn't realized existed, made her thrust her face upward, closer to his, as he stood towering over her. "Yet you expect me to defend myself to you."

He said nothing. Her back rigid, Miranda turned and walked calmly up to her room.

* * *

Anger. Fury. Rage.

As he slept in the guest room that night, Rolf felt them all invade his dreams. Miranda's face became Adrianna's. For the first time Rolf saw the differences. Adrianna's nose had been narrower and pointed at the end rather than turned up slightly like Miranda's. Her lips were not as full, her eyes duller and rarely showering him with sparks the way Miranda's had tonight. Miranda...insulted and fighting mad at his implications.

Adrianna. He thought of her and of the way, when faced with an accusation, she would simply concoct a lie. He recalled that she'd done exactly that to him. Accused him of murder in order to save her brother. The result had been his exile and very nearly his death. Indeed she had cost him his entire world, his family, everything he'd ever known.

Miranda assumed that, because of what he was, he'd raped and murdered innocents. It hadn't been until that final voyage that he'd—

Rolf sat up in bed, eyes flying wide, fully awake now. He'd been struggling for the memory of the last voyage to no avail. Now, suddenly, it came to him without effort. He'd sailed from Norge a condemned man, *úrhrak,* outcast, and his anger had driven him to behave like one. In a rage he'd led his crew of misfits on a rampage along the coasts of England and the Shetland Islands, along the coasts of Francia and Normandy.

As he thought of it now, Rolf wished the memory had evaded him a bit longer. He'd allowed his anger at Adrianna to completely overwhelm his mind and to command his body. He remembered and he covered his face with his hands and groaned softly.

The clash of steel on steel, the screams of terrified women, the wide-eyed children. Oh, Miranda had been wrong about the rapes and murders she'd accredited to him.

Rolf's upbringing had taught him better than to force himself on a woman, or to kill a man without cause. Men had died, all the same. Those who were foolish enough to fight the Plague of the North. Rolf and his men had swept through the wealthiest villages, taking what they wanted. They'd taken spoil from peoples who had never wronged them, and Rolf's upbringing had taught him better than that, as well.

His father, had he known, would have been appalled. But Rolf had been wronged, vilely so. He'd had his vengeance. He'd plundered his riches. By the time the *drakkar* was on its way across the fickle North Atlantic for the second time, he'd amassed enough gold and silver to suit a king, enough iron to forge blades for an army.

He'd determined he would build his own village in the midst of the Skrælingar, south of the barren wilderness in which he'd secreted his first cargo. In Vinland. He'd trade for what his people needed, trade with the civilized lands within easy sailing distance. If they refused to trade, he'd raid, instead. He'd be prosperous and wealthy, and his name would once again be on the lips of kings, this time uttered with fear of his vengeance rather than with good will for his friendship. His friendship, he'd believed at the time, had meant so little to his high-placed allies that they hadn't even stooped to help him when his life was in peril.

And now, with hindsight, he saw that he'd been wrong to let his rage so fully rule him. Thor had seen that he was punished. For truly, had not the ship been so laden with chests of booty, she might have made it to the shore.

Miranda couldn't sleep. She'd known it before she'd tried but she'd tried anyway. She'd done all there was to be done—chosen the clothes, talked to the funeral director, ordered the flowers, contacted all the relatives she could think of. She'd even arranged to have Erwin Saunders give a eulogy. Her father hadn't been much for religion. Few scientists were.

Still she kept getting the feeling there was something she had forgotten. Something important. It wasn't until her eyelids grew heavy, toward dawn, when she hovered between sleep and wakefulness, that she remembered what. Her father's last words to her had been a plea. Read the journal. The real one. And then he'd said something that made no sense. Jules Verne.

Too tired to think and too wide-awake to lie still, Miranda got up. She didn't bother dressing. She wore an oversize football jersey, a gift from a student, and she figured that was enough. Darryl and Rolf had done an admirable job of picking up the ransacked house while she'd been dealing with the funeral arrangements. They'd left the study, probably so as not to disturb her while she'd been in there. She would have done it herself, but it had seemed such a poignant reminder of her father that she'd had to get out of the room all at once. Now, though, she felt able to tackle it. She wanted to smell the scent of his pipe tobacco clinging to the curtains and the carpet. She wanted to run her hands over the supple leather of his swivel chair, to hear it creak as it used to whenever he sat down or rose, or even moved.

She began by replacing the desk drawers, and sorting through the items that had been dumped from them before they'd been tossed to the floor. Reverently she picked up notepads and pencils, a favorite lighter. The antique pistol lay on the floor, its pearl-inlaid grip marred with scratches. She stroked the tiny gun, tears blurring her vision as she replaced it in the drawer.

The desk restored to order, she moved on to the bookshelves. Volume after volume had been scattered over the floor. One by one, she picked them up and slid them back onto the shelves. When she held in her hands an old edi-

tion of *Around the World in Eighty Days,* she paused, and
her father's odd words came back to her. "Jules Verne,"
she whispered.

She yanked the leather chair closer to the desk, sat down,
and opened the book. Only instead of the pages and illus-
trations she remembered, the book had been filled with
lined sheets, each one covered in her father's spidery script.

She cursed herself for leaving her glasses upstairs, and
didn't want to risk waking Rolf to go and retrieve them.
Instead, she bent the desk lamp's long neck lower, and
squinted as she began to read.

Chapter 10

When she finished an hour later, Miranda shivered.

Her father, never satisfied with the Inuit version of things, had longed to know more even before they'd discovered Rolf in that cave. He'd believed so completely that they would find him that he'd already begun work on the next step. He'd researched every historical account he could find until he'd found one that fit. Of that much, Miranda had already been aware.

The rest of what she found came as a complete surprise to her. The man known as the Plague of the North had not always been so, her father noted. In fact, he'd been considered one of the wisest men in his country. He'd been called upon by Knut the Great not only to fight by his side in battle, but to act as translator in sensitive discussions with other European leaders. He'd been respected and trusted implicitly.

And then he'd brutally murdered one of Knut's emissaries in Norway at a crucial time in history. The man had been beaten to death, and the information he'd been gathering for Knut came to a stop. As a direct result, Knut's archenemy, Magnus, had gained the Norwegian throne.

With his banishment, the once-honorable aid to a great king became the Plague of the North. Lawbreaker. Ruffian. Thief. Murderer.

Here Russell had noted that, despite popular belief, most Vikings did not go around raiding and plundering at random, but only in serious efforts at political and commercial expansion, or colonization of new lands, or in retribution for some serious wrong they felt they'd suffered. A few notorious renegades had broken the code, and history had recorded their deeds more thoroughly than those of their more honorable counterparts.

The exiled man, however, was ruthless. He and his band raided villages along coastal Europe. He robbed people of their stores and their valuables. Then, suddenly, he vanished.

The recorded description of the criminal shook Miranda even though she knew what it would say. From the time they'd found Rolf, she'd known he had to be the legendary Plague of the North her father sought. She simply hadn't been so enlightened as to the details of his crimes. He was described as large, much larger than most men of his time. His hair was golden and worn very long. His face was covered by a reddish gold beard, and his eyes were the blue of a winter sky. He carried with him a magnificent sword known far and wide as Vengeance, and with it, the legend went, he was invincible. He raided in the manner of the Berserkers, wearing no helmet or armor of any kind, and often barechested, as if daring his enemies to strike a killing blow.

At the end of the hand-penned notes, a notation, "C:\ plague," was written in red ink, followed by the word, "Biblio."

Miranda shot to her feet and ran into the basement, flicking on lights as she went. Every disk in their files had been taken in the burglary. But according to what she'd read, this information was stored in the hard drive. She switched on the computer and typed in the path: C:\ plague. The screen went black. In seconds it lit up once more. "This file is password protected." Miranda typed Biblio at the command prompt and tapped the Enter button.

Then she sank slowly into a chair as she scrolled through page after page of her father's words. Dazedly she realized she was reading a synopsis. He'd been working on a book— a book about the Plague of the North. A book about Rolf Magnusson. It appeared he'd been trying to delve into the past more deeply than ever before. He'd asked himself questions. Why does one of the most respected men in his country suddenly commit murder and go on a transAtlantic spree? What became of all the stolen goods? Her father theorized that more than one trip had been made across the Atlantic. He based that supposition on the period of peace between one raiding spree and the next. The ship had been laden with plunder, he wrote, and that plunder had been carried across the North Atlantic. It had been hidden away before Magnusson and his cohorts returned to the coasts of Europe with a vengeance.

"He was an intelligent man," Russell had written. "A genius, by all descriptions. Too intelligent to continue in this manner on the basis of a mere tantrum. I believe he had a plan, and I further believe he may not have been guilty of treason and murder to begin with. The accounts I've seen of the tale tell only of a single witness against him, the daughter of a Norwegian noble. The nobles of Norway were the ones who placed Magnus on the throne. Furthermore, if Magnusson were guilty of treason against Knut, he'd no doubt have received a pardon the moment Magnus took the throne. He did not. The why of that puzzles me.''

The text of the synopsis went on for page upon page. Russell had planned to return to the site and search for the missing treasure before the agreement with Canada expired next August. He'd wanted to search for the sunken dragon ship, as well, to learn if any part of it still remained. The sword, with the word "Vengeance" carved in runic symbols upon its hilt confirmed his theory that the respected Rolf Magnusson of Norway and the feared Plague of the North were one and the same man, and he wanted to find every clue he could uncover as to why.

So did Miranda.

Was she presently living under the same roof as the crazed Berserker who'd plundered three villages in a single night, leaving forty dead men in his wake? Leader of the raiders who penetrated the most heavily guarded fortresses in all of England, and looted them to the bare walls?

"Miranda."

She leapt to her feet and spun around. No. There was more. There had to be more. Her father had sensed it. Miranda knew it. What?

Rolf's gaze narrowed, then heated as it moved down her body, tracing the shape of her lengthy, unclothed legs. She saw his lips thin and felt the force with which he lifted his gaze up again to meet hers.

And then he frowned. "Why do I see fear in your eyes? Only a few hours ago you would have fought me to the death, I believe. I angered you enough to do so, no doubt."

"What do you want?" She bit the question off too quickly, too impatiently. She didn't fear him. She'd simply managed somehow to suppress the knowledge about who he had been. The account of all the deaths and destruction attributed to him, written in her father's own words, had been a sharp reminder. It had shaken her. She'd had enough of death.

"I wish to know what I have done to frighten you. I did not take you for a woman easily frightened."

"I'm not—"

"What is this?" With a quick movement, he pushed her aside and peered at the computer screen. Reading the words there, he scowled and whirled to face her. "Plague of the North, is it? And you, no doubt, believe every word this . . . machine tells you?"

"Th-they are my father's words. He—"

"He judged me by rumors, stories. He could not have known the truth."

She shook her head quickly. "He didn't judge you at all. He questioned everything he learned. It was his way. Look." Returning to the screen, but careful not to turn her back to him fully, she scrolled back to the questions she'd just read and stepped aside to allow Rolf to do the same.

When he finished, he looked away and blew an exasperated sigh.

"Well?"

He only looked at her, his expression tired. "What?"

"Is it true? Are you the same man who raided those villages?"

He met her gaze, his own unwavering. "I am."

Miranda averted her head. She'd been so hoping he would deny it. She just couldn't look him in the eye.

"You are disappointed? I thought you had already branded me as a murderer, a plunderer, a rapist."

"Are you?" She looked up quickly, wishing there could be some plausible explanation for what he had done, fearing there wasn't. Fearing that the certainty inside her was no more than wishful thinking.

He looked her up and down, and finally shook his head. "Believe what you will." He turned to go. "I will leave here in the morning."

"Wait." He faced her again. She cleared her throat. "I don't want you to leave."

His brows went up as he studied her. "You wish for the Plague of the North to remain sleeping beneath your roof, Miranda? Why, when you fear me, do you wish me to remain?"

"I told you, I'm not afraid of you." She stiffened her spine and stepped closer to him as she spoke. She couldn't let him leave; it was that simple. She sensed that if she didn't convince him she wasn't afraid, there'd be nothing she could do to make him stay.

"You are a poor liar, Miranda."

"It's not a lie. I honestly don't think you would hurt me." Oddly enough, it wasn't until she spoke the words that she realized how true they were.

His eyes narrowed. "A woman who reacts to a kiss as you did to mine is afraid."

She shook her head. "That was no kiss. It was an attack, and you're too intelligent to pretend you don't know the difference."

"Correct. I know the difference. Shall I demonstrate?"

She felt herself stiffen, and though she didn't mean to, she drew away slightly. His breath escaped him in a rush. "You fear me. I will go."

He turned from her for the second time, and Miranda felt self-disgust rise through her. Because of her ridiculous reactions she could easily lose the chance of a lifetime. Desperation made her voice louder, harsher, than necessary. "It isn't you! Dammit, Rolf, you can't assume I'm afraid of you just because I don't want you touching me."

He stopped in the doorway, but didn't turn. "What then am I to assume?"

She sighed, pushed a hand through her hair, wished for her wire rims to hide behind when he turned slowly to face her as he awaited her answer. "I just...don't like to be touched."

He pursed his lips thoughtfully, then observed, "That is untrue. You did not mind so much the embraces of Saunders or young Darryl. You found comfort in the touch of Travis. Even in my repulsive embrace you relaxed." He glanced again at the electric blue screen behind her. "But that was before you knew of my crimes, was it not?"

She closed her eyes. "Listen to what I am saying. It is not you. When you held me in the hospital, I did find comfort." She was disconcerted. She hadn't given that odd reaction much thought before now. "More even than when Fletcher hugged me. But that was different. You touched me then only to give comfort, not to—" She bit her lip and looked down.

"Not to what, Miranda?"

"Look, I just don't like men, okay? Not in *that* way."

He scowled and his head tilted to one side. The movement of his head sent his long hair sliding down over his shoulder. "You...prefer women?"

"No!" She pressed two fingertips into her forehead, grimacing. No help for it, she had to blurt the truth. Remaining in that posture, eyes tightly closed, she did just that. "I'm frigid, Rolf. I don't like sex. In fact, I adamantly *dislike* it."

He stepped closer, his expression hard. "Then, you have known men before me?" Always he had to end with that "before me" comment. It shook her to the bone. "How many, Miranda?"

"Enough to know my own mind." She turned from him back to the computer. She'd pretend she had to finish reading her father's notes. Anything.

But Rolf caught her shoulder, his hand surprisingly gentle as he turned her to face him once more. "How many?"

She swallowed the lump that came into her throat. She did not want to discuss this. It would only resurrect the memory she'd murdered and buried. "One." There, it was said. Maybe he'd leave her alone now.

"Only one? You base this certainty about yourself on the touch of one man?"

Bitterness welled up in her like the sea at high tide, and she forgot that she was going to say no more on the subject. "One was plenty, believe me."

His gaze moved rapidly over her face, as if he was trying to read every nuance of her expression at once. "Was it—"

She shook her head hard and fast. "No. I won't discuss this with you. Not anymore. I've told you I'm not afraid of you. I've asked you to stay. Will you or won't you?"

He considered her question for a long while before he answered. She knew he was debating whether to drop the subject of her problem with sex and she prayed he would. Already her stomach churned and her hands trembled slightly.

He drew a deep breath. "I cannot stay."

Miranda felt a fist tighten around her heart. "Why?"

"Because I am not of your time, Miranda. I do not think the way your people think. I cannot allow a woman to provide for me. My garments, my food, my bed. I must find a way to do for myself."

She blinked. She hadn't taken time to think about his pride, or to wonder how it might be faring in all of this. "The silver you gave me is worth more than I make in a year, Rolf."

"You no longer have it," he countered. "You gave it to Travis."

"Just to study. He is an expert in old coins. He won't keep them."

"Nor will you. Your university will put them out for the world to view. Foolish waste of good silver."

"Rolf, I'm not going to let you leave. I need you. I need your help."

"In what?" The skepticism in his voice was evident.

"In answering the questions my father asked. In finishing the book he was writing about you. I can't do it alone. You are the only one who can help me."

"That is foolish. Writing words on paper will not pay for the food you eat."

"Yes, it will. Publishers will pay a great deal for this book when it's finished. Especially if we locate the relics to back it up. And I need your help to do that, as well."

"Relics? I do not—"

"The treasure you and your crew amassed on that first set of raids, that you carried across the Atlantic and hid before going back for more. Do you know where it is?"

Doubt clouded his face. "What could remain after so much time?"

"You were preserved. Why not the treasure?" She paced across the floor, turned and retraced her steps. "And the ship. I need to know precisely where the ship was when it went down. Can you tell me?"

Rolf watched her intently, wondering at the sudden change in her. Where before she'd seemed weary, saddened by the loss of her father and slightly afraid of him, now those feelings slipped from her countenance like ice thawing in the hot sun of summer. Her steps brought her to a stop in front of him and her eyes widened as she awaited his answer.

He cleared his throat, sensing the import of what she asked of him, not wishing to disappoint her and see the soft

light fade from her eyes. "I might." He scratched his head,
giving the matter much thought. "I cannot tell by using
your maps, as I am unfamiliar with them. No, nor by trav-
eling northward by land," he added, recalling the shape of
this continent on the globe she'd so recently demolished.
"But from the sea..." He stroked his chin and strode toward the window. He pushed it open and inhaled the familiar scents of the ocean. "By sea I believe I could take
you there." He faced her again, nodding firmly.

"If you can do that, Rolf, it will be worth more than you
can imagine, more to me than if you gave me every bit of
that treasure." She turned from him, staring into empty
space, seemingly seeing nothing, he thought, but oh, how
her eyes sparkled. "This would make up for everything, for
losing the Ice Man, even." She faced him again, hurrying
to him until she stood so close her warm breathing bathed
his chin as she tipped up her head. "Will you stay? Will you
help me finish what my father began? It would mean so
much to him... and to me."

He would. He could deny her nothing, not when she
looked at him in such a way. Did her heart turn out to be as
rotten as Adrianna's, no doubt Rolf would again be taken
in by it. There was no helping it.

He looked down her body, his gaze moving over the unbound shapes of her breasts beneath the thin layer of cloth.
He could see them so clearly there. He wished to touch
them, to learn their shape, their weight... their taste. Her
long, slender legs, bare from midthigh to unclothed feet,
held his attention for a very long time. He wanted to press
his lips to that supple skin on her thighs.

"Rolf?"

The sound of her voice made him look up again, but he
only became lost in the wondrous mane of her auburn hair,
which floated about her as untamed as a windstorm. How
he longed to bury his face in that unruly silken mass, to in-

hale its scent, to feel it touching his skin. He shuddered and forced himself to speak. "I will help you, Miranda. I owe you as much. There is one thing I would ask in return. Nothing too difficult. A token, really."

She smiled, her excitement showing in her heightened color. Her cheeks glowed as if they'd been vigorously rubbed with rose petals. "What is it?"

"A kiss," he replied.

She sighed in despair, dampening his enthusiasm. "Rolf, I've already explained to you, I don't—"

"I understand. I do not expect you to respond or to feel any... attraction to me. I only wish to be certain you no longer fear me, Miranda. I cannot remain unless I know I am not frightening you each time I come near you. Do you allow me to kiss you, and do I not feel you recoil in utter revulsion, or see you grow pale and ill at my touch, then will I know you fear me no longer."

A convincing reason for a kiss, he thought. Especially considering he'd made it up this very moment. In truth, he did long to feel her lips beneath his. And more, to feel her response to him, for he thought she was wrong about herself. He had seen the hint of a flame in her eyes before he'd frightened her so badly with his brutality. He'd felt the heat in her gaze as it had moved over his body. He wanted more than anything to believe his behavior hadn't extinguished that flame for good.

He looked at her face now as she struggled with unseen demons. "I don't know," she said, and her voice was very soft. "If I ask you to stop, will you stop right away?"

"On my sword, I will stop."

Her lower lip trembled, but she nodded. "All right, then."

She braced herself as if preparing to be struck rather than kissed. Rolf lifted his hands to her shoulders and immediately her eyes flew wide. Damn, but she feared him, despite her words to the contrary.

"It isn't you," she whispered fiercely, as if sensing his thoughts. "Could you do it...without touching me?" Her gaze slanted to his hands resting on her shoulders as she made her request.

Rolf contained his frustration and lowered one hand to his side. With the other, he hooked only his forefinger beneath her chin and gently lifted it. He lowered his head, and as he did, he felt a new purpose. No longer was he eager only to satisfy his own inexplicable thirst for her mouth. Now he also longed to erase that haunted, wary look from her eyes. He wanted to prove to her, because his pride would not allow him to tell her, that he was not the ruthless killer she believed him to be.

His lips touched hers lightly, brushing their satin surface briefly while every fiber in his being yearned to crush them beneath his. He indulged himself only by allowing his mouth to open slightly, that he might capture her full lower lip between his lips and suckle it softly... oh, so softly, not to frighten her. His free hand began to move upward, but he stilled it with a supreme act of will. He released her lower lip only to capture its mate and taste its sweetness, as well.

She didn't move away from him. In fact, her eyes tremulously closed, her thick lashes resting upon her cheeks like frightened birds, ready to take flight at a moment's notice. With the tip of his tongue, Rolf traced the shape of her lips. When he slipped it between them, to touch the tip of hers, she did not pull away. He caressed her tongue and then the inside of her mouth. He felt himself grow uncomfortably hard. The restraint was killing him. He wanted to put his arms around her and pull her tight against him. He wanted to force her mouth open wide and plunder the sweet moistness within. He refused to allow himself anything beyond this tiny sip. And when a moan of suppressed desire leapt from his mouth into hers, her hands came up to press lightly against his chest.

Rolf lifted his head, keeping his forefinger still hooked beneath her chin so he could search her eyes. They were wide, but not with fear or revulsion. With something else . . . something that might almost have been . . . wonder.

Chapter 11

Miranda stood very still for a long moment, her hands resting lightly upon his chest, her eyes still searching his. There was so much there she hadn't seen before. The ice blue depths grew darker the deeper you looked, just like the sea itself. His lashes were not golden or honey or wheat, the three colors she saw in his hair. They were darker, a rich sable brown, as were the smooth, full brows above them. And those very eyes in which she'd allowed herself to become immersed were plunging themselves into her own just as searchingly.

She blinked, breaking the spell under which she seemed to have fallen. Never in her wildest imaginings had she believed he could be so gentle. It was a shocking contrast. He was big, with a raw power and masculinity that was almost frightening. Yet he could kiss her with the tenderness of a poet, with a touch lighter than a springtime breeze rippling the surface of the bay, far from shore. A touch so tender... She shook her head in wonder. It had been so tender she hadn't been afraid. In fact, she'd enjoyed the kiss. When her hands had planted themselves against the muscled wall of his chest, she hadn't intended to push him away. She'd been ready to pull him nearer. Only his soft groan had prevented her from doing just that.

She was surprised. She hadn't believed she could ever want a man's kiss again. She'd wanted his, she realized slowly. She'd wanted it very much. Maybe she still did. Recalling the reason for the experiment in the first place, she cleared her throat. "You see? I'm not afraid of you."

His lips curved slightly upward at the corners. "No, you are not, are you?"

She smiled her answer. "So will you stay?"

"I cannot leave now, Miranda, even do you ask me to go."

She was taken aback. He was being utterly ridiculous, of course, offering her a compliment as he no doubt thought she would expect after such a tender encounter. "You d-don't—" My God, she was stammering like an idiot! She drew a calming breath and ordered herself to be sensible. "You don't have to say things like that."

He reached out to thread his fingers through her hair. *"þu ert unaðsfögur."*

A tiny chill ran up the back of her neck at the depth and resonance of his voice as it caressed her with those foreign words.

"Wh-what?"

"You are beautiful, Miranda."

She shook her head automatically. When she did, her cheek touched his fingertips as they moved through her hair. She chided herself because she wasn't altogether certain she hadn't done it deliberately.

He responded by stroking the side of her face. "Adrianna was the most beautiful woman in Norge. Never did she doubt it, though she had only a precious disk of polished steel in which to see her reflection. You have a houseful of glass mirrors, and yet you fail to see what is there.''

Again she shook her head. ''If your Adrianna knew how beautiful she was, it was probably because people were constantly telling her so.''

Rolf disagreed. ''Might men have noted her beauty less, had she any other virtue? Might they not fail to note yours only because there is so much more in you to praise than mere beauty?'' She frowned up at him, unsure what he meant. His seawater eyes narrowed. ''So much more. I believe I've only begun to see it.''

Rolf took a seat in the rear of the large, crowded room, leaving Miranda to move forward alone. The body of her *faðir* lay within a box of polished hardwood. He wore fine garments, though to Rolf the colors appeared dull and the fabric plain. In his time brilliant crimson and scarlet or bright blues, threaded with gold, had been favored for such solemn occasions. Cloaks of wonderful, shimmering cloth from the East were not uncommon among those able to afford them. But times had changed, he thought as he regarded the people crowded into the room, filling every chair. All of them wore somber colors—black, brown, gray, midnight blue.

Miranda was dressed in a black skirt that hugged her hips and legs, stopping just below her knees. Her legs were encased in a whisper-thin fabric she called nylon, and on her feet she wore shoes with pointed toes and spikes poking from the heels. Her shirt—blouse, she'd called it—was white, with tiny buttons of pearl and a thin border of lace at her throat and wrists. The blouse's neck was high, and she'd fastened a brooch at its center, an oval of onyx with a female face silhouetted in white. Her hair she'd gathered high and loose, so that her auburn curls spilled freely in a coppery cascade.

She was beautiful. Even with her eyes red rimmed and swollen behind their shields of glass, and her nose shiny, she was beautiful. Rolf glanced at the other women in the room and found none to compare. His glimpses were fleeting, though, for he did not wish to have his attention diverted for too long. Though he'd broken away from her side, he'd done so only to allow her to grieve privately as seemed the custom of her people. She would have the seat of honor near the finely crafted box, as was fitting. He would allow her the time to bid her father farewell in her own way. He knew well the import of the occasion.

In his time, all would gather around a pyre. The fallen warrior would be dressed in his finery and laid upon satin carpets and cushions. A great leader was ofttimes laid within his *drakkar,* and the ship itself placed upon the pyre. His weapons would be placed at his side, along with offerings of meat and fruits and mead. If a slave girl, or even a wife, wished to go with the fallen one on this final journey, she would drink the *nabid,* and submit to the ceremonial murder.

When all stood in readiness, the warriors surrounding the pyre would begin to beat their shields with clubs, as the eldest son of the fallen, stripped to his bare flesh, walked backward to the pyre to toss a torch over his shoulder upon it. As the blaze took hold, the others would light smaller torches and toss them in, as well. Even after Christianity forbade cremation, the ritual was kept by many Norsemen. In burning, the spirit of the dead man was freed at once to journey toward Valhalla and receive its final reward. Rolf had never understood the Christians' preference for tossing their dead into the earth to rot slowly.

Rolf shook off the memories, though for a moment he could smell the acrid smoke, see before his eyes the fire lighting the night, hear the pounding of the shields. He felt a pang of homesickness, but forced it away and resumed his observation of the burial customs of Miranda's people. A somber, quiet occasion, he thought. They would all die of shock to see the boisterous funerals of his time.

Miranda stood for a long time beside the body of her father. Rolf wondered at the look of the man in the box. His skin color had not altered in the least, nor had he swelled as the dead are wont to do, especially in warm weather. The man looked to be in better health now than he had upon his deathbed in the hospital.

Miranda leaned over, and her soft hand covered the still one within the box. She whispered something no one else could hear, then pressed a kiss to her fingertips, and her fingertips to his unmoving lips. Rolf felt a hard blockage take form in his throat and a hot stinging at the back of his eyes. She straightened and moved toward the chair that had been placed near the box. Before she sat, though, she turned and quickly scanned the room. In a moment her gaze found his and she came toward him.

She said not a word as she reached him, only extended her hand. Rolf took it, rising and following where she led. She drew a chair from the rest and placed it beside hers. She sat down now, still clutching his hand so that Rolf had no alternative but to sit beside her.

As Erwin Saunders took his spot near the front and began to speak in slow, measured tones about the fallen man, Rolf felt Miranda's grip on him tighten. He squeezed her hand in return, glancing down to see the fresh moisture gathering on her lashes. The lump returned to Rolf's throat. Truly she honored him, by allowing him to sit beside her, to be the one with whom she shared her grief.

The only one, he noted a short time later, as the ceremony ended and the mourners filed past her. Each one touched her, either pressing a hand to her shoulder, hugging her, kissing her or simply taking her hand. She dried her eyes for them. For them she forced a false smile and spoke brave words. Even for Fletcher Travis, though he hugged her harder and longer than most others, she kept her sadness hidden.

Only when they were alone, in her small car, did she succumb to her grief. Rolf sensed it building inside her as she drove. When she pulled the machine to a stop on the path that led to her home, she trembled visibly, then lowered her head onto her arms, resting across the steering device.

He touched her shoulder. "Miranda—"

"I'm sorry," she said, her voice shaking and weak. "I don't know what's the matter with me. I never cried like this when my mother died."

"Because you sensed your father needed your strength." She lifted her head, looking at him through rivers of tears. "You cry now, perhaps, for both of them. You cry because you know you can."

She sniffed and nodded. "You see so much." She wiped her tears away. "I'm just sorry you had to see me like this."

"Do not be sorry, Miranda. Perhaps it is you who are in need of strength now. Do you wish it, I would give of my own."

She glanced at him through dewy lashes, her lips trembling. "Didn't you know? You already have. I couldn't have survived this day without you."

He slipped his arms around her slender frame, pulling her across the seat and against his chest. He held her hard, willing her pain to leave her. "The day has not yet ended, *astín mín.* Give your grief to me."

Her arms curled around his neck and she clung. Her tears soon soaked the front of his shirt, but he cared not. He would cry them for her, were it possible. His body absorbed the trembling of hers as she wept. And it seemed only natural, when he cupped her head in his hand to tilt it back and lowered his mouth to hers, to capture her sobs, as well.

She didn't compress her lips when his mouth covered hers. She let them remain parted, as if she wanted his gentle invasion. Her hot tears dampened his face as Rolf complied. He drank from her lips and then from the honeyed recesses beyond. He tasted her tongue hungrily as his compassion became only passion. The flames ignited within him, and he forgot that he'd been holding her to give comfort. He licked at the silken interior of her mouth, and with a low groan, he tightened his hold on her body. He shifted slightly in his seat, pressing her backward and leaning over her in his eagerness to quench the thirst raging within.

Miranda's eyes flew open. She drew a ragged breath and twisted her head from beneath his demanding mouth. Her hands, formerly clutched around his neck, became fists that pummeled his chest. "Get off me!" she cried in a hoarse, panic-filled voice. "I can't... breathe. Get off me!"

Frustrated and confused, but seeing the sudden fear in her eyes, Rolf quickly straightened. She flew from his arms, collapsing against the opposite door, breathing as rapidly as he was, though he doubted hers was a result of arousal.

He watched her for a moment. Her shoulders were trembling uncontrollably. "Forgive me, Miranda. I did not mean..." He groaned. "I am sorry."

"No." She faced forward as if forcing herself to do so. She drew several deep breaths and it was as if she measured them, forced them to calm her. "I'm the one who should be apologizing. I'm a fool to think you would ever..." She shook her head, not finishing the thought. Instead she said simply, "Thank you... for stopping when I asked you to."

Rolf felt a fury slowly begin to stir to life deep within him. So, she had been afraid he wouldn't. She'd suddenly realized she was in the arms of a murdering, raping villain and she'd panicked, thinking her fate sealed. No doubt his restraint surprised her. She hadn't expected the Plague of the North to respect a woman's wishes when she said no.

She turned her back on him and shoved the door open. Her unsteady steps took her away from the car, but she did not go into the house. Instead she veered around it and vanished from his sight.

Rolf swore loudly, slamming a fist into the seat. He'd been a fool yet again. He'd begun to allow himself tender feelings toward another beauty with a heart of stone. He'd let himself believe her lies, when she'd so cleverly convinced him she had no fear of him. In truth, she wished only to use him to find what she sought.

He wrenched his door open and took the same path she had. She would soon learn that Rolf Magnusson was not a man to be used. His steps broad and quick with his anger, he followed the path to the rocky bluff above the sea. And there he found her, seated upon the ground, her knees drawn to her chest. She faced the sea, and the sun was slowly sinking behind her. He heard her sobs as he drew closer, and in spite of his anger, his heart twisted in his chest. Seabirds sang in loud discord as he approached her. But when he parted his lips to condemn her, he found no sound would emerge.

"I'm sorry, Rolf."

He grated his teeth. Sorry, was she? For lying to him? For using him to reach her own goals? Or for her frightened reactions to his touch? "You needn't fear I will kiss you again, Miranda. You've made your feelings known to me, though you deny them with your lips."

She shook her head, not turning to face him. "You're wrong about that. It wasn't you—"

"No more lies."

She did face him then. "Rolf, it isn't—"

"*Stodva*. You need not continue in your charade. You fear me. It is clear. I will find your precious treasure for you, since I have given my word. And when it is found, I will take my leave of you, your house, your very life. I will make my own way in this world of yours. Have no doubt, Miranda."

She rose to her feet. "It was the car, Rolf. That damned tiny car, and—"

"Do you continue to speak falsely, my leave will come sooner."

She closed her eyes slowly. "You're not going to believe me, no matter what I say, are you?"

He said nothing. It pained him to know her heart, when he'd wished so much to believe she found solace in his arms. A small sound from far above drew his gaze upward, and he saw a silvery bird, the likes of which he'd never seen.

Her voice was hoarse when she spoke. "It's an airplane. A ship that sails in the skies."

Rolf shook his head in wonder. "Your people travel by such ships?"

"Yes. It is faster than any other way. And safer than the car, believe it or not."

Rolf lowered his gaze to hers as the bird ship vanished from sight. "Your world is filled with wonders, lady. Still, I believe I would rather sail in my own sort of ship." As he spoke, he looked out toward the sea.

"You love it, don't you?"

He nodded. Then stiffened as her hand closed on his upper arm.

"You have to let me explain, Rolf."

"*Nei*. I do not." He allowed his gaze to travel once more over her lovely, tear-stained face before he turned and walked to the house alone.

* * *

Two days after the funeral, Miranda sat beside Rolf in front of Erwin Saunders's desk at Beaumont.

She leaned forward in her seat, forgetting for the moment the things that had been troubling her. Rolf had treated her coldly, had been distant toward her, since her stupid reactions to him in the car. He honestly believed she was afraid of him, and he refused to allow her to explain. But she had to push those thoughts aside. She needed to make her points clearly and forcibly. "Don't you get it, Erwin? That is what the person who broke in was after. Not the Ice Man, but whatever clues we might have gleaned from him. He must have known what Russell knew, who the man was, what he was accused of doing. He knew there was a massive treasure involved, and he wants it."

Saunders shook his head. "How could anyone have known? You said the information was in a coded file in the computer. Russell was obviously keeping it to himself."

"Anyone could have figured it out the same way my father did, by following leads and tracking down records. And the very fact that he had the information so well hidden proves to me that he suspected someone else might be after it."

Saunders stroked his goatee thoughtfully. "You might very well be right."

"I know I'm right. Furthermore, we don't have any idea how much more this person knows. We have to locate the two sites involved before he does, or we'll lose any chance we ever had to complete the work my father began."

"Miranda, what makes you think we can find either the shipwreck, or the missing booty? We don't have a clue . . . unless there was something in that hidden file." He stood quickly, coming around the desk with a light in his eyes. "Miranda, did your father think he knew where—"

"No." The man seemed to sag before her eyes, but he straightened quickly when Miranda added, "But Rolf thinks he can locate both of them."

Saunders's gaze met Rolf's, and there was no doubting the skepticism there, or the hope. "How?"

"I am not certain of finding the lost treasure," Rolf said slowly. "Landscapes change." Saunders opened his mouth to interrupt, but Rolf quickly continued, "Of the *drakkar,* I have no doubt I can show you precisely where she rests, though I wonder whether anything remains."

Again, Saunders uttered the one-word question. "How?"

Rolf shrugged. "It is only a matter of being familiar with the old methods of navigation, of knowing the most likely landings, of studying the currents, the winds."

"It would be best if you could simply show me the site, mark it on a map or—"

"Impossible. I will not know it until we are there."

"We'll have to go by ship," Miranda observed. "It doesn't have to be a large one. But we are going to need a RCV and sonar equipment. It isn't going to come cheaply."

"That's an understatement, Miranda. Do you know what a submersible remote cam-video costs?" Saunders drummed his fingers on the desk thoughtfully. "Of course, we might be able to borrow one from another university. I hate to, though. The fewer people who know about this the better."

"Do you think the board will approve funding?" Miranda sounded apprehensive.

"The board." Saunders breathed the words on a rush of air. "Time is of the essence here, isn't it? No, I don't think we can wait for Harry Kirk and his board to mull this over. We need to act now, before the agreement with Canada expires in August and we're forced to get permission all over again."

"Does that agreement cover offshore explorations, Erwin?"

Saunders shrugged. "It doesn't say 'land only.' That's as good as an okay in my book. I could get outside backing. Just proceed with the project and get permission later."

Miranda stood slowly, shaking her head. "Erwin, you could get into a lot of trouble—"

"You think they're going to care, once we find it?" Saunders's face glowed with heightened color. "Are you sure you can do this, Magnusson? What experience do you have? I don't even know your credentials."

Miranda spoke before Rolf could so much as part his lips. "Rolf's an expert, Erwin. He's mostly self-taught, but there is no denying his abilities, I guarantee it. If you want to waste time checking his background, I suppose—"

"No. We need to act right away. If you vouch for him, Miranda, then I'm sure he's legitimate." Saunders rose, again stroking his beard, apparently lost in his own thoughts. "You go on now. I'll take care of everything." He seemed to snap out of his reverie for a moment as they moved toward the door. "Remember, not a word to anyone. We have no way of knowing whom we can trust."

Miranda looked at him doubtfully. "Erwin, I don't know about doing this without consulting Harrison. He's the dean, after all, and I don't want—"

"There'll be no risk to you, my dear. I'll take full responsibility for any repercussions, I promise you. We have to do this." He studied her face. "For your father," he added quickly.

Miranda became certain all at once and she nodded firmly. "Yes, you're right. Call me as soon as the arrangements are made."

One week later, Miranda stood on the deck of *Mermaid*, a former minesweeper built for the British Royal Navy in

1942. She'd been acquired by an oil company in '67, and fitted with sonar transmitters and receivers, as well as two submersible remote camera videos for use in monitoring underwater pipelines.

Mermaid was now the property of Cryo-Life Industries. It galled Miranda that once again Saunders had gone to the company for funding, and it baffled her that they had agreed. He must have dangled before them the hope of finding another Ice Man, or perhaps suggested they might still locate the original one, to gain their cooperation so readily. It galled her still further that Jeff Morsi would accompany them as Cryo-Life's representative.

Still, she had other worries besides Jeff Morsi's infuriating presence. She turned to look at Rolf standing at the rail. The sea wind blew his golden hair back off his shoulders, and he leaned into it as if in ecstasy.

Miranda frowned. He hadn't so much as touched her since that time in the car. She hated herself for panicking the way she had. It was ridiculous for her to think, even for one uncontrollable moment, that Rolf could hurt her, could force her the way— She stopped the thought. That was in the past, and she had to find a way to leave it there. She'd discovered something about herself since Rolf had come into her life. She was not as immune to the touch of a man as she had once thought. When he touched her, when he kissed her, she felt things she'd never felt before. Longings, desires, tiny flames igniting throughout her body. She was sure no one else could inspire those wonderful feelings in her. No one ever had. But Rolf could. And now he was angry or hurt, and mistrustful of everything she told him. She was afraid she'd lost the only chance she would ever have to feel like a woman.

Of course, she couldn't blame him. She'd reacted like an idiot. God, if it had been anywhere else, she might have been all right. Why the car? Why did it have to be in that tiny damned car?

For a moment she wondered just why she felt so certain he wouldn't hurt her, knowing what she did about him. He'd admitted to being the dreaded Plague of the North, to ruthlessly raiding coastal villages, to robbing and quite probably raping and killing.

No. She felt a sudden conviction that it wasn't so. No man capable of such atrocities could caress her as tenderly as Rolf had. She tried to recall every word her father had written on the subject, to trace in her mind the source of the rage which had driven him to violence so long ago.

He'd been a trusted friend of Knut... right up until the charge of treason and murder, and then the exile. There'd been only a single witness against him, she recalled reading. The daughter of a nobleman. And, as her father had noted, it had been the nobles who usurped the throne of Norway, and handed it to Magnus.

That was all in the past. The needs of the present demanded her attention now. The preparations were complete. The equipment had been checked and double-checked, the plans gone over. They only awaited the last few members of Erwin's handpicked crewmen and then they could depart. There was nothing pressing to be done at the moment, except talk to Rolf. She could think of no excuse to put it off, though his attitude this past week had been discouraging in itself.

She came up behind him, entranced by the waves of his wind-whipped hair. He knew she was there before she said a word, and he turned slowly, leaning back against the rail and eyeing her. "There is something on your mind?"

She stood near him, head tipped back. "I want to talk."

He shrugged lazily. "Talk, then."

"You're angry with me."

His gaze was hooded. She found herself sorely missing the changing colors she'd seen in the depths of his eyes before he'd chosen to hide them away. "You are mistaken. I have no anger toward you, lady."

"I think you do. And I know it's because of the way I reacted that time in the car, when you kissed me. But it isn't fair of you to refuse to let me explain. I just want a chance to make you understand."

He shrugged again, refusing to answer her.

"Would it matter if I told you that my reaction had nothing to do with you? It's me. I have certain... problems, things in my past that I haven't dealt with. I can see I need to face them now, and I will."

The veil over Rolf's emotions lifted a little to reveal the heat of anger in his eyes. "You thought I would rape you. You were so afraid that your heart thundered in your chest." He stared hard at her. "You deny this?"

She bit her lip. "It was a brief panic, that's all. It would have happened no matter who had been kissing me. It wasn't you."

He shook his head. "You found yourself in the passionate embrace of a barbarian. It is little wonder you felt fear."

"You aren't listening." She sighed deeply. "It isn't you. Something happened to me once, and—"

"Will you tell me of this thing that so troubles you?"

Footsteps approached, then passed, and Miranda glanced over her shoulder to see Jeff Morsi striding across the deck. She could easily imagine what Rolf might do to him if he ever found out. Swallowing hard, she faced Rolf again. "I can't. I'm sorry. You'll just have to trust me. I'm telling you the truth."

"Trusting you is difficult, Miranda. I once trusted a woman so like you as to be your twin. My reward was betrayal, and nearly death."

"Adrianna," she whispered. He said nothing, but she turned his words over and over in her mind. "Was she the one who accused you of murder?"

He pursed his lips, and finally gave a curt nod. "Her *broðir*, my friend, stood accused. She betrayed me to clear him."

"Did he do it?"

"Are you so sure I did not?"

"It isn't impossible, you know," she went on, ignoring his comment. "The nobles put Magnus on the throne. They could have been plotting to frame you from the start."

Rolf released a laugh that sounded more like a bark. "Then I am twice the fool. I never suspected—"

"Were you in love with her?"

He shrugged again, averting his gaze. "Half the men in Norge were in love with Adrianna."

"That is no answer."

"It is the only answer you will get, lady."

She felt mulish the way she pressed on. "Why was your exile carried out even when Magnus took the throne? I would think he'd have approved of your supposed treason against Knut."

"Magnus was no fool. He knew where my loyalties lay." Rolf turned as he spoke, staring once again out to sea.

"Then the charges were false. You just said it. You were loyal to Knut."

"Stodva." He uttered the word without inflection. "Cease this interrogation, Miranda, and come to the point. What is it you wish to know?"

"Only the truth, Rolf. What made you do what you did? Which of the crimes attributed to the Plague of the North are true, and which are embellishments added by generations of storytellers?"

He sighed, nodding as if he suddenly understood something previously beyond his grasp. "I am *útlendur maður*, an outsider, unproven. You wish to hear me defend myself against the charges, to listen as I confess my crimes or attempt to explain them away. I will not do it, lady. Believe of me what you will. Judge me by whatever evidence you choose, be it the words of those who are now ashes in the wind, or the man you see before you. Do not ask me to convince you of the one or the other." His gaze remained on the horizon and his last words sounded like a dismissal.

Miranda sighed hopelessly. He didn't need to convince her of anything. She already believed him innocent of the murder, and incapable of the brutalities of which he'd been accused. She'd only wanted the details and... All right, she admitted to herself, perhaps she'd wanted a little reassurance, as well. She'd wanted confirmation that she wasn't letting her growing fondness of him interfere with her common sense. Why couldn't he grant her that much, at least?

She lifted a hand toward him, but let it fall when she heard her name shouted. She turned to see Fletcher Travis jump from the small gangplank and trot toward her, and she couldn't stop the smile that leapt to her lips. "Fletch! What on earth are you doing here?"

He grinned in return, coming toward her and leaning on the rail as Rolf did. "Hey, you didn't think you were going to sneak off on some grand adventure without inviting me, did you?"

She gave him a teasing look. "Since when do shipwrecks interest the famed numismatist?"

"Since his favorite archaeologist is sneaking off to locate one, that's when," he quipped. "Besides, I'm an archaeologist, too, and furthermore, there are liable to be some pretty interesting coins if you find the site."

"Oh, we'll find it," she said softly, glancing toward Rolf. "Make no mistake about that."

* * *

Rolf saw the emotion in her eyes as she expressed her faith in him. Would that it were genuine. He knew too well it was not. She feared and quite possibly despised him. She believed him capable of heinous crimes, and even of violence against her. It tore at his gut that she could think it of him even now. It tore at his pride that she'd asked him to defend himself against her assumptions. He wouldn't. Let her think what she wished. It mattered not to him.

Oh, but it did. How very well he knew that it did!

"Hello, Rolf, how are you?"

Travis's arm was resting around Miranda's shoulder when Rolf relunctantly faced the man. Rolf's glare must have penetrated, for the man lowered that arm all at once and offered a friendly smile that seemed genuine.

"*Gott kvöld*, Travis. I am eager to be away," he answered honestly. "Will you be accompanying us?"

"Unless you have objections," Travis said. His tone of voice conveyed little meaning, but in his steely eyes Rolf saw more. Something the man was not saying.

"You are welcome to join us, do you wish."

"Good. I, uh, have my luggage to bring aboard. Mind giving me a hand, Rolf?"

Travis wished more than Rolf's aid in carrying, and Rolf knew it. He nodded, and the two men walked away toward the gangplank, leaving Miranda behind at the rail. At a small car near the dock, Fletcher picked up two suitcases and handed one to Rolf. "I wanted a word with you, away from Miranda."

Rolf nodded. "*Já*, I discerned as much."

"I might be overreacting, but I'm worried." He slammed shut the trunk from which he'd taken the cases, turned, and set his case on the ground. "This entire expedition is being kept very quiet."

"With reason. How did you learn of it?"

"I overheard Jeff Morsi and Erwin Saunders discussing it as I entered Erwin's office yesterday. You know, it's highly unusual to keep something like this under wraps."

"There is a possibility of great wealth to be found. Miranda believes the one who broke into her home was seeking information about the missing treasure, as she calls it. The secrecy was to keep that one from learning of the trip and attempting to sabotage it, or to steal the treasure for himself."

Travis nodded. "That's all just fine, but suppose he already knows about it?"

Rolf frowned. "Explain yourself."

"I'm just saying, what if the guy already knows about this trip? What if he's just waiting for you to lead him to the site? What then? With so few people knowing what you're up to... Do you see what I'm saying?"

Rolf considered this possibility. "If the man wishes to steal the plunder, he might wait until it is recovered and take it from us. It would sorely aggrieve Miranda."

"And what if it isn't the treasure itself he wants? What if it is only the credit for locating it he's after?"

"I do not understand," Rolf admitted.

"If Miranda pulls this off she'll be in demand by every university from here to Alaska. She'll gain the respect and standing in the scientific community that most people work their whole lives to achieve. That kind of acclaim is worth more than the plunder."

Tilting his head, Rolf studied Travis. He needed to look down only slightly. The man was nearly his height, and solidly built. A worthy opponent, but a valuable ally. "You are saying there may be one who wishes to claim it was he who located the *drakkar,* and the treasure it holds? But to do that, he would need to silence—" Rolf stopped suddenly, now understanding Travis's alarm. To claim the credit, all who knew the truth must needs be silenced. Rolf feared not for himself, but for Miranda.

"Now you see why I've decided to come along," Fletcher said, bending to pick up his case once more. "It's a far-fetched scenario, but not impossible."

"The villain would likely follow by sea," Rolf said, turning the possibilities over in his mind. "He would need stop us before we could tell anyone of the find. Perchance he has implanted a spy among us, to keep him abreast by means of that magical box Miranda calls radio."

"Magi—" Travis glanced up, frowning, but let the matter drop. "You're right, there might be a rat on board. We'll keep a sharp eye on those crewmen Erwin hired."

Rolf nodded his approval. "It is good that you wish to protect Miranda. I accept your help with gratefulness."

"Protect her," Travis said thoughtfully. "Yeah, and maybe I ought to add that it's *all* I want. She's my friend, Rolf. That's all. I love her, but like a sister. You got that?"

Rolf shot the man a suspicious glance. "Why think you I care?"

Travis's dark brows went up. "You're kidding, right?"

Chapter 12

Rolf stood once more in the prow, leaning into the night wind. He felt as if it were his body knifing through the deep blue waters, his breath stirring the air. This time no sails. No oarsmen. Only the dull throb of the ship's heart, pulsing with energy, moving them along like a great living thing, kind enough to carry them all in her embrace. He felt as if he'd come home. Here, in the chill air, in the dark of night, he forgot, for a few precious moments, about Miranda and what she thought of him.

His respite was all too brief. For in the fickle way of the sea breeze, voices carried in odd patterns. "Looking for me?" Jeff Morsi's words were laden with suggestion.

"What do you think?" Miranda's voice trembled, though it seemed she sought to make it biting.

Rolf straightened from his position on the rail and turned slowly. They were not in sight. Probably somewhere on the starboard side.

"I'm not an idiot, Miranda. I think you're looking for your muscle-bound boyfriend."

Rolf listened for her ardent denial, but heard none.

"Does he know what a cold little bitch you are, I wonder?"

"Jeff..." It was little more than a whimper. Rolf frowned hard and started toward the sound of their voices.

"Or have you changed?" Morsi went on. "I wonder—"

"Jeff, don't—"

"Oh, come on. Just a little experiment. I'm dying to find out what he sees in you."

Rolf came upon them. Miranda's back was pressed to the rail. Morsi's arms entrapped her there. As he leaned over her, his face drawing nearer to hers with each second, she arched backward until it must have been painful. Rolf almost smiled, waiting for her to deliver a little pain of her own. Surely she would kick the bastard in his vulnerable groin, or stomp his foot, or pummel his chest. Any moment now she would coolly threaten to rip his heart out, did he not desist.

She didn't. Her face went white and Rolf heard her strangled efforts to breathe combine with her choking sobs. Even from where he stood, he saw her body tremble. What was wrong with the woman? Was she going to stand there and allow this? Apparently she was, for Morsi leaned closer and caught her mouth beneath his. He quickly moved his arms from the rail on either side of her to capture her head in his hands as he cruelly kissed her.

Rolf lunged forward, gripped Morsi by one shoulder and whirled the man around.

"Rolf." Miranda had time only to gasp his name before she spun, lowered her head over the rail and retched violently.

"This is a private conversation, Magnusson. Do you mind?"

"I mind a great deal." Rolf swung a fist at the bastard's face, but Jeff was ready. He ducked quickly and as he rose drove a fist into Rolf's stomach. Rolf took the blow admirably well, he thought. He clenched his stomach muscles in the instant before the fist landed, and though it hurt, he managed not to flinch. The reaction, or lack thereof, had the desired effect. Morsi paused to peer slowly up into Rolf's face, a stunned look in his eyes.

Rolf hammered him with one blow. Jeff Morsi crumpled to the wooden deck.

Rolf began to reach down to him, but before he could, Miranda launched herself from the rail and into his arms. His anger abated slightly as he closed his arms around her. She was shaking, her entire body rippling like the water's choppy surface. "If you touch her again, I will kill you, Morsi. Make no mistake." Rolf scooped Miranda up into his arms.

"No, Rolf. D-don't say—" She hugged his neck, burying her face there, stammering as she tried to speak. By Thor's justice, why did she react this way?

"It is said." Rolf turned away from the beaten man, unsure whether his promise had been heard or not. Morsi lay very still, blood trailing down his neck.

Rolf carried her to his cabin, closed the door and turned the lock. The light still burned, just as he'd left it, filling the small cabin with an amber glow. He laid her upon his bed as gently as he could manage, then straightened and took a step backward. For a moment he only stared at her, trying to fathom the reason for her failure to act in her own defense. He wondered what might have happened had he not heard her voice. How far might that villain have taken his demented game? Rolf's anger simmered anew.

"Explain yourself, woman."

Miranda's gray eyes widened and she blinked away the tears that had begun to coat them. "Wh-what?"

"Why do you allow Morsi so much?"

She shook her head, bewildered and wounded by the look in her eyes. "Allow him? Rolf, he didn't ask. He had me cornered. You saw him. How can you—"

Rolf shook his head and blew a loud sigh. He walked away from her across the cabin and back. Standing close to her again with hands on hips, he searched her eyes for an explanation. "You recall the time I first kissed you? Despite my size, my strength, you crushed my unclothed foot and wrenched yourself from my arms. The next time I made a move toward you, you threatened me with a blade large enough to eviscerate me. The time after that, you offered to make a large hole in me with your little gun, and proceeded to demonstrate that you could carry out the threat. In your car you pounded my chest with your fists. I do not—" He stopped suddenly as some odd constriction formed in his throat.

He found he could scarcely force the words from his lips, but he made himself. He hadn't been aware how much more he wanted from her than simply to bed her. He wanted to have her as his exclusively, he realized now, to have the *right* to kill Morsi for touching her.

"Is it that you prefer his touch to mine? Am I so much more detestable to you that—"

She sat up quickly. "Is that what you think? Did it look to you like I *wanted* his filthy hands on me?"

"You did not seem to fight his touch, Miranda. Not the way you do mine, at least."

"If you thought I was enjoying myself so much, why did you interrupt?"

The bitterness and the anger in her voice stunned him. He knew full well she hadn't welcomed Morsi's touch. He was only reacting to his unfounded jealousy. Yet he couldn't seem to stop himself. "I'll not trouble myself again, lady."

She lowered her head, such sadness in her expression that

he wished he could recall his impulsive words. She rose from his bed, her gaze on the floor as she moved toward the door. When she reached for it, Rolf's hand shot out to grip her wrist. "Wait."

Her head came up, eyes glittering with anger. She wrenched her wrist from his grasp, slamming her other palm into his chest with such force he actually staggered backward. He stood there, searching her face.

"You see why I am confused, Miranda? I am twice Morsi's size. Where was this ferocity when he was mauling you?"

The anger faded. Her face became softer, her eyes seeming to search inwardly. "I...was too afraid. I wanted to fight him, but I—" She stopped, slowly shaking her head.

"Are you not afraid to strike out at me? Miranda, I am a powerful man. I could do you a good deal more harm than that puny dog could."

Her eyes met his and she denied his words quickly. "No, you couldn't. You wouldn't. Maybe that's the key to my reactions. I lash out at you because I feel safe in doing so. I know you won't hurt me."

Rolf drew his brows together in bewilderment. "He is a civilized man of your time. I am a murdering barbarian from the past. How is it you feel safe with me?"

She lifted her gaze, her eyes haunted. "Every age has its barbarians, Rolf. Even mine."

"Do I see him touch you again, Miranda, I do not believe I can stop myself killing him."

She almost smiled at the warmth that spread within her at the ferocity in his tone. Surely this was what every woman must crave—a man like this one, ready to kill for her at a moment's notice, even though she prayed he wouldn't take it that far. "Then you didn't mean what you said...that you wouldn't bother helping me next time."

"I meant none of what I said to you. I was angry."

"Why?"

He turned from her, pushing both hands through his golden hair, lifting it from his shoulders as his fingertips raked his scalp. "I dislike the notion that you might prefer another man's touch. Or even that you might loathe the touch of another less than you loathe mine."

Miranda was stunned by his admission. "Really?"

He nodded, facing her again with a grin that was slightly sheepish. "I was not aware you honored me by feeling safe in battering me."

She swallowed hard, licked her lips. "I don't loathe your touch, Rolf."

His brows rose in disbelief. "No?"

"No," she said, shaking her head.

"But in your car—"

"It wasn't your touch that frightened me," she forced herself to say.

"I do not understand."

"I know." She wished she could explain, but she couldn't. Not unless she wanted to see Jeff tossed overboard and Rolf behind bars. Reluctantly she gripped the door handle. "I should go."

"Nei." Rolf placed his hand over hers. "You will sleep here tonight."

As propositions went, she thought, it wasn't exactly poetic. "I'm not sure I'm ready for—"

"It matters not. You say you trust that I will not harm you. I know it to be true. Of Morsi, I am not so certain. He looks at you with anger, with rage." He stared so intensely into her eyes she shuddered with the force of his gaze. "Will you tell me yet what went between you?"

"Between . . . Jeff and me?"

He nodded curtly. "You intended once to wed him. Why did you not?"

She looked away. "Marrying Jeff would have been the worst mistake of my life."

"On this we agree." Rolf cupped her cheek, turning her to face him. "You did not part as friends."

"No. The truth is, we were engaged for six months. During that time we ... well, we slept together. I never ... I didn't—" She broke off lamely. It was difficult to speak so frankly about something she'd never discussed with anyone.

"Morsi was not able to pleasure you," Rolf filled in with uncanny insight.

She nodded, feeling the blood rush to her cheeks. "I was ashamed, so I hid it. I ... I pretended."

"Ashamed? Why, Miranda?"

"I thought I must be frigid. My father was constantly telling me that I wasn't like other women. That a career was all I needed in my life. That a husband and a family could never make me happy. My time with Jeff was ... was my last-ditch effort to prove him wrong. Instead it seemed like I'd only confirmed what my father had been saying all along." Miranda crossed the room, sinking onto the edge of the bed. "I got tired of pretending and decided to tell Jeff the truth." She averted her face from Rolf's all-seeing gaze. "He didn't take it well."

With an expression of deep concern, Rolf came to her. He caught her chin, tilting her head up as he searched her eyes. "Miranda, what—"

"Would you mind if we didn't talk about it anymore right now? Please, Rolf?"

Eyes narrowing, he nodded at last. "I do not trust Morsi. Will you stay here tonight, under my protection?" She hesitated, not because she was thinking it over, but because he'd asked her, rather than ordered her to stay. Mistaking her pause, he hurried on. "I'll not rest do you return

alone to your cabin, Miranda. You may rest upon my bed.
By my sword, I will not touch you. Only watch over you."

"Yes, all right. I should go to my cabin for a night-
gown, though." She rose as she spoke, but found her legs
oddly watery. Whether from reaction to Jeff's assault or
nervousness, she didn't know.

"Your knees wobble too much to walk, and I've no desire to leave you unguarded while I fetch the garment for
you. Here." He handed her the oversize robe she had
bought for him, and promptly turned his back to her.

She began unbuttoning her blouse, but her fingers trembled and she swore softly at her clumsiness. He faced her
at once. In two steps he stood before her. His hands closed
on the front of her blouse and he gently released each button. His gaze dropped to the swell of her breasts, now visible above the lace-edged cups of her bra. He cleared his
throat and turned away once more. "You may wish to
consider making me sleep beyond the door, lady. Plague of
the North or not, a man would have difficulty remaining
honorable when you lie so close."

She peeled off the blouse, shimmied out of her slacks and
pulled on the robe. Tying the belt around her waist, she said
simply, "I trust you." She slipped into the bed and pulled
up the covers.

Rolf faced her again. "It amazes me that you do. I am
still unsure I believe it." He took an extra blanket from the
foot of the bed and threw it over his shoulders like a cape.
When he'd settled down directly in front of the door, Miranda studied him, feeling guilty for making him sleep on
the hard floor.

"Well, it's true. I trust you. If you want to share the bed,
I won't object."

He closed his eyes as if in pain. "Think before you speak,
woman. Have you not yet realized how much I want you?"

She sat up, tilted her head to one side. "You do? I can't understand it."

He laughed very deep in his throat. "That you have no idea how desirable you are only makes you more so, Miranda. Do you allow me in that bed, you'd do well to sleep with your gun beneath the pillow. The blade, as well, perhaps."

She smiled a little. "You underestimate yourself. You wouldn't touch me if I objected."

His blue eyes raked her. "There is much about yourself you do not know."

"Like what?"

"There is a fire that burns inside you, lady. I have felt its heat. I think, perchance, you would not object at all."

Chapter 13

She studied his face, feeling the warmth of his gaze and sensing the desire behind it. "Do you really believe that?" she asked, shaken by his observation.

"I do."

She shook her head quickly. "Rolf, some women simply don't respond—"

"This I know. You are not one of those women, Miranda."

"How can you know that? I told you, I'm not inexperienced. I never felt anything with Jeff."

"When Morsi kissed you, you felt nothing?"

Her gaze fell to her hands clenched in her lap. "No. Nothing."

"And when I kissed you?"

Her gaze rose slowly then and locked with his. "I . . . I felt . . ."

"You see, lady? The problem before was in him, not in you."

She took that in with silent wonder. Could he be right? For so long she'd considered herself immune to desires of the flesh. It boggled her mind to think she might not be. But she had begun thinking it, and to know he thought it, as well, gave added credence to the idea. When Rolf had held her, had touched her, she realized that she *had* felt something...something powerful. A tingling awareness throughout her body, a tight ball of longing deep within her. She drew a deep breath and held it. She wanted to explore these new feelings. She wanted Rolf to be the one to guide her. No one else would do, for no one else made her feel this way.

"Rolf?" His head lifted once more. "I want you to kiss me again."

He rose to his feet, the blanket falling from his shoulders like a cascade. Slowly he came to the bed and lowered himself onto its edge. She waited, sitting straighter as he leaned forward, his arms braced on either side of her. His lips came to hers lightly, teasingly. He nibbled the lower one, suckled it softly. Then his arms closed around her and he kissed her deeply. His tongue swept into her mouth as it had done before, and it elicited the same response.

Miranda considered the sensations crashing through her, trying to analyze each one. Her arms crept around his neck and she pressed herself closer. When his head lifted from hers, his eyes glittered with unmistakable passion. Her voice hoarse, she whispered, "My God, you're right. I do feel it."

"It is only a whisper of what you could feel, Miranda. Do you allow me, I would show you."

She licked her lips tasting him on them. She nodded once, and closed her eyes as she waited. His strong hands slipped beneath the covers, tugged the belt loose. They returned to her shoulders and pushed the fabric down over her arms. Her eyes fluttered open to find his hooded and focused on her breasts.

"You are beautiful, Miranda." He slid the back of his fingers downward over her breasts. When the roughened skin skimmed her nipples she sucked in a breath. She felt them harden as he turned his hands over to cup her in his palms. Then, so gently she marveled, he rolled the taut crests between his thumbs and forefingers. A shudder rocked her, and as her head tilted backward, his moved lower. His lips closed over one nipple and she gasped again. Tenderly he suckled her, and in a moment Miranda realized that her hands had gone to the back of his head to hold him closer. Rolf lifted his head, a look of wonder in his eyes. "You wish me to stop, Miranda? Speak it now, if you do."

Too breathless to speak, she shook her head from side to side.

He pressed her gently back until she was lying flat. Slowly, giving her time to object, she thought, he pulled the covers from her. She wore nothing now, and she squirmed inwardly as his heated gaze moved over her from head to toe with agonizing deliberation. "How did I ever mistake you for Adrianna?" he whispered. "Her beauty pales beside yours."

Again he leaned over her, suckling her breasts, nibbling them, flicking his tongue over her nipples until she was panting with a longing she'd never felt before. One hand slid lower, his palm flat on her belly. His fingers tangled in her soft curls, then circled down, until they parted her. He touched a hidden spot with his forefinger and her eyes flew wide at the surge of sensation.

Slowly he lay down beside her, his right hand still sending spirals of heat through her. His lips lingered over her throat; his tongue laved her skin. He caught her earlobe in his teeth and worried it softly. His fingers moved lower, leaving that magical place he'd discovered to slip easily inside her. She felt the dampness there and wondered at it.

But as his fingers probed more deeply, she tensed with the anticipation of what was to come.

"Relax, my lady. I only seek to show you pleasure, hmm? Relax and allow it. Do not think or worry. Only feel. Feel my touch. Never would I harm you. You need only tell me to stop, and I will."

She closed her eyes and his mouth traced a path along her jawline to find her lips again. He kissed her harder this time, demanding greater access, thrusting his tongue deep within her and touching off fires all through her.

When he moved again to her breasts, she writhed with pleasure and yet she felt fear. He must have sensed it, for he stopped and searched her face. "Miranda...let me pleasure you. By the gods, I will not harm you. I will not remove a stitch of my clothing unless you ask it. I swear by Thor's hammer."

She had no clue how he could continue making love to her without removing his clothes, but she consented with a brisk nod. He was pushing her to a realm beyond the one she knew. Her body was taking over, sending urgent messages to her brain.

Again he resumed his exquisite torture of her breasts until her nipples throbbed with longing. But his mouth left them to the chill air and moved downward. His tongue traced wet paths over her belly and probed her navel. She whimpered with suppressed desire as he persisted, licking a hot trail over her abdomen.

Her hips moved against her will, and then his hands were gripping them, pulling her around sideways and toward the bed's edge. Vaguely she realized he'd shifted position until he was on the floor, kneeling. He gently spread her thighs open and bowed his head between them.

She felt his mouth, his hot breath caressing her most intimate spot. Then his fingers parted her and his tongue touched her in ways she'd never dreamed of. He pressed his face to her, as if he, too, were deriving the same exquisite pleasure he was giving to her. He drank from her, like a man dying of thirst, desperately. Her fingers tangled in his hair. His hand moved upward, arms reaching until he caught her nipples again in his merciless fingers.

Moving his mouth away only slightly, he spoke with an air of command. "Give me your sweetness, Miranda. Let it go, for I must have it." When his tongue dipped again, fiercely thrusting and swirling and tasting her, Miranda felt something inside her give way. She cried out as myriad explosions went off in the core of her. The final drafts he drank from her brought convulsive spasms of ecstasy. She shook from head to toe with the force of her release.

She was still trembling when he lifted himself to lie beside her. She curled into his arms and felt their warmth and strength surround her. As she cuddled nearer, she felt, too, his arousal pressing against her. He'd shown her pleasure, given her release like nothing she'd ever known; revealed to her a knowledge about herself that would change her entire life. He'd asked nothing in return. More than before, she knew she could trust this man. He had kept his word to her, despite the obvious difficulties. It was so opposite what Jeff had done to her.

She focused on Rolf, instead of on the ripples of reaction still shuddering through her body. She felt the thundering of his heart, heard his ragged, shallow breathing. He held her tightly, almost desperately. He was in a thoroughly aroused state, she realized. She could give him release. She could give to him as unselfishly as he'd given to her. She marveled as the truth hit her. She wasn't afraid anymore.

He rolled away from her suddenly, sitting up and thrusting one hand through his hair. She gripped his shoulder when he started to rise. When he glanced down at her, she shook her head. "No, Rolf. Don't go yet."

"I must. I'm a man, Miranda. Not a god. Do I not leave you now, I will be unable to—"

"Stay."

He searched her face. "You are grateful for this lesson I have taught you."

"Yes." She reached up to his bare chest and ran her hand over it. "And eager for another lesson."

His eyes closed briefly. "Speak plainly, woman. Do I touch you again, I may not stop so easily."

"I don't want you to stop." She met his gaze without flinching. "Make love to me, Rolf."

He studied her face for a long moment. "As you wish it, lady." He stood, still holding her gaze. He removed his jeans carefully, then the briefs beneath them. He hesitated as her gaze moved lower. The state of his arousal alarmed her, but only momentarily. "Are you certain?" he asked, still standing, exercising obvious restraint.

She swallowed hard. "You would never hurt me."

"I would die first," he told her. He lowered himself onto the bed beside her. He rested on his side, facing her. She believed him.

Shyly she slipped one hand lower to touch him. His soft moan told her how this affected him. A moment later, his arms were around her. His mouth possessed hers with a new urgency and he rolled her onto her back, covering her body with his own.

Miranda's hands moved over his back as she returned his kiss. She traced the hard contours of him, felt the heat of his tight skin. At the heart of her she felt him nudge her moistness and she parted her thighs for him. Already the fires were burning brightly. She found herself more than ready for him when he entered her.

Carefully he moved deeper. She arched her hips upward. Rather than discomfort she felt excitement as her body stretched to fit him. He withdrew slowly and began

again, inching inward. His hands slipped beneath her to cup
her buttocks, holding her to him so he filled her more
completely this time.

His gentle rhythm held, though she sensed the effort it
cost him. His body shook with it. As the ship rocked gently beneath them, Miranda felt the recurrence of the pattern she now recognized. The tightening within her, the heat
searing her wherever they touched. His pace increased, his
movements growing quicker, less delicate. She caught her
breath when she knew she was once again on the brink of
ecstasy. Her gasp reached him even now, and he paused.
"Miranda?"

She tightened her grip on his shoulders and moved her
hips, sheathing him heatedly within her. "Please, Rolf,"
she muttered. And when he responded with more urgent
movements of his own she moaned softly, "Yes. Oh, yes."

She felt the tension mount in him even as she sensed the
same within herself. They moved in unison, seemingly an-
ticipating each other's needs with psychic perception. Finally he thrust more deeply than before and she knew he'd
found release for the throbbing inside her. That knowledge pushed her over the brink, as well, and she clung to
him with every part of her. His lips found hers, and when
he moaned with pleasure, it was into her mouth.

He collapsed on top of her then, his weight a warm burden, one she wouldn't willingly relinquish. "Miranda." He
lifted his head and his eyes widened. His hand came up, and
with his thumb he stroked a tear from her cheek. "I hurt
you!"

"No." She shook her head quickly. "No, you didn't hurt
me, Rolf. Not at all." She smiled and raised her head off
the pillow to press her lips to his.

"But you cry." He obviously didn't understand.

"How can I explain?" She sniffed and tried to stifle the
urge to shed more tears. "It's as if part of me was dead, or

asleep as you were for so long. You've awakened that part.
I feel truly alive, more than I've ever felt before." She gazed
at him in wonder. "How can I ever thank you?"

He smiled, the concern leaving his face. "Let me hold
you in my arms until the dawn, *ástin mín.* It will be all the
thanks I need."

She snuggled nearer, silently rejoicing as his arms tightened around her and his shoulder pillowed her head.
"What does that mean?"

"What?"

"*Ástin mín?*" She repeated the phrase he'd used, and felt
him stiffen beside her.

"I said that?"

"Mmm-hmm." A sweet lethargy was stealing over her,
a peace such as she'd never known before. "What's it
mean?"

"If it has an English equivalent, I am not aware of it."

"Oh." Her eyes closed.

She slept curled in his embrace, every so often snuggling
closer. Rolf didn't sleep at all. He held her, constantly
aware of every aspect of her. The touch of her skin against
his, the deep, steady pattern of her breathing, the scent of
her. It was not her thanks he wanted, he acknowledged at
last. It was her heart. And while he had given her physical
pleasure, he knew he did not have that.

All he'd really accomplished, he realized grimly as night
moved toward dawn, was to awaken the sleeping temptress
inside her. Now that she knew her own desires, she would
feel free to explore them with other men. Hadn't young
Darryl explained that today's women were free to give
themselves to any man they chose? Miranda herself had
said that a husband would interfere with her career.

A husband? Had he really been fool enough, even for a
moment, to let that thought enter his mind? What could he

give to a woman like Miranda? He possessed nothing of value, save his sword. And why would she want a man like him, ignorant of this world, uncertain how to make his own way within it?

No. He must keep in mind always that the night they had shared meant little to her, apart from the things she'd learned about herself. She would place little importance on it. For Rolf, it seemed, the matter was quite different. The experience for him had been a revelation, too. For he had not known the depth of his feelings for her. Now that he did, he nearly wished he'd remained on the floor.

He glanced down at the woman in his arms, her face resting on his chest, her hand gripping his upper arm as if to keep him by her side. No, he couldn't regret bedding her. Though she was aware only of her own sexual awakening, Rolf knew he'd experienced one of his own, for never had sex been as moving or as potent as it had been tonight.

As they continued north, it became necessary for them to wear their heavy overcoats on the open deck, even though the sun burned bright and long into the night. It set only briefly, sinking only slightly below the horizon, still casting a glow in the sky. As the *Mermaid* charged steadily through the waters between Greenland and Helluland, or Baffin Island as it was now called, Rolf remained in the prow almost constantly. Icebergs here were common, and deadly. A man must be alert for them, always. They harbored a fondness for slipping out of the mists and into a ship's path.

They'd just crossed the invisible wonder Miranda called the Arctic Circle, when Rolf saw the familiar shape of the coast—ice mountains sloping sharply downward, then stretching into flat vast tundra as far as one could hope to see. The cool wind bit his face, despite it being summer, and Rolf imagined himself momentarily transported back in time. He felt again the pitch and roll of his *drakkar,* once more heard the harsh cries of his men and shivered in the sea spray.

A sharp crack sounded behind him, and he whirled, half-expecting to see the mast crashing down upon his helpless crewmen. He realized the sound had just been in his mind when he saw only Miranda, looking concerned, and Fletcher Travis, at her side as always.

"Rolf?"

He turned back to face the rail, unwilling to let her see the weakness in his eyes. The memories were too fresh. For him, the horror had occurred only a matter of days ago. He had no real sense that nine hundred and fifty-nine years had come and gone. "Tell your friend to drop anchor, Miranda."

He heard quick steps leaving the deck. But when he turned she remained, alone now. "Fletch went to tell Paul."

Paul. The man who piloted this vessel was now as friendly with Miranda as every other male in her reach apparently wanted to be. To the others, the man was Captain Potter. To Miranda, he was Paul.

She touched his arm. "Are you all right?"

It was not her fault she treated everyone with such kindness, Rolf thought in self-reproach. He had no right to become jealous of every man she knew. He had no right to become jealous at all. Not having that right made him jealous all the more. "Why do you think I would not be?"

She blinked and stepped to the rail. Her gaze moved over the pale blue waters, over the chunks of blue-white ice floating everywhere. "Growlers," Captain Potter called them. She looked beyond to the jagged shores, as Rolf watched her. "You were this close?"

Rolf stood right next to her. He couldn't help wishing to be as near to her as possible, whenever he could manage it.

"Nearer. See that small finger of ice? That is near the place where my *drakkar* went down."

She gripped his arm and stared, her expression pained. "That's only about five hundred yards from shore."

He nodded. "That ridge, see it?"

She looked where he pointed, and nodded.

"It was there the Skrælingar stood."

"The *Inuit,* Rolf. Skrælingar is a derogatory term. To use it is to insult them. They are not weaklings, by any means."

"They must not be, to have survived so long here in this wilderness. What does Inuit mean?"

"It means 'the people.'"

He continued his tale. "The People stood there. Their dark-colored fur clothing showed clearly against the snow beyond them."

"Were you blown off course by the storm?"

He shook his head. "*Nei.* We chose this place for its remoteness. Our plunder could be transported south easily enough when we'd established a defensible fortress. We planned to build in Vinland."

Her head snapped around suddenly. "Leif Eriksson's Vinland?"

"*Já.* Eriksson was there."

"And you?"

"Of course. I wouldn't have chosen it without first seeing for myself. Until we built there, we saw this as the safest place for our bounty."

Her brow creased in thought. "The cave where we found you isn't far from here." She pointed south, toward the craggy, treeless hills. "The expedition there is still going on. There's a little village of dome tents and scientists." She licked her lips. "Is there any chance of them finding it?"

"My plunder? No, they will never find it, Miranda." He took her arm. "Come, we will instruct your Captain Potter to ease us in nearer the shore, and show him where dangerous reefs and fingers of ice lie just beneath the surface. I know them all.''

Paul knew his stuff, she had to give him that. He manipulated the remote camera skillfully, keeping his eyes on the video monitor. Miranda stood crowded against him, with Fletcher at her side, and Erwin and Jeff crammed on Paul's opposite side, all craning their necks to see.

They'd been here for hours. It was a painfully slow process. Rolf rarely left the ship's rail. He stood there, staring down into that icy water as if time didn't exist. It pained Miranda to see him so tormented. But he wasn't accepting any comforting just now. Respecting his need to be alone, she'd come back in here. She'd monitored the sonar receiver, but her lack of experience left her with little idea which blips were hunks of ice, stone formations or sunken dragon ships.

''Bing-go.'' Paul said it softly, and it took a moment for her to realize his meaning. Her gaze moved back to the screen.

The dark shape protruding from the murky bottom of the sea on the monitor's screen was completely encrusted with sediment. Still, there was no mistaking that shape, not when one knew what one was looking for. It was the carved dragon's head, the *drakkar's* daunting prow.

''We've found it,'' she whispered. Then louder. Then everyone was speaking at once and Fletcher folded her in a crushing embrace and kissed her face repeatedly in his excitement. When he released her, she was whirled around and into Paul's arms for a similar celebratory hug.

Chapter 14

Fletcher Travis slapped Rolf's shoulder. "Good job, damn good. I still don't know how the hell you did it, but—" He broke off at Rolf's quelling glance, then Rolf sensed Travis's gaze following his own. Miranda stood amid the others, being hugged first by Erwin Saunders and then various members of the crew.

Travis smiled rather uneasily and shook his head. He stepped nearer Rolf and kept his voice low. "Look, no one's doing anything improper here. Don't look so glum. Go hug her yourself if you want to. It doesn't mean anything."

"It matters not to me," Rolf lied. "I am only glad she's overcome her aversion to physical contact with men."

Travis seemed not the least shocked by Rolf's remark. "It's the excitement, Magnusson. Don't read more into it than that. Miranda isn't that kind of woman." His tone was no longer so kind.

"Perhaps she wasn't. People change."

"What is that supposed to mean?"

"Only that Miranda seems to be thoroughly enjoying the attentions of those men."

Travis shouldered Rolf out of the doorway where they'd been standing and onto the open deck. "You bastard," he said in a still, even voice. "Make another remark like that one and I'll knock you on your oversized backside."

"Are you certain you're able?"

"You care to find out?"

Rolf watched the man for a long moment, tempted to break his neck just to teach him a lesson. But he couldn't. He liked Travis, despite the man's blindness where Miranda was concerned. "As it happens, I do not. Take me at my word, Travis. Do not attempt to bed her. I won't allow it."

"Bed her?" The man's dark brows rose in shocked surprise. "Bed her? Where the hell did you get a phrase like that? Look, I told you before, I have no romantic feelings for Miranda. I don't have the least interest in taking her to bed."

"You don't?" Rolf shook his head, confusion beginning to whirl in his brain. "Why not?" From what Rolf could see, every man aboard the *Mermaid* was biding his time to mount Miranda's newly awakened body.

"What kind of a question is that?"

"A logical one, I think. Look at her. The way she glances up from the corners of her eyes. The way she moves. She is beautiful."

"Son of a—" Travis chuckled with delight. "You're in love with her. You big jerk, you're in love with her. Why didn't you say so?"

Rolf looked away grimly. "You know nothing."

"I know Miranda. And believe me, she isn't the least bit interested in Paul Potter or Erwin Saunders or any of those others. Anyone with two eyes in his head ought to be able to see she despises Jeff Morsi. I've already told you, she and I are only friends. There's never been a hint of anything romantic between us. To tell you the truth, I never thought of Miranda along those lines. I see her as a scientist, a colleague.''

"If she has no interest in them, then why does she embrace them that way?'' Rolf glumly eyed the still-celebrating group in the corner.

"Look, now Paul has his arms around Erwin. See how hard Erwin just squeezed him?''

Rolf's face began to clear. "Like men celebrating victory after a hard won battle.''

"Exactly. They're excited. This find is a major one, especially after the disappointment of losing the Ice Man.''

Rolf felt like a fool. Why was such a simple explanation so obvious to everyone but him? The woman was driving him from his senses without doubt.

She chose that moment to join them, and the smile she'd been wearing died slowly as she approached. She touched Rolf's shoulder so gently it was painful. What was happening to him? Where was his warrior's strength now? How could the simple sight of a woman in the arms of another cause him such agony?

In self-disgust, he jerked from her touch. Her eyes clouded as she searched his face. "Leave us alone, would you, Fletch?'' She spoke without looking away. Travis muttered something about forests and trees and then he was gone.

"Rolf, what is it?''

Such innocence in her eyes. Might Travis have been right? But again, what if he wasn't? Rolf's feelings for Miranda had rapidly grown deeper than he'd realized. Her betrayal would cause him considerable pain, more even than Adrianna's had. So much more it didn't bear comparison. He needed to distance himself, to somehow convince himself that he could get along without her. For he knew, beyond any doubt, that he would have to do just that. Hadn't she told him there was no room in her life for a man?

"Talk to me," she said softly. "Is it something I've done?"

The goal for the moment, he decided at once, was to hide from her his pathetic weakness. Surely if she, a mere woman, could share what they'd shared and walk away unscathed, then he, the Plague of the North, could do the same.

"It's this place, isn't it? The memories ... This must be hell for you." She slipped her arms around his waist and lowered her head to his chest.

He ordered his arms to remain at his sides. They disobeyed, closing around her as if commanded by some greater force. He bowed his head and immediately the cool sea wind brought the scent of her hair to his nostrils. Yes, he thought grimly. He did, indeed, feel as if he were a prisoner in Hel.

The sky was gray, but not dark; for a short time in July, the sun here never sank completely below the horizon. Fletcher was assisting Miranda in lowering the small motorboat from its hoist and into the calm, cold waters.

"Miranda, it is a mistake to go ashore." Erwin Saunders shook his head and gestured with his hands. "We all agreed it was best to keep this undertaking a secret until we have it secured."

"I really don't see the need for secrecy now that we've found it," Miranda countered, her tone as patient and reasonable as she could make it. This would be the biggest find Erwin had ever been personally involved in, and she could understand his concern. His lack of hands-on participation in recent expeditions had been commented about more than once in her presence. She imagined he was worried about job security. "The more people who know about it, the less likely someone else will be bold enough to try to take it from us."

"That's your opinion. I believe the opposite is true. This person has already committed violence twice in his quest for this very site. He won't hesitate simply because of public opinion. Miranda, please." His voice was harsh, nearly desperate.

"I agree with Erwin," Jeff Morsi put in. "Cryo-Life would be furious if someone decided to try something. I say we keep quiet until we have the retrieval operation well underway, and a lot more bodies around for security."

Miranda sighed her exasperation. She caught the glance that went between Rolf and Fletcher, and she wondered at it. "All right, Erwin, I won't breathe a word to anyone about what we're doing out here. That wasn't my purpose in going ashore, anyway. I just wanted to show Rolf the cave where we found hi—the Ice Man. That's all."

She saw Fletcher's deep frown and the way he glanced sharply at Rolf all of a sudden. Had he caught her slip? No. That was ridiculous. Who would even consider such a far-fetched notion?

Saunders still stubbornly shook his head. "There are too many people camped around that site. There'll be a lot of questions and you're the worst liar I know."

"Come with us if you don't trust me." She knew her words were short. All she'd wanted was to give Rolf some time away from the ship and from all the eyes aboard. He needed time to deal with the memories that must be attacking him even now. And time to open up and share some of his turmoil with her. She wanted to know exactly what was bothering him. He seemed as tense as the still summer air before a thunderstorm.

Saunders looked at her for a long moment, apparently trying to reach a decision. "I guess I have no choice," he finally muttered.

They headed for shore in the small boat—Rolf, Miranda, Jeff and Saunders. Miranda heard Fletcher tell Rolf that he intended to stay aboard the *Mermaid* to "keep an eye on things." Miranda wondered about the secret the two of them seemed to be sharing, but dismissed the notion as the boat neared the shore. Jeff handled the helm, angling southward slightly to bring them to land as near as possible to the site. He had to negotiate the waters slowly, to avoid the countless blue-white ice chunks that dotted the surface.

Miranda had no idea why Jeff had insisted on coming along. He seemed loath to let any of them out of his sight. Maybe he was as concerned about theft as Erwin was, but Miranda suspected he had an ulterior motive.

She was sorely disappointed that the two had come along. She'd wanted it to be just her and Rolf, alone together. There were so many things she wanted to say to him. She wasn't even sure what things exactly, but she knew they had to talk. Their relationship had changed now. At least on her part it had. What they'd shared last night had been far more than sexual . . . unless he didn't see it that way. Maybe that was why he seemed so distant today. Maybe he didn't want her reading more into it than a simple one-night stand.

At the shore, Rolf tugged the boat up out of the water without aid and then looped the rope around an outcropping of rock. There were no trees to tie to. They were north of the tree line. Nothing much grew here. There were only the craggy, glacier-formed hills to their left and the endless, flat tundra to their right.

Saunders glanced uneasily toward the rocky hills and the crop of dome tents nestled nearby. "I'll remind you again, Miranda, not a word about our mission."

"Don't worry yourself," she snapped. "Rolf and I are going straight to the cave. You two can do what you want." She snatched up the backpack beside her and slung it over her shoulder.

She hiked away, skirting the tents and heading up a sharp incline toward the cave's entrance. She knew Rolf followed, but she was in no state to walk in companionable silence with him just now. She was unsure of his feelings, confused by his apparent hostility toward her and more than a little hurt by it. Erwin's attitude had nettled her still further until now she felt like swearing at someone.

Still, all of her disquiet faded when she stood at the opening in the ice. The crew left behind had widened it, so it was a much simpler matter to step in than before. Even so, her heart quickened its pace and so did her breathing. Her palms, despite a temperature below thirty degrees, began to dampen with sweat inside her heavy-duty gloves.

An archaeologist with claustrophobia was like a pilot with acrophobia, the way Miranda saw it. She clenched her teeth and slipped the pack from her back. She bent over it, unlacing the flap and removing the items they'd need. Two helmets with lamps attached, a length of rope and a pair of carabiner links, to go with the ones on the belts they both wore at their waists, and an extra flashlight just in case. She plopped on her helmet and fastened its chin strap. She slipped the flashlight into one of the deep pockets of her overalls and looped the rope, carabiners attached, over her shoulder. By the time she finished, Rolf was standing behind her, scanning the cave entrance with narrowed eyes.

"What is it? Do you know this place?"

He shrugged. "I am unsure. The ice—"

"The glacier moved in after the shipwreck, Rolf. It might not have looked like this the last time you saw it." She handed him a hard hat and he scowled. "Put it on," she said firmly, "or we don't go in. And be sure and fasten the chin strap, or the entire helmet is useless."

Rolf nodded and obeyed. Miranda reached up to the top of his hat and flicked on the light, then did the same with her own. Drawing a deep breath, she slipped over the lip of ice and jumped lightly to the floor below.

She stepped aside and in a moment Rolf landed beside her. He straightened and turned slowly, the light of his helmet moving over the stalactite-covered ceiling, pausing on the glasslike needles sprouting like vegetation from one of them.

"Helictites," Miranda said softly, some of her irritation with him fading as the familiar thrill of discovery began coursing through her. "They're formed by seeping water. Look." She turned her light on another of the crystalline bushes growing upward from one sloped wall, seemingly in defiance of gravity.

Rolf remained silent, nodding as she spoke, but making no comment. She led him through the passage, reminding herself that she'd been here before and hadn't suffered a single bout of panic. It was not a small, cramped crawl space, but a wide, arching passage, with plenty of room to breathe. She'd be fine.

After entering the massive room, Miranda paused, and pointed to the flat stone table. "That's where we found you."

When Rolf glanced around the room his eyes widened as if in recognition. "This? This is where they put me to rest?" He sounded incredulous.

"Yes. Right there, on that flat stone." She couldn't help but recall her odd reactions to her first glimpse of him. "I stood at this spot, only facing the other way," she told him.

"This is not credible."

Miranda shivered, and prickles ran along the back of her neck as they had once before. "I got this weird feeling all of a sudden, as if someone was standing right behind me. And I turned and saw you lying there." Her voice softened as the memory came flooding back.

"Miranda, are you certain it was this cave—"

"I fell to my knees when I saw you." She took a deep breath and sighed. "It was as if they just turned to water. And I think even then I had the most profound sense of sadness that you were not alive."

Rolf stood perfectly still, his gaze narrowed, raking the cave's interior. "How could they have known?"

"I think I was meant to find you here. I know it isn't scientific or logical, but I honestly believe it. I think that somehow all my father's work was truly just to lead me here, to you, though he never knew it."

At last Rolf drew his gaze from the room around them and met hers. He lifted a hand toward her face. "Miranda, do you mean to say—"

At that moment a violent explosion rocked the ground beneath their feet. It felt like the entire world was quaking and Miranda fell to her knees much as she had the first time she'd set foot in this cave. Fear gripped her with fists of ice as the roar ripped through her eardrums, to be followed by a low, ominous thunder that matched the racing of her heart. Beneath her knees the uneven stone floor clawed at her through the heavy overalls and wool underwear. Her palms vibrated where they were pressed to the ground. Fragments of stone rained down onto her back and the rumble grew louder.

Buried. She was going to be buried alive, here and now. All of a sudden she couldn't catch her breath. She gulped desperately, dragging little but dust into her lungs.

Then strong hands gripped her shoulders and hauled her to her feet. Rolf put his arm around her shoulders and, bending them both low, ran with her. She thought he spoke, but she couldn't hear. She was only aware of her fear, of the grim certainty that she was about to be smothered by the earth that surrounded her, and the knowledge that she didn't want to die so young. Not when she'd just begun to come alive.

Dirt and dust rained so thickly it was impossible to see even with the headlamps still glowing. The showering stones grew steadily larger and she sensed that in seconds the entire cave would fall down upon them. Her panic overcame her and she would have frozen in fear had Rolf not propelled her along at his side. He released her, pushing her down as he shoved with all his might at the stone table which had once been his bier. She couldn't make sense of his actions, not until the stone moved. Rolf's face tensed with the strain, and he bared his teeth as he pushed, and without thinking at all about it, Miranda rose and pressed her hands to the stone, as well, shoving with all of her strength.

It moved a bit farther. Rolf pointed and Miranda obeyed without question, slipping down into the opening the rock had concealed. Her fear of this small, dark area was secondary to the fear of remaining where she was and being buried.

She felt a stone ledge under her feet, and then she ducked her head beneath the huge table above. Waiting for Rolf to join her, she fought a fit of violent shaking that engulfed her body. She screamed aloud when he disappeared, instead. A moment passed, a moment in which she felt certain she'd lost him. But then he returned, carrying the length of rope in one hand. He must have gone to get it from the floor where she'd fallen with the first jolt. He squeezed through the small opening to join her.

"Rolf, what—"

"No," he shouted above the roar, swinging one arm out to snag her around the waist. "Do not move. There is no floor. I must lower you down." He aimed the beam of his light downward. She gasped when she saw how near she stood to the edge of the small protrusion of stone that held her. He pressed the carabiners linked to the rope into her hand. The air was thickening with dust and a lot of rubble was falling on him through the small opening. "Get down, Miranda. We'll be buried soon."

She snapped the locking carabiner to the link on the belt at her waist. Rolf didn't anchor his end of the rope. He only braced himself and held it in his hands. Miranda trusted him. She pushed off from the side and quickly rappelled down the sheer stone. She tried not to imagine what kind of debris was pounding Rolf's body from above. She moved as fast as possible, and the second her feet were on solid ground, she cupped her hands and shouted up at him, "Rolf! Come on, hurry!"

His form came hurtling down from the darkness above. He landed with a terrible impact, tumbling forward and then lying still. He made no move to get up. Miranda rushed forward, falling to her knees beside him, her heart in her throat. She gripped his shoulders and shook him hard. "Rolf, come on. Get up. Get up!"

He opened his eyes. "Can you never stop giving orders, woman?" Slowly he maneuvered himself up onto his knees, a difficult thing to do, she imagined, since her arms were wrapped tightly around his neck as he attempted it.

She pulled back just enough to scan his face by the light of her helmet. "Are you all right? Please tell me you're all right."

"I am, but are you?" His hands cupped her head, molding her hair to it, he held her so tightly.

"Yes. Fine." She hugged him and he cradled her to his chest.

"Thank the gods, Odin and Thor and Tyr for their mercy. I feared they would punish my foolishness by taking you from me, Miranda."

"What—"

"Later. We will speak of these things later. Now we must not." He stood slowly, lifting her with him.

Miranda began to get her bearings and to believe that, perhaps, she wasn't going to die just yet, after all. It was cooler in the cave where the temperature remained steady year round. She put it at twenty degrees Fahrenheit or a little less. Still, with the absence of the cruel Arctic wind, it wasn't the same chilling cold as outside. The stone walls were smooth and black, much like the ones above. They were rough and uneven, with otherworldly columns protruding down from the arching stone above, narrowing at their middles, widening again as they stretched to the floor like sentries standing guard. But there were newer speleothems, as well. Unlike the ones at the entrance above, which had been formed long before the glacier had rendered the cave airless, many of these appeared to be in the process of formation. Which meant this was a well-ventilated area...which in turn meant there must be an opening somewhere.

Finally, she thought, her brain seemed to be functioning on all eight cylinders again. "Rolf, how did you know about this place?"

"The better question would be, how did the Skr—the Inuit know?"

She could hear him much more clearly now. Apparently the falling rubble had sealed the hole through which they'd descended, and maybe the avalanche above was nearly over, as well. "Are you telling me you've been here before," she asked. "Before the shipwreck?"

"Yes. Miranda, the secrets of this cave were to fund my village, and then my city. They were to make me a respected leader, or at least a feared one. It was to be my revenge."

She studied him, her mind jumping far ahead of his words. "Go on. Are you saying this is the place..."

"*Já*"

She swallowed hard. "This is where you stashed all the plunder? My God."

"Miranda, the sound I heard before the cave fell in, it was not natural. Not the sound of falling rock or the splitting of ice."

She nodded, recalling the initial roar and the violent shock wave. "I think it might have been some sort of explosive."

"Another of your modern weapons?"

"They can be."

"We were not far from the entrance, Miranda. Someone has decided to kill us both." Rolf touched her face again, then moved his hand to stroke her jawline, then her neck. "I have never been so afraid...afraid you would be hurt or..." He shook his head. "Never have I had such a weakness, Miranda."

Miranda covered his hand with her own, then wished she wasn't wearing gloves. "I would have been killed if you hadn't been here." She swallowed hard and looked around her, her light moving with her head. "Then again, we're not out of here yet."

"Do not be afraid," he assured her. "I will see you to safety, Miranda, do I need dig us out with my hands."

She smiled at him, taking some comfort from his words, but not nearly enough. A shudder went through her. "This was deliberate. I guess Erwin was right."

Rolf tilted his head. "Your Fletcher Travis believes someone may wish to steal not the treasure itself, but the credit for locating it. Does this theory make sense to you?"

Miranda considered for a moment, then sucked in a sharp breath. "If Fletch is right, they'd have to get rid of everyone who knew better. Including Fletch and Erwin."

Rolf nodded. "And who knew precisely when we entered this cave, Miranda?"

"Only Erwin...and Jeff. Jeff!" She bit her lip. "He lost all credibility in the scientific community when he went to work for Cryo-Life. He didn't care then. He only wanted the money they were willing to pay him. But it began to gall him after a while, the lack of respect. If he could claim credit for this find..."

"You'll not prevent me from killing him this time, Miranda." Rolf picked up the rope that lay coiled at his feet. He must have tossed it down just before he'd jumped. He wound it up quickly as Miranda released the carabiner from her belt. He looped it over his shoulder, clasped her hand in his, and started forward.

For some time he didn't speak, only guided her farther along the uneven rocky floor. They were shrouded in absolute darkness. The only areas visible at all were those where the beams of light from their hard hats cut through the pitch-black cave as they moved along. Directly ahead of them she heard the sound of rushing water. She stiffened, the proximity of the fickle sea leaping into her mind, but Rolf inexorably pulled her onward, never slowing his pace.

They rounded a bend, and immediately ahead of them a waterfall tumbled and splashed into a dark frothy pool at their feet. Breathless, Miranda could only stare, awed by the simple beauty of the spectacle. She strained to see through the dark, and thought the pool was actually a stream, which wound and twisted its way down another passage to the left.

Rolf shone his beam downward, then leapt easily over the water to land on the other side. There seemed no obvious reason to be there. He stood with his back to a wall, upon a narrow ridge of black stone, beside the waterfall. Trusting him nonetheless, Miranda leapt across to join him.

She caught her breath as he drew her back until she was pressed flat to the cool stone wall, then slowly he sidestepped and took them right behind the cascade. Miranda watched the curtain of water flowing down in front of her and felt the oddest sensation of having just stepped through the looking glass. Her surprise increased when Rolf seemed to disappear through the wall at his back. Her breath caught in her throat, for his hand still clutched hers and he was pulling her through with him.

It wasn't a wall, after all, but a hidden fissure within the wall. Beyond it, Miranda thought, was the treasure of Ali Baba. As Rolf moved the beam of light around the chamber she saw the remains of what were once trunks and chests. The iron bands on most had rusted to nothing, with bits and pieces here and there still showing their original shape. The wood, too, had rotted, leaving little but black piles of mulch where it had been. Amid these remains were heaps of tarnished silver, piles of gold, relics of every imaginable kind. There were chalices and goblets, necklaces and jeweled bracelets, headdresses with— Miranda moved closer, leaning over one piece in question —yes, diamonds, rubies, sapphires. Daggers with jeweled hilts and mounds of ancient coins littered the floor. Brooches of gold, silver combs, strands of pearls and golden chains. Silver bowls, rings, belt buckles, golden plates and bronze sculptures. And those were only the few things she could identify from the light of the beam. There were many more, oh, so many more. The piles of treasure, their chests long gone, lined the entire chamber.

She was nearly speechless with wonder. To a person in her profession, this was a dream come true. She glanced at Rolf, suddenly aware that, from his point of view, this all belonged to him. "If we tell the authorities, they'll take this all away from you, Rolf. This will be considered the property of the government of Canada. Beaumont University might get to study it for a time, but then it would have to be returned. Do you understand that?"

"You speak as if there is another choice," he said in a low, steady voice.

She blinked. "Well, I suppose you could try to smuggle some pieces out of the country. Sell them to an unscrupulous dealer or collector somewhere. Believe me, just a few of these treasures would give you all the money you could hope to spend in a lifetime."

"And you would not reveal my actions?"

She answered thoughtfully. "No. Of course I wouldn't. It's just that we can't tell anyone your role in this discovery without admitting who you are, and we can't do that."

He searched her face, seemingly trying to see through to her soul. "And if it were learned that you helped me in this way?"

She averted her gaze quickly. "It . . . wouldn't be good."

"I believe, Miranda, that your . . . career . . . would be at an end. Would it not?" She shrugged. "And yet, you would still allow me to take what I wanted?"

"It's yours," she said quickly, though she knew it wasn't true.

He shook his head slowly. "*Nei.* It never was." She glanced up at his odd words, but he showed no inclination to speak any further on that subject. "Morsi had no idea what he gave up by sealing us in here."

"No. But I guess he must have decided he had to get rid of us before we announced finding the ship," Miranda said as her mind began working to find a way out of their predicament.

"The Inuit must have seen my men and me as we left this place that first time. They returned my body here, since it was the only place they connected with me."

"Why do you assume they saw you leaving, and not entering?"

"Entering, we carried the chests. Had they seen them, no doubt they'd have searched until they found them."

She swallowed hard before asking the next question. "Is there a-another way out?"

He met her gaze squarely, his eyes glittering in the darkness. "There once was." He turned his head so that the beam of light danced on the opposite wall, then slid lower.

Miranda gasped when she saw the tiny tunnel, black and small, only large enough to crawl through on hands and knees. Her hands began to shake and she averted her gaze. Rolf gripped her trembling hand and pulled her toward the little hole.

She stiffened, planting her feet as a full blown panic attack swept over her like a hurricane. "I can't go through that."

"Miranda, there is no other—"

"I can't!" Already her lungs felt as if they were constricting. "I'd rather stay here."

His hands closed on her shoulders. "Miranda, if you stay, you will die."

Faster and faster came her breaths. Yet she wasn't inhaling deeply enough to sustain her. Her heart raced. She could feel the pulse pounding in her temples. "I . . . can't. I can't, Rolf. Please . . . you go. Just leave me. I can't. . . ."

"Why?"

His voice didn't just ask for an answer. It demanded. She pressed her palms to either side of her head and spun away from him, removing her hard hat as if that would ease her breathing. *I'm not going in there. I'm not. I won't do it and nothing he says or does can make me do it.*

Chapter 15

"Why, Miranda?" he repeated, more gently this time. "Where does this fear come from?"

She shook her head. It wasn't as if she could talk about it, especially not to him. The question itself was eliciting the memories, though she fought to block them out. "We were in his car when..." she heard herself blurt. She forced herself to continue. "We—we were in his car when I told him I couldn't marry him. That damned tiny car."

"Morsi," Rolf uttered in a low voice.

She moved on shaking legs toward a stone outcropping, and sank onto it. She stared straight ahead into the dark, the images of that long-ago night flashing inside her mind. Why did she have to recall it all so vividly? Why now? "He asked me why. I told him. That was my mistake. I shouldn't have told him."

She heard Rolf moving nearer. He stood behind her and his hands closed over her shoulders. "You told him his touch left you unmoved."

She swallowed hard and lowered her head. Her eyes closed tightly. "He was angry." She recalled his expression, illuminated only by the car's dashboard lights when she'd admitted she'd been faking her response to him from the start. He'd looked murderous. He'd *been* murderous. "And then he stopped the car."

"Miranda—"

"And . . . and he locked the doors," she whispered, but she was barely audible. Her throat convulsed painfully. Forcing the words out hurt her. "And then . . . he hit me." Her fists clenched until her nails nearly pricked her palms right through the gloves. If she hadn't been wearing them, she would have drawn blood. "I couldn't get away from him. The front seat under me, the locked door at my back, my shoulders jammed between the dashboard and the back of the seat. Him on top of me, raping me. I couldn't move. I couldn't breathe." As she spoke her breathing began to quicken again with the memory. "I honestly thought he was going to kill me."

She wrapped her arms around herself and bowed nearly double. It seemed to Rolf as if she was trying to protect herself from the memory.

He would kill Jeff Morsi. The dog would die slowly and painfully. Rolf knew that beyond any doubt. He wished in vain he had not left his sword behind at Miranda's home. But that would come later. For now, he had to bring Miranda into the present once more. He had to make her see that the danger was past. His arms went around her shuddering body and he pulled her into his lap as he sat on the cool stone floor in front of her. He held her hard, to be sure she knew he was there.

"I was so afraid, Rolf. So afraid and repulsed, and so ashamed."

"The shame belongs to him, Miranda. Not you."

"No. I shouldn't have let it happen. I should have tried harder to stop him, fight him. But he hurt me. God, how he hurt me. When it was over, I was sick. I couldn't stop throwing up. I could barely walk." She sobbed in his arms, and Rolf held her more tightly.

"Miranda, I understand now why you questioned me. Will you listen while I give you the answers you sought?"

She sniffed and nodded, her head still resting weakly against his chest.

"I was a boy of ten when a neighboring village was besieged by an enemy of the local Jarl. The sister of my mother, a woman still in the prime of her beauty and only recently wed, was raped by the marauders. Her husband, my uncle, was murdered before her eyes. She came to us, no longer the happy, lovely woman I knew, but a hollow-eyed ghost. All of my mother's comforting did little good. She took her own life less than a week later."

She shuddered in his arms. "Why do men do it?"

"No *man* takes a woman by force. Only a cowardly dog would act in such a way. This lesson I learned at a youthful age, and never did I forget. Later, in my rage, I put aside many of my father's words, but the lesson of my aunt Helga I remembered always. I have never forced myself on a woman, Miranda. I am sorry I did not assure you of that sooner."

She swallowed hard. "Why didn't you?"

He thought her shaking was subsiding a bit. He held her harder. "Because it wounded my pride to be asked to defend myself against such a charge. Perhaps I wished you to believe in me without my explanations."

Her head lifted, and in the glow of the light beams her tears glittered like diamonds. "I did, you know," she whispered. "If I hadn't, I never would've been able to let you make love to me."

"I ask too much of you, Miranda, to believe in my innocence when I refuse to explain. I was enraged after my exile. My king and my friend, Knut the Great, turned his back on me. My country banished me. I felt I had no more to lose. I was determined to build a great city to show them all my worth. For that, I needed gold and silver, iron and steel. So I put aside the ways of my father. I raided every coastal village I came upon. Yet my men knew that rape and murder were forbidden on pain of death. The only blood to stain our swords was the blood of those foolish enough to defy us. For those few brave men, Valhalla awaited." He paused to allow her time to consider. "I was not guilty of the crime for which I was banished."

"I know that," she said.

He lowered his head and pressed his lips into her hair. "Do you also know that I would die before I would let harm come to you, Miranda? Do you know that I would use my sword to remove the fingers from my hands before I would cause you pain?"

She lifted her head and stared into his eyes, shadowed now in the dim light. "Do you mean that?"

"I can prove it to you, lady. For do you choose to remain here, I will remain, as well. I will die at your side, rather than take the path to escape and leave you behind."

She shook her head and he thought her eyes widened. "I can't let you do that."

"Nor can you stop me."

She drew a long, slow breath and squared her shoulders. "How long is the passage?"

"Not long. But I must warn you it becomes smaller before it grows larger again."

She closed her eyes tightly and he saw her catch her lower lip in her teeth.

Stroking her silken cheek, he whispered, "Nothing will hurt you, Miranda. I will be close to you all the time."

"I know."

"Are you ready, then?"

She nodded, but he felt her body trembling. The merciful thing to do, he thought, would be to knock her unconscious and drag her to safety before she awoke. The very thought of raising a hand to Miranda caused Rolf's stomach to heave. He couldn't do it. Did her life depend upon it, he could not harm her deliberately.

Questions raced in his mind, but he held them back. Now was not the time to ask her the things he longed to know. Why, for instance, she had not taken steps to see that Morsi was punished for his acts? Surely her society had laws providing for the protection of its women. He simply could not fathom the reasons a woman like Miranda, a woman intelligent, capable and respected by all who knew her, would allow herself to be wronged in such a way without seeking retribution. It baffled him. It seemed so foreign to her character.

Rather than question her in her agitated state, he rose, setting her easily on her feet. He retrieved her helmet from the floor and placed it upon her head, fastening the chin strap securely. Taking a firm hold on her hand, he drew her to the small oval opening in the stone wall. He released her hand and slipped his legs into the tunnel. Once inside, he rolled over onto hands and knees. Facing her, he extended a hand. When she took it, he moved farther back into the darkness. The cold stone touched his sides. Only inches of space separated him from the stone above. "Come, Miranda. Come to me now."

He heard her movements, and saw the approach of her light. Her grip on his hand tightened as she crawled toward him. "Look only at me," he instructed. "Nothing else." She said nothing, but he heard the quickened pace of her breathing. He touched her face. "Come with me, Miranda. It will be over within a few moments, I promise you."

Awkwardly he crawled backward, keeping his senses attuned to her, feeling the heat of her body, hearing the brush of her knees over the stone as she crawled toward him. He moved slowly enough so she was never beyond his reach.

The tunnel sloped downward, then leveled off. The passage narrowed until Rolf had to stretch his legs behind him and push himself backward lying flat on the stone. Miranda could still crawl, but he knew the ceiling must be pressing down on her back, the walls against her sides when she moved slightly off center. Her breathing became harsher and she stopped moving. Panting, she fought to speak. "I . . . can't. I can't go—"

Rolf reached out to cup her face in his hands. He brought his head close to hers, touched her lips with his. "No harm will come to you, Miranda. Nothing here can hurt you. There is only you and me. Nothing else."

"I—" she fought for air "—I want to go back!" He heard the tears in her voice, the overwhelming fear.

"It is farther back than it is to the outside now, Miranda. Trust in me, if you can. Here. Hold my hand." He gripped her hand in his again and pushed himself backward with the other. Her hand felt as cold as the stone, even through the glove. It trembled violently, but she came with him all the same. He thought there could be no measure of the courage it took for her to forge ahead when she was nearly paralyzed with fear. He wished for greater strength, for unnatural speed, as he kept pushing himself backward. He spoke to her constantly as they struggled on.

Finally the tunnel widened again. A few yards more and its breadth was enough to accommodate them both, side by side. Rolf turned himself around and drew her up beside him. He was able to get up on his hands and knees again. "It is not much farther," he assured her. He wondered that she didn't faint with the rapid pattern of her breathing. He felt icy moisture dotting her face when he touched it again, and wished he knew a way to ease her torment.

At last they rounded the final bend in the passage. His light beam found the half circle of the tunnel entrance and then the snow and ice beyond. He heard her gasp deeply, and her pace increased. Rolf stayed at her side until they crawled out into the biting wind.

He stood then and helped Miranda to her feet. Instead of standing on her own, she collapsed against him without warning. His arms encircled her to hold her upright. The hammering of her heart alarmed him. He flicked the button to extinguish his light, then hers. Easily he scooped her up and began trudging down a snowy slope toward the village of tents and scientists that seemed so out of place in this barren land.

The place was oddly silent and seemingly abandoned. Rolf crouched low to enter the first tent he came to, and once inside, he lowered Miranda to the folding cot near the back. The tent was warm, a little heating device eliminating the chill. He tugged a blanket over her and knelt beside her, searching her face in the light of a lantern someone had left ablaze. "Are you all right, lady?"

She nodded, pressing a hand to her chest and forcibly, he thought, regulating her breaths. "I'm sorry. I'm such a coward."

"No, Miranda. You have the courage of a warrior. I've known few men in my life who could face such a powerful fear and conquer it."

"I couldn't have . . . if you hadn't been there. You saved my life, Rolf."

"If I did, then it is no more than you did for me." He watched her face for a long moment, feeling an unnatural tightness in his chest. He hadn't realized the might of the feelings for this woman until tonight. When he recalled his thought to curb his fondness for her, to avoid the pain she would cause him in the end, he nearly laughed at his own ignorance. It was too late for him to hope for mercy. It would kill him when she told him to go, when she continued with her life without him.

Miranda sat up slowly, one hand pressed to her forehead. "Rolf, we have to stop Jeff. Erwin and Fletch are both in danger now."

"I will go. You remain here, warm and dry. Rest here. Where are the others you spoke of?"

"Probably heard the explosion and are all at the original entrance trying to determine the cause." She threw back the cover. "I'm not staying here. We have to go. Quickly, Rolf. I pray we're not already too late." She got to her feet and came toward him. "My God, if I'd come forward about what he did to me two years ago, Jeff might be in jail right now. If anything happens to the others..."

Rolf's questions leapt to mind again. "Why did you not, Miranda?"

She shook her head, her eyes focused on the floor. "I was afraid."

"Of Morsi?"

"Yes, and of the stigma that would be attached to my name. No matter how much evidence there is in a rape, Rolf, there are always those who refuse to believe the victim, or who somehow find a way to claim it was her fault. I didn't think I could bear that." She bit her lip. "I was wrong. But I kept silent. He hadn't hit me in the face, and the other bruises were easy to hide." She looked up at him quickly. "I can't back down in fear of him this time, Rolf. I have to come with you."

"Please, Miranda, stay. I will not allow you to put yourself at risk again."

She lifted one hand to his face. "I'm going with you. I'm afraid—" She broke off, and shook her head.

"Afraid of what?" he prompted.

She lifted her gaze to his. "Afraid that if I let you go, I'll lose you. That's not something I can allow to happen."

He stared at her concerned face, trying hard to see the meaning behind her words, but failing. She couldn't mean that she had come to care for him. He knew he was unworthy of such a magnificent woman. Before he could argue with her further, she slipped past him out of the tent, and trudged determinedly over the frozen ground toward the sea. "Fletch is alone on that ship, and God knows where Jeff is."

Rolf caught up with her only as she was climbing into a small and battered-looking metal canoe. "They've got to have already gone back to the *Mermaid*," she said breathlessly. "The boat is gone." He knew her fondness for Erwin Saunders, and her greater love for Fletcher Travis. He felt a sharp concern of his own for Travis, for he'd grown to like and respect the man.

Rolf shoved the small craft into the sea. He stepped into it, sitting quickly as it wobbled. Miranda handed him a short, stubby paddle. She sat with her back to him holding a similar one. "Like this," she told him, lifting the paddle to demonstrate the proper grip. "You paddle on that side, and I on this. Ready?"

Rolf dipped his paddle as she did hers and pushed the water away behind them. He had to adjust his stroke right away, for his was so much more powerful than hers that the craft began to veer to the right. He soon mastered the rhythm. The sleek little craft knifed quickly through the mercifully calm sea. Soon they bumped against the hull of the *Mermaid*.

Rolf had no idea what Jeff Morsi's reaction would be to see them both alive when, no doubt, he'd thought them dead and buried. He only knew that he would not allow the dog to harm Miranda, or to draw another breath now that he knew how much harm he'd already done.

* * *

The rope ladder still hung over the side of the *Mermaid*. Rolf easily scaled it, then stood watch as Miranda climbed up to join him on the deck. He held her waist in his large hands as she clambered aboard. He tied no line to keep the little craft from drifting. Better to let it go and not announce their presence, Miranda guessed.

Miranda's heart leapt into her throat when she heard footsteps. Rolf's arm came around her fast and sure and he drew her into the shadows. The steps passed. Rolf held on to her hand, and together they moved down the shallow stairs to the area housing the cabins.

Rolf moved steadily, silently, in the direction of Jeff's cabin. Miranda tried to swallow her fear. Rolf stopped outside the door. He pressed her back against the wall and signaled her to stay there. Then he slammed open the door and leapt inside with murder in his eyes.

Miranda braced herself. Nothing happened. Only silence came from the room, and she turned, unable to stay still another second, and went inside. Jeff Morsi's body lay crumpled on the floor, a neat round bullet hole between his eyes. She screamed. She couldn't help it. She turned into Rolf's ready embrace and sobbed uncontrollably.

"What the hell—"

At the sound of Erwin Saunders's voice, Miranda tugged free of Rolf's grip. Relief washed over her when she saw him. "Thank God," she breathed, moving forward automatically to embrace him. "Thank God you're all right," she sobbed. "We were afraid Jeff had killed you."

"Jeff had—" Saunders tensed and held her away from him, searching her face. His hard expression eased at once, and he hugged her once again. "And I was certain he'd killed you, Miranda. I tried to go for help, but he forced me back here at gunpoint."

She sniffed, and wiped her tears away with a finger. "He wanted the credit for everything," she concluded. "Oh, Erwin, what happened here?"

"There, there, child. Calm yourself. Everything is fine now. Come, both of you. To your cabin. I'll fix you a warm drink and explain everything. The authorities have already been notified. They're on the way."

She walked beside Rolf, his arm firmly around her. In her cabin, she slipped out of her overalls and damp clothing, and donned fresh woolen underwear, a heavy sweater, sturdy denim jeans and a warm coat. Rolf changed, as well, and by the time they'd both finished, Saunders had returned with mugs of hot buttered rum for each of them.

Miranda sipped hers gratefully, feeling its warmth sing through her veins. Rolf's drink was half-gone with his first swallow. Then he faced Saunders. "How did Morsi expect to achieve this without help, Saunders?"

Saunders waved them both into seats, while he continued standing, watching them, his face seemingly concerned. "He had help. I've learned of the entire plot. It's all very involved."

Miranda sipped her drink again. Rolf downed his. "Who killed him?" Rolf asked.

"His partner. Guess the selfish bastard wanted all the credit for himself." He stroked his beard, his gaze glued to Rolf's face.

"Who?" Rolf pressed a hand to his forehead, blinked a few times, and shook his head as if to clear it.

"Would you believe . . . Fletcher Travis?"

"*Nei.*" Rolf began to stand. As he did, Miranda saw two of him all at once, and her head was swimming. Odd. Probably shock.

"Not Fletch," she mumbled, her tongue feeling thick and awkward.

"No, not Fletch," Saunders agreed. "Did I tell you about his accident? He took a blow to the head and fell overboard a little while ago. Damn shame he was so clumsy."

"No!" Miranda leapt to her feet, and instantly sagged to her knees.

Rolf leaned over to help her, but sank instead to the floor beside her. He turned an angry glare on Saunders. "You . . . poisoned the . . . drinks."

"No, not quite, but close enough. You might have also guessed the identity of Morsi's partner by now, or I should say, ex-partner." He stepped back as Rolf's arm swung out toward him. He reached for the door, stepped through it. "Morsi wouldn't admit to stealing the Ice Man, Miranda, so I can only assume you did it. Care to tell me where it's hidden while you still can?" She didn't answer. "Ah, well, no matter. I'll find it. Have a nice nap, you two. I'll be taking steps quite soon to insure it is a permanent one."

Miranda saw Rolf's head fall forward, his eyes droop closed, just before her mind went blank and her body limp.

Chapter 16

When she opened her eyes, Miranda knew something was different. She felt the cool air and the constant spray of water on her skin. She felt the sun's heat gradually warming her chilled flesh.

She sat up suddenly, rocking the small boat. She gripped its sides and looked around her, eyes wide. "Oh, my God," she whispered hoarsely.

Everywhere, in any direction she looked—water. Deep, dark blue, ice-cold water. Its surface was a study in ripples and lines, and gentle, ever-moving swells lifted and lapped at the small craft. Far, far away, the brilliant orange ball of fire seemed to rest on the water's surface. There was nothing else in sight. No land, no ice. She didn't even see a sea-bird circling in the distance. She had time to be grateful for the overcoats they still wore before panic took root, colder than the sea that surrounded her.

A low groan brought her head around. Rolf stirred, but didn't open his eyes. He lay slumped in the rear of the boat, near the motor, his head cocked at an impossible angle, one arm bent beneath him. Carefully, so as not to tilt the little boat, she crawled to him, gripped his shoulders and attempted to make him more comfortable. When she tugged his arm out from under him, he grunted. It must have hurt. His eyes flew open and slowly he seemed to focus, first on her, then on the small boat and the limitless sea surrounding them.

He sat up slowly, his gaze returning to Miranda. He rubbed his left temple with his fingertips. "He put something into the drinks," he said finally. "A sleeping powder." Miranda shook her head in denial as the truth hit home. "It was not Morsi alone who tried to kill us, Miranda." Rolf shifted, lifting himself onto the soft padded seat in the stern. "It was Erwin Saunders, as well."

Again she shook her head. "But why? He was my friend, my father's friend—"

"*Nei*. He is a man with much greed and a great hunger for glory. He wished to retain all credit for the discovery of the *drakkar*. And perhaps he meant to find the treasure, as well, to take a goodly share of it for himself. You yourself told me what a simple matter it would be to sell a few pieces, and acquire more wealth than one could spend in a lifetime." As she desperately sought for another explanation, he touched her face. "Travis said it would have been the greatest achievement in your father's career, or in yours. He said you would be in such great demand by universities, you would be able to name your own price."

She nodded, and studied his face. "I just can't believe money and acclaim would be so important to him that he would try to kill—" She stopped short and glanced out to sea once more. "Is he going to succeed this time?"

Rolf laughed. It began as a low rumble deep in his chest and gained momentum until he fairly bellowed. Finally he wrapped his arms around her and hugged her hard. "My sweet lady, your friend picked a poor method to execute the Plague of the North."

He turned toward the stern again, touched the motor. "No doubt this contraption was the first thing to be disabled." To give proof to his theory, he attempted several times to start the thing, but found it uncooperative. He then found the bolts that held it in place and twisted them free with his fingers. Gently he eased the motor up and, with a shove, tossed it into the freezing waves where it disappeared.

Miranda choked back a sob, but too late not to have him notice the small sound. He turned, frowning at the tears that shimmered in her eyes. He eased her up onto the seat at the bow and knelt beside her. "No tears, Miranda. Not only do they cause me unspeakable pain, but they rob you of precious water. You need to conserve what you have in your body." He put his hand on hers. "Have you so little faith in me?"

She sniffed and blinked away her tears. "It hurts me to be so betrayed by someone I once cared for. That's why I was crying."

He nodded. "I know that pain, lady. I've had much experience in that pain." He was silent for a long moment. Then he took the seat beside her, one hand gripping hers tightly. "But he never truly felt anything for you, you know. Or for your father."

"No. He must not have."

"He was pretending all along, even earlier, when he funded the expedition to find me."

"He must have been laughing at us then. He thought it was all madness. But when we found you, he couldn't wait to cash in. I wonder how much of Cryo-Life's backing went into the budget, and how much went into Erwin's pockets."

"He used your father, Miranda. He used you."

She felt her spine grow tense. "He caused Russell's heart attack. He broke in that night, searching for the true journal, the one we found in the computer."

"No doubt." Rolf studied her face as Miranda felt her heart begin to pound, pumping the blood that no doubt colored her cheeks right now. Anger burned a hot path through her veins. Her hands clenched with it. "Although I am sure he didn't intend for your father to die," Rolf added.

"He might as well have. He killed my father and now he's trying to kill us. Damn him, Rolf. Damn him, he'll pay for this!"

When she turned toward him he was smiling very slightly. "Much better. Your eyes glitter like silver when you are angry, Miranda. I much prefer silver to the diamonds in your eyes when you cry."

Her anger was unabated but she filled with warmth toward him. "I think I know how you must have felt after your exile. I don't know what stings more than betrayal. Especially when the traitor is someone you loved."

"In my case, it was little more than a young man's lust. At the time, though, it was the nearest thing to love I had known." He shook his head. "There is no excuse for what I did. Since the object of my wrath was not available, I sought my vengeance upon the innocent coastal villages of Europe."

"I feel angry enough to raid a village or two myself at the moment."

He chuckled, obviously amused at the image. Then he looked around. "We are drifting at the whim of the currents. Not a safe prospect. We need power, and direction." He grabbed one of the two oars from under the seat. "Behold, a mast." He dragged out the other oar and then set them both down beside him, and rummaged beneath the seats for more tools. He emerged at last with a length of rope and a first-aid kit. He tossed the latter to her. "See if there is anything of use in this box." Then, with the oars crossing over one another in his lap, he began wrapping the rope around them in an X pattern.

He took his time and worked carefully, sometimes unwrapping and rewrapping when he felt it hadn't gone just right. "I will need your shirt. You can keep the coat, but your shirt and mine will be our sail."

Miranda caught her breath. He was truly amazing, her Viking. "You won't need the shirts, Rolf. You can use this." She held up the folded square of impossibly shiny material. At Rolf's frown, she explained. "It's supposed to be very warm. You wrap it around you in case of emergency. It's a sort of blanket." As she spoke she unfolded it, but clutched it to her chest when the wind threatened to rip it from her hands.

Rolf nodded in approval. "Very good, Miranda. Have you any ideas for a rudder?" As he spoke, he painstakingly tied the corners of the blanket to the crosspiece and the main mast. This finished, he laid the newly formed sail to rest, instructing Miranda to hold it lest the wind blow it away.

She watched in wonder as Rolf tore the cushions from the rear seat and pulled a small dagger from his boot. Slowly, steadily, he chipped away at the wooden board. It took the better part of an hour for him to carve a small jagged hole in the seat. He thrust the bottom of the oar-mast into this, tested its stability, and added two lengths of rope to anchor it in place.

No sooner had he raised the sail than Miranda felt the wind pushing them rapidly through the water. She felt the thrill of success sing through her veins, but not for long. Only a moment after she squinted directly into the rising sun, she caught her breath. "Rolf, we're heading east. Shouldn't we be going the other way?"

"You'd have made a fine oarsman, woman." He hurriedly disconnected the rope anchoring one side of the sail. Then he slowly turned the sail until it angled to one side. When the boat rocked dangerously, the wind pushing it sideways, he pushed the outermost edges of the sail closer together, until the thing was pointed, rather similar to the triangle-shaped sails of today's sailboats. Their direction changed gradually, until they moved away from the sun. Rolf anchored the sail and relaxed for a moment. "We travel west by southwest," he told her. "And we still need a rudder."

Miranda dumped the contents from the first-aid box. "This is plastic. You could cut it to the right shape with your knife."

Rolf took the box from her hands, turned it over slowly. He nodded. "Yes, it might work. He retrieved the dagger and went to work once more, stopping periodically to leap to his feet and readjust the sail. Miranda realized it would be frightfully easy to tip over, especially sailing against the wind as they were, and having to cut the boat in and out of it.

Yet she wasn't afraid. Instead she felt an odd excitement stirring within her. She silently thrilled with each demonstration of Rolf's skill and her blood churned with the adventure of it all. The challenge.

All day they skimmed over the waves. Rolf used the position of the sun to gauge them, sailing toward it rather than away once it passed its zenith. Rolf sat on the floor of the boat, behind the sail, so he could maneuver the sail and the rudder simultaneously. They spoke little.

Miranda was cold and her head ached with the aftereffects of whatever Erwin Saunders had drugged them with. She was hungry and before the day waned, terribly thirsty. She spoke of none of this, though, since she knew Rolf must be feeling the same things she was. She racked her brain to think of a way she could boil the water and capture the purified steam.

They sailed past huge icebergs, and once Miranda spotted the dorsal fin of what she swore was a whale, far off in the distance. The day seemed to last forever, but finally, after what must have been eighteen hours, the sun dipped below the horizon. Her eyes widened. "Rolf—"

"*Já*, we have moved to the south. The current pulls us rapidly southward. We will find the warmth as well as the shore, Miranda. I'll not have you dying of the cold." As the sun sank just out of sight, Rolf lowered the sail, and dropped the anchor over the side. He came to the fore where she huddled in her coat, and sat down beside her.

"Are we stopping for the night?"

"No. Only until the stars appear to guide us. The anchor should keep us from drifting too far, though it will not hold us steady. At the moment we are in a southwesterly bound current, so if we drift, we drift in the right direction."

She snuggled closer. "Put your arms around me, Rolf. Hold me."

He did, and she immediately felt warmer. "Are you afraid, Miranda?"

"No. Strange, isn't it? But I'm not. Aside from a few minor discomforts, I'm enjoying this."

"You are a woman of odd tastes. You enjoy being cold, hungry, thirsty?"

"I enjoy facing insurmountable odds and beating them, although today you've done most of the beating." She shifted her position so she could look up into his face. She ran a hand over his stubble-coated cheeks and chin. "Ahh, your beard is coming back. Soon you'll look like you did when I first saw you."

"You change the subject. You wish to take part in beating these odds you speak of?"

She thought about it a moment. "Yes. Ever since you convinced me to crawl through that mouse hole I've begun to feel differently. Not like myself. More . . . I don't know . . . confident, stronger. You know?"

"When once a man conquers his strongest foe and yearns to repeat the battle, this is the mark of a true hero." He looked at her intently. "It was one of my father's favorite proverbs. The fear of that tunnel was your strongest foe, my lady heroine, and now you are eager to conquer all others. I think you like adventure."

She shrugged. "Maybe I do."

"Then you will learn to man the sail and the rudder, and give my tired arms some time to rest."

She tensed in his embrace. "I'd better not. I might get us both killed."

"It isn't so bad. I've died before, remember?" At her look of absolute shock, he smiled, his amused face clearly visible in the pale sub-Arctic night. There would only be a very short period of real darkness. "I was kidding, as you say, Miranda. You have not enough faith in your own abilities. You are a strong, intelligent woman, with more courage than some warriors I have known. You will manage."

She did. He'd known she would. Rolf sat behind her, his arms around her, guiding her hands as she got a feel for the wind in the sail and the rush of the sea on the handmade rudder. He pointed out the stars they would follow, and told her their names in his native tongue.

She was nervous at first, but as she relaxed the knack of handling the boat came to her, as he had sensed it would. "Feel the wind caress the sail, Miranda? There, that gentle change, feel it?" She nodded and easily adjusted the sail to accommodate the shift in the wind.

"This is incredible," she whispered. Her hood blew back and her hair whipped around Rolf's neck. He took his hands away from hers to replace it but she put a hand on his arm. "No, leave it. I want to feel the wind."

He looked into her eyes with understanding. Had he not stood upon the deck amid raging storms simply to feel the power? Instead of replacing his hands on hers, he lowered them, encircling her narrow waist. She was doing well, sensing instinctively what was needed and when. Rolf would know if she made a mistake and he would right it before any harm was done. For now, he'd let her maneuver the boat in the gentle wind and easy current. He leaned over and whispered in her ear, "You are not *in* the boat Miranda, you *are* the boat. You are one with the wind and the water and the wood. You see?"

She nodded. "Yes. And with you."

Rolf blinked in astonishment, but realized at once she was right. He was feeling it—too, this union of spirits. The sense of uniting with nature was a familiar one to him. That of uniting with another soul was foreign, and for a second it shook him. Then he thought it over more carefully and he knew that was exactly what he'd felt when he'd made love to her. Union. He hadn't been inside her; he'd been a part of her. They'd been as one mind, one body. He'd sensed her pleasure, her needs, much as she'd seemed to sense his. It had been beyond any experience he'd had in lovemaking, and he knew it had been the same for her, as well. Just like sailing. Just like becoming one with the sea and the wind and the ship. Blessed union. Consummate understanding. He hadn't believed such a thing was possible between two human souls.

His hands rose higher, and he slipped them beneath her coat and then her blouse, cupping her breasts, squeezing them, stilling when her tender nipples blossomed to his touch. They pressed to his fingertips as if pleading for attention and he gave it without hesitation. He bent his head to nuzzle her neck with his lips.

"Your hands are cold," she whispered, tilting her head backward to ease the way for his mouth.

"You wish me to stop?"

"Never."

He angled his head around farther, so he could taste her lips. They were dry, but he moistened them for her. The sweetness they protected was as succulent as ever and he drank deeply of her for a long time. "I want you very badly, Miranda."

"But..." She struggled for words against her rapid breathing. "The sail..."

"Trust me," he muttered, nibbling her earlobe like an exotic fruit. He moved his hands to the snap of her jeans, and in a moment he was shoving them down over her hips, underwear and all. He ran his palms over the warm, bare curve of her buttocks, then threaded his fingers forward, finding her hot center already open and moist.

She made a sound deep in her throat when he probed her. "Do not close your mind, Miranda. Keep it open to everything. Not just me, but the sea and the wind, as well. Feel it all." She nodded, and Rolf removed one of his hands so he could free himself of the constraints of denim and zipper. He throbbed for her, and in a moment he lifted her slightly and lowered her over him. He knelt, sitting back on his heels, her lovely rounded buttocks pressed tight to his lap, her sweet, narrow passage tight around him. Her thighs parted and her knees supported most of her weight, a situation Rolf wished to remedy. He did, slipping his hands beneath her thighs and lifting her.

Immediately her weight shifted. He lifted his hips until her entire body was supported only by his manhood. He gripped her waist and pulled her down harder, feeling himself penetrate more deeply inside her. When she would have fallen forward, he lifted his hands, holding her and cupping her breasts at the same time. He moved his hips rapidly, plunging into her again and again.

At the first hint of his growing aggression, she stiffened and lifted her body as if to move away from the intruding shaft of heat that invaded her. But he held her to him with gentle firmness and plunged as deeply as was possible. "Surrender, Miranda," he growled deep in his throat. "Feel." Again he thrusted himself into her. "Tell me, is it pain you feel, or pleasure?"

Breathing ragged, she replied, "It's just... so tight, and... and so deep."

Her words drove him to the brink of madness, and he quickened the pace of his thrusts. He was not surprised when she joined in his efforts to increase the depth to which he could caress her, slamming her body harder and harder down onto him. When she neared release, he knew. He felt the way her body tightened around him, the sudden rush of her honeyed fluids coating him, the fit of trembling that engulfed her. He held her harder, giving himself over to every sensation. To the rocking of the boat beneath them, to the breeze caressing their bodies.

She cried out as her body began to convulse around him in a rhythmic massage. Rolf exploded into a million searing bits of sensation as he poured his essence into her. He remained within her for a long time as the desperate throbbing eased in both of them, slowed, and cooled. Finally he eased her from his lap and righted her denims before his own. As soon as he settled back once more, she snuggled into his embrace, her body nestled between his legs, her back pressed to his chest. Her head came to rest just beneath his chin and he bent his own to kiss her hair.

She tilted her head up a little to see him. "I'm in love with you, Rolf."

He blinked rapidly. In love with him. He knew the significance of her declaration, yet he doubted the truth of her words. "You believe there is a chance we will not survive this voyage, Miranda, so you say things you would not say otherwise."

She shook her head, but he only smiled softly and continued. "It flatters me that you might think yourself in love with me, but we both know it is only the situation. You will soon be the most respected, sought-after scientist in your field. You will have achieved the goal you have worked your entire life to reach. There is no room in your life for a barbarian from the past."

She opened her mouth to speak, then bit her lip. Her head moved very slightly from side to side. "You're wrong, but I can see I won't convince you of it with mere words. I suppose it can wait."

The wind shifted abruptly, and Miranda sat up fast, moving the sail to the right and reaching for the rudder almost from instinct. Truly Rolf could almost believe they were one. A shame that she would never be able to devote herself to him above her career, her science. For only that would do. He couldn't have her if she placed more import upon the work than upon the two of them together. He felt too strongly for her to settle for that. And anything else, he knew, was not possible.

For now, though, he would revel in her nearness, her closeness to him, body and soul. He held her to his chest, breathed her scent, and gazed upward into the growing darkness. Truly he felt content here with her like this, he felt. As if, after a very long voyage, one fraught with confusion and loss, he'd come home to her welcoming embrace.

He almost wished to prolong their voyage together, for when it ended, so would this closeness between them. At the thought of that, a warm tear escaped from Rolf's eye and rolled in silence down his face.

Chapter 17

Miranda slept, though she wasn't sure exactly when. As she slowly opened her eyes, a cold dawn greeted her and the sea rolled less gently than it had before. Frigid waves lapped at the sides of the small boat and rocked it frighteningly. Rolf manned the crude sail with expert hands, but his face seemed drawn and tired.

She'd told him she loved him last night. She recalled his tender caresses, his soft-spoken Norse words, his fevered lovemaking. He hadn't said he returned her feelings. Far from it. He'd argued that she would have no room in her life for him. He was wrong.

She straightened and stretched her arms above her head to work the kink from her spine. Shuffling into position, she removed his hands from the sail and replaced them with her own. As his blue eyes scanned her face, she forced a tremulous smile. "Rest for a while, Rolf. I'll take over."

He smiled tiredly. His hands came up to cup her face and he leaned over to press his lips tenderly to hers. Without a word he settled back and closed his eyes. In minutes his deep, steady breathing told her he slept. That he trusted her enough to pilot the tiny vessel while he slept sent a wave of warmth through her, and she took great care to keep them on course, checking often to see that the sun remained behind her right shoulder.

Hunger pangs stabbed at her. She shivered constantly now, unable to get warm even in the folds of her heavy coat, dampened as it was with sea spray. Her throat cried out for water and she was sorely tempted to scoop a handful of seawater to her lips. She resisted that impulse, knowing it would do her more harm than good. She forcibly closed her mind to the physical discomforts and focused only on the boat, the sail, the sea, striving to experience again that oneness she had felt last night. More and more, though, she felt only despair. She truly began to wonder if she'd ever set her feet on solid earth again.

Rolf rested only an hour by Miranda's guess. He stirred awake too soon, she thought, and again took the sail. Miranda wrapped her arms around his waist and rested her face against his broad shoulder. "You should sleep more, Rolf. You've been awake all night."

He released the rudder long enough to stroke her hair. "There will be time for sleep later, *astín mín,* when we reach the shore.

Her head came up quickly. "What shore?"

"The same one I found many times in the past. The place I planned to build my city, Vinland, with its forests and sweet grasses, lies farther to the south. And a great distance still farther, in the land you call Maine, is another place Leif Eriksson visited, and I after him. We will find land before then, I know. I know not how far, but I think we will see it by nightfall."

His certainty bewildered her and he must have seen the doubt in her eyes. "You forget, Miranda, I have sailed these waters many times, with no aid from your compasses and maps. The stars last night showed me the way. The skies are fair. We will soon see land again.''

"Rolf, we have no idea how far Erwin took us. It could be hundreds of miles to land, any kind of land, let alone some that's inhabited.''

"We are with the *straumr*, the current, now, Miranda. By nightfall, I promise.''

That assurance was all that got her through the day. She kept scanning the horizon until her eyes ached. It was nearly full dark when she felt his hand grip her shoulder and followed the direction of his gaze. A seabird swooped down, emitting its piercing cry like a welcome, and ascended again to the skies with a small fish clamped in its oversize bill. Her heart raced, adrenaline giving her new-found energy.

An hour later they sighted a beautiful shape of land protruding from the sea. Another hour after that, Rolf skillfully guided the small boat around two densely forested and apparently uninhabited islands, and into shallow waters along the coast, which swelled in a gentle green mound up from the sea. At an Inuit fishing village, with its clusters of neat houses and occasional house trailers and its rows of bobbing fishing boats, Rolf dragged their small craft out of the water. The place smelled of conifers and fish entrails.

Someone spotted them and then several men rushed toward them, exclaiming in accented French and something that sounded like Inuktitut. Miranda stepped from the boat unaided, trying to judge exactly where they were, staring at the hills and forests in the distance. Then Rolf turned to help her. The moment his strong hands closed on her arms, darkness descended and she slumped into his embrace.

If he'd thought the journey had been difficult to this point, Rolf now saw their time in the little boat as a fond memory. The Inuit—and he was certain that is who these people were, by their sun-darkened skin and exotic almond eyes—had definite ideas about how to care for Miranda, though Rolf had refused to let them take her from his arms. He'd been guided to a sled, which was pulled by another, one with a motor like a car. The ride was gut-wrenching and cold despite the friendly sun and the blankets they'd both been draped with. But at the end of that ride, there had been another, far more harrowing journey.

Tensed to the breaking point, Rolf had clung to Miranda in the silvery-winged bird-ship as it carried them right into the skies. At least this time the man at his side spoke in Miranda's tongue, though his words were strangely accented. Rolf was fairly certain they were being taken to a hospital where Miranda could be cared for properly, and for that he was grateful.

At last he'd been forced to surrender her. Only two hours after tugging the boat onto the shore, Rolf watched helplessly as Miranda was placed upon a table with wheels and pushed down a corridor and through a set of doors. This place had the same pungent aroma and white-coated people filling its halls as the first hospital Rolf had visited. The place where Miranda's *faðir* had died. It had the same hushed quality and the same clean, orderly appearance. Rolf slumped into a chair to wait, only to find himself approached by a stranger.

The man introduced himself as Le Blanc and held up a badge, which meant very little to Rolf. "Can you tell me what happened?" Unlike the others he'd spoken to so far, Rolf found this man's speech easy to understand.

Rolf nodded, supposing this Le Blanc must be in some position of authority here. "There is a group of scientists at the place you call Baffin."

"Baffin Island? You mean the expedition team that uncovered that Ice Man?"

"Já," Rolf said, nodding hard. "The woman, Miranda, is one of them. She located the sunken *drakkar*...the dragon ship of the man she called Viking, and the place where his treasures were hidden." He recalled again Miranda's courage in the cave, and his heart twisted painfully in his chest. His gaze turned toward the place they had taken her. "Will she live?"

"I'm sure she'll be all right. I heard the doctors say it was a mild case of exposure...too much time in the cold." The man pulled a notepad from his shirt and printed words upon it with a pencil. "You said her name is Miranda?"

"Miranda O'Shea," Rolf told him, his voice flat. "And the man who attempted to kill her is called Erwin Saunders."

The man's head came up slowly. "Tried to kill her?"

"Já, and me, as well. We were given a beverage with some kind of sleeping powder. We woke upon the small boat, far away from shore. The boat's...motor...had been disabled."

Le Blanc narrowed his eyes. "Why do you think this man wanted to murder you?"

"He wished to claim it was he who discovered the ship and the treasures it held. He was, I believe, envious of Miranda's wisdom, and fearful she would replace him in his position at the university."

"Do you have any proof of all this?"

"My word. Miranda's, when she wakes. Saunders killed Jeff Morsi with a gun, but has likely put the body into the sea by now. And Fletcher Travis..." Rolf shook his head, pressing his fingertips to his brow and closing his eyes. "I fear he has killed Travis, as well." Rolf got to his feet. "I have told you all I know. I will go to her now."

Le Blanc stood, as well. "Maybe you ought to let them have a look at you."

"I am well." Rolf turned and started down the hall.

"They're not going to let you in there," the man warned.

"They will not keep me out." Rolf strode away, and pushed the doors open.

"Damned if I don't believe you," he heard the man mutter before the doors swung closed again.

Hours later, as he held on to her hand, Miranda's eyes opened, and Rolf's throat tightened painfully as his limbs turned weak with relief. He leaned nearer her, only to have her arms encircle his neck and her lips press to his face. No words passed between them as they embraced. Rolf held her hard to his chest, buried his face in her silken hair, breathed her scent. Would that he could remain just so for all time.

When she finally straightened, she searched his face, her own eyes dark with concern. "What's happening?"

"The authorities of this...Canada...were unable to find Saunders. The *Mermaid* has gone. I am told, Miranda, that Saunders is expected at Beaumont today. He has scheduled something called a . . . press con-fer—"

"A press conference." Her eyes narrowed and Rolf saw the tightening in her jaw that boded not well for the one who had caused it. "No doubt he's going to announce his discovery. I wonder how he'll explain our deaths?"

"Your police will be there, Miranda. He will be taken, though I would much prefer to inflict my own justice this time."

She started to smile, but it died utterly all at once and her eyes swam beneath an onslaught of moisture. "What about...Fletch?"

Rolf stood and moved away from the bed. He heard the sob that caught in her throat as he reached for the door. He pulled it open, then turned to watch Miranda's eyes light up when Travis entered. He had a white bandage wrapped around his head and one hand was heavily bandaged, as well. He held a wooden walking stick as he limped into the room.

"Fletch!" Miranda leapt from the bed and threw her arms around him. For once, Rolf felt no jealousy. His own reaction to the man's appearance had been much the same. "What did you . . . how did—"

"Easy, Miranda. I'm not exactly myself." As she stepped away, she seemed to note his injuries for the first time. Travis only smiled crookedly. "When I heard the explosion I was half-crazy to get to that cave. Someone hit me from behind and tossed me overboard. I should've been watching my back."

"Are you all right now?" Her concerned eyes moved over his bandaged head and hand, then lit on the cane.

"A little frostbite, a few stitches in the noggin. Nothing serious. I was about to leave the hospital in St. Anthony when your Canadian cop, Le Blanc, tracked me down. I caught the first flight down here."

She frowned. "Where are we, Rolf?"

"A hospital in a place called St. John's in Newfoundland. They brought you here because it is the best hospital in the area. We came by way of one of your wondrous bird-ships, Miranda. I wish you had been awake."

She smiled at him, her eyes brimming with emotion. "You flew? You must have been scared to death."

"More afraid of losing you than of sailing in the bird-ship."

She stepped up to him and slid her arms around him. He held her tight for a long moment. Then she turned, still in his embrace, to face Travis once more. He was looking very strangely from one to the other. Miranda stiffened. "It's just that he's never flown."

"No doubt," Fletcher replied, one brow lifting higher than the other.

"How did you end up in St. Anthony?" Rolf sensed she was trying to change the subject.

"I swam for the shore, passed out at some point, but I must have made it. The Inuit inhabitants pulled me out of the surf." Travis slanted a sly glance at Rolf. "Seems to me they're making a habit of doing that. First Rolf, now me."

Rolf froze, Fletcher's meaning clear. Miranda's grip around his waist tightened.

"I'm just glad they took me to the nearest dome tent and turned me over to the Beaumont expedition. Sure beats the hell out of being dragged into some cave and left for dead for the next nine centuries, huh, Rolf?"

"Fletcher . . ." Miranda began.

"Hey, don't look like that. I'm not saying a word to anybody." He glanced at Rolf once again. "Who the hell would believe it? No, I'd probably end up in a psychiatric ward wearing a brand-new jacket." He smiled at the two of them and turned to go.

"Thank you, Travis," Rolf said softly.

"Don't think I won't expect some form of compensation, big guy. I'll be bugging you to tell me stories until you're ready to throw me back in the sea."

"No chance of that, my friend," Rolf replied with a wide grin.

Again, Rolf flew. This time holding Miranda's hand and enjoying the novel adventure, rather than clinging to her limp form and fearing for her life.

She'd insisted they leave at once to be present for Saunders's press conference. It seemed she did not trust in the police to see justice done. Or perhaps she simply wished to witness the event firsthand.

Either way, a short time later they found themselves in a crowded room, which was slowly being lined with police officers. A crowd of men and women holding flashing lights and odd devices of all sorts milled around a platform where Erwin Saunders stood speaking. Rolf, Miranda and Travis lingered unseen at the rear and listened to the lies he spewed so easily.

"I had no choice but to shoot Jeff Morsi. He would have killed me just as he did my peers, numismatist Fletcher Travis, our own archaeologist Miranda O'Shea and her friend, an Icelandic historian called Rolf Magnusson. Their bodies, I fear, may never be found since he tossed them into the sea. And he did all of this from simple greed, I'm afraid. They knew that it was I who tracked down the exact locale of the sunken ship, and Morsi was determined to take the credit."

Miranda lunged forward then, despite the hand Rolf reached out to stop her. "If you're finished, Professor Saunders, perhaps the press would like to hear the truth now."

A rumble went up from the people around her. Her name was whispered, then shouted, and the blinding lights flashed like explosions. Saunders turned white. His mouth gaped and he sought words but found none. A second later, he bolted, but was easily grabbed by the police officers who had been silently waiting. Miranda watched his capture, rage visible in her eyes. She stepped up to the podium and addressed the crowd.

"It was Rolf Magnusson who located the ship. Fletcher Travis and I knew it, and that is why Erwin Saunders tried to kill us all. Jeff Morsi was Erwin's accomplice in all of this. Erwin shot him because he didn't want to share the credit . . . or the spoils."

"She's lying!" Saunders's hoarse cry was so obviously desperate that few in the room gave it heed. Instead, questions were shouted at Miranda, who waved them aside.

"I'm sorry. No questions. I promise the details will be forthcoming."

She stepped down amid shouted questions and made her way toward Rolf, who waited to fold her into his arms. He swelled with pride for her strength and her courage, and yet as he saw the way the people in the room sought her attention, his heart grew heavy.

Truly his time with Miranda had come to an end. No longer would she need his strength, for it seemed she had found her own. Her goal would be reached with this latest adventure. She would be as sought after as Saunders had hoped to become due to this discovery. Rolf had remained long enough to assist her in finding the ship and the treasure. She didn't need him any longer. It was time, past time, for Rolf to make his own way in this world.

"Which offer will you accept?"

Miranda replaced the receiver and faced Rolf. He carried two cups of steaming cocoa. He really did have a weakness for chocolate, she thought idly. He'd been oddly distant since they'd returned three days ago. Not that there had been much chance to be otherwise. Reporters had hounded their steps. The telephone had rung off the hook, one call with word that Paul Potter and the rest of the shiftless crew Saunders had hired had been located and were in custody. Offers from the most prestigious universities in the country had been pouring in steadily. And not just for her. Many sought the expertise of Rolf Magnusson, the man who'd used some sixth sense, as far as they could tell, to find the sunken ship and then the treasure within the cave. He'd volunteered that information, observing the treasure had never really been his to hold.

"What do you think I should do?"

He shrugged, handed her a cup and took a seat opposite her. He stared into the crackling fire on the hearth. "You have reached your goal. You are the most sought after, the best, as you said you wished to be. The choice is yours, *astín mín.*''

She shook her head. He was her choice. But how could she make him see that? "Those were more my father's dreams than my own." She drew a deep breath and sighed. "I don't want to be the head of any department. I don't want to be tied down to a classroom and a university and a desk. It would bore me, after all we've been through." He studied her in silence. "Rolf, you've had offers, too. You have a great deal of knowledge, and people would like for you to share it."

"*Nei.* I, too, would soon grow bored with it. Fear not for me, *astín mín.* I will find my way in this world of yours. These jobs they offer, there are too many complications. They wish to know where I came upon my knowledge of the past."

"You are self-taught. You've proven your abilities. No one will make too much fuss."

"I am not a citizen of your country. There are laws. How will I explain my past, or seeming lack of one? No, it will be easier to find a simple job, to earn my way with my hands. I am strong. I will manage."

"There are ways around the laws, Rolf." She straightened her spine and lifted her chin as she gathered her courage. "We could—" She broke off as the doorbell sounded. Angrily she set her mug aside and went to answer it. She was growing more frustrated by the minute. The man seemed determined to leave her, and that was not something she thought she could bear.

Harrison Kirk, Beaumont's Dean, came in slowly and patted Miranda's shoulder with one hand as he shook the other. He approached Rolf and greeted him warmly. "Sorry to intrude. I know it's been hectic."

"It's all right, Harry. Come in. Cocoa?"

He held up a hand. "No, thank you. I just wanted to check in, see if you've decided what to do."

She turned, studied Rolf's expectant face. *Astín mín,* the words he used more and more often when he addressed her, echoed in her ears. Last night she'd looked them up in her Islensk dictionary. My love. Did he toss such endearments around lightly, or did he mean it?

Time to find out.

"Yes, as a matter of fact, I have. I'm turning down all offers, yours included."

Rolf frowned until his pale golden brows met over his Arctic blue eyes.

"Turning... Miranda, dear, what are you saying?"

"I don't want to tie myself down, Harry. I can't be head of anyone's department. I want to be in the field, with my hands in the dirt and the excitement in my heart." She tore her gaze from Rolf's surprised one and faced Harry squarely. "If Beaumont will continue funding my expeditions, I'll stay on for now. But on a project-by-project basis."

Harry looked shocked. "You can't be serious. Do you know what you're turning down?"

"I'll manage. My father had begun work on a book, you know. The life story of the man they called the Plague of the North. I think I'll finish it." She glanced up at the stunned dean and smiled, feeling free and unfettered for the first time since... since that night she'd spent with Rolf in the little boat with nothing between the two of them and the sea and the wind. "Well, Harry? What do you say? We could begin with an excavation of a site right here in Maine, proving Leif Eriksson's explorations extended much farther south than previously believed."

Harrison's eyes widened and took on an excited gleam. "You...you are serious, aren't you? You want to...to free-lance?" He said the word as if it were distasteful, then bit his lip. "You really think you can find evidence of Norsemen in Maine?"

"Rolf can. Of course you realize we're a team now. I can't work without him."

"You can't?" Harrison seemed confused, but Miranda ignored him, her gaze returning to Rolf's.

"No, I can't. I can't work without him...I don't think...I could live without him."

Rolf rose slowly, his eyes never leaving hers. "Miranda, consider your words. I cannot take second place to your work, much as I would like to do so."

Miranda stepped forward until she could reach up and run her palm down the side of his face. "I would never ask you to, my love," she replied softly. "I love my work, but it's only a shadow compared to the way I love you."

Harrison Kirk stepped awkwardly back, gripped the doorknob, cleared his throat, shook his head. "I'll, um, come back another..." He gave it up and ducked outside, closing the door behind him.

"You are giving up a great deal, Miranda."

"No. I'm trying to keep what I want most in the world. Don't leave me, Rolf. Stay with me always. Be my..." She bit her lip and forced her gaze to hold his as she said it. "Be my husband."

His smile was quick and brilliant. "This world of yours puzzles me always. Is this another new bit of progress, that a woman might propose marriage to a man?"

She shrugged. "It's done, though not often." She slipped her arms around his neck. "What is your answer?"

He stroked her hair away from her face with gentle fingers. *"þu ert unaðfödur, astín mín,* Miranda. Lovely Miranda with the courage of ten warriors and the beauty of a Valkyrie. I will care for you, cherish you, love you always. I am a fortunate man, truly blessed by the gods, to have you as my wife."

He bowed his head to kiss her deeply, with a fierce possessiveness in which she reveled. In his embrace, in his love, Miranda found that part of herself that had so long eluded her. She clung to it and silently vowed she would never let go.

* * * * *

MILLION DOLLAR SWEEPSTAKES (III)

No purchase necessary. To enter, follow the directions published. Method of entry may vary. For eligibility, entries must be received no later than March 31, 1996. No liability is assumed for printing errors, lost, late or misdirected entries. Odds of winning are determined by the number of eligible entries distributed and received. Prizewinners will be determined no later than June 30, 1996.

Sweepstakes open to residents of the U.S. (except Puerto Rico), Canada, Europe and Taiwan who are 18 years of age or older. All applicable laws and regulations apply. Sweepstakes offer void wherever prohibited by law. Values of all prizes are in U.S. currency. This sweepstakes is presented by Torstar Corp., its subsidiaries and affiliates, in conjunction with book, merchandise and/or product offerings. For a copy of the Official Rules send a self-addressed, stamped envelope (WA residents need not affix return postage) to: MILLION DOLLAR SWEEPSTAKES (III) Rules, P.O. Box 4573, Blair, NE 68009, USA.

EXTRA BONUS PRIZE DRAWING

No purchase necessary. The Extra Bonus Prize will be awarded in a random drawing to be conducted no later than 5/30/96 from among all entries received. To qualify, entries must be received by 3/31/96 and comply with published directions. Drawing open to residents of the U.S. (except Puerto Rico), Canada, Europe and Taiwan who are 18 years of age or older. All applicable laws and regulations apply; offer void wherever prohibited by law. Odds of winning are dependent upon number of eligible entries received. Prize is valued in U.S. currency. The offer is presented by Torstar Corp., its subsidiaries and affiliates in conjunction with book, merchandise and/or product offering. For a copy of the Official Rules governing this sweepstakes, send a self-addressed, stamped envelope (WA residents need not affix return postage) to: Extra Bonus Prize Drawing Rules, P.O. Box 4590, Blair, NE 68009, USA.

SWP-S594

HE'S AN

AMERICAN HERO

He's a man's man, and every woman's dream. Strong, sensitive and so irresistible—he's an American Hero.

For April: KEEPER, by Patricia Gardner Evans: From the moment Cleese Starrett encountered Laurel Drew fishing in his river, he was hooked. But reeling in this lovely lady might prove harder than he thought.

For May: MICHAEL'S FATHER, by Dallas Schulze: Kel Bryan needed a housekeeper—fast. And Megan Roarke did more than fit the bill; she fit snugly into his open arms. Then she told him her news....

For June: SIMPLE GIFTS, by Kathleen Korbel: For too long Rock O'Connor had fought the good fight to no avail. Then Lee Kendall entered his jaded world, her zest for life rekindling his former passion—as well as a new one.

AMERICAN HEROES: Men who give all they've got for their country, their work—the women they love.

Only from

INTIMATE MOMENTS®

Silhouette®

CONARD COUNTY

continues...

Once again Rachel Lee invites readers to explore the wild Western terrain of Conard County, Wyoming, to meet the men and women whose lives unfold on the land they hold dear—and whose loves touch our hearts with their searing intensity. Join this award-winning author as she reaches the POINT OF NO RETURN, IM #566, coming to you in May.

For years, Marge Tate had safeguarded her painful secret from her husband, Nate. Then the past caught up with her in the guise of a youthful stranger, signaling an end to her silence—and perhaps the end to her fairy-tale marriage.... Look for their story, only from Silhouette Intimate Moments.

It's those rambunctious Rawlings brothers again!
You met Gable and Cooper Rawlings in IM #523
and IM #553. Now meet their youngest brother,
Flynn Rawlings, in

by Linda Turner

Fun-loving rodeo cowboy Flynn Rawlings
couldn't believe it. From the moment he'd
approached beautiful barrel racer Tate Baxter,
she'd been intent on freezing him out. But Tate
was the woman he'd been waiting for all his life,
and he wasn't about to take no for an answer!

Don't miss FLYNN (IM #572), available in June.
And look for his sister, Kat's, story as
Linda Turner's thrilling saga concludes in

THE WILD WEST

Coming to you throughout 1994...only from
Silhouette Intimate Moments.

IT'S OUR 1000TH SILHOUETTE ROMANCE, AND WE'RE CELEBRATING!

JOIN US FOR A SPECIAL COLLECTION OF LOVE STORIES BY AUTHORS YOU'VE LOVED FOR YEARS, AND NEW FAVORITES YOU'VE JUST DISCOVERED. JOIN THE CELEBRATION...

April
REGAN'S PRIDE by **Diana Palmer**
MARRY ME AGAIN by **Suzanne Carey**

May
THE BEST IS YET TO BE by **Tracy Sinclair**
CAUTION: BABY AHEAD by **Marie Ferrarella**

June
THE BACHELOR PRINCE by **Debbie Macomber**
A ROGUE'S HEART by **Laurie Paige**

July
IMPROMPTU BRIDE by **Annette Broadrick**
THE FORGOTTEN HUSBAND by **Elizabeth August**

SILHOUETTE ROMANCE...VIBRANT, FUN AND EMOTIONALLY RICH! TAKE ANOTHER LOOK AT US! AND AS PART OF THE CELEBRATION, READERS CAN RECEIVE A FREE GIFT!

YOU'LL FALL IN LOVE ALL OVER
AGAIN WITH
SILHOUETTE ROMANCE!

$\mathbf{V}$ *Silhouette*®

CEL1000